~~~~~~~~~~~~~~~~~~~~~~~~~~~~~~

"Wherever science fiction goes exploring, there also terror may travel along. In the present book alone you will find examples from such categories as interplanetary flight, life on other worlds, aliens from deep space invading earth, travel in time or in other dimensions, imaginings of our own world in the future, dangerous inventions, and unknown 'natural' horrors on (or in) our own planet of today."

—From the Introduction by Groff Conklin

~~~~~~~~~~~~~~~~~~~~~~~~~~~~~~

# SCIENCE FICTION TERROR TALES

was originally published by Gnome Press.

# SCIENCE FICTION
# TERROR
# TALES

Edited by

**Groff Conklin**

PUBLISHED BY POCKET BOOKS NEW YORK

SCIENCE FICTION TERROR TALES

A *Pocket Book* edition
1st printing . . . . . . . . . January, 1955
4th printing . . . . . . . . . . April, 1970

This original *Pocket Book* edition is printed from
brand-new plates made from newly set, clear, easy-to-read type.
*Pocket Book* editions are published by Pocket Books, a division of
Simon & Schuster, Inc., 630 Fifth Avenue, New York, N.Y. 10020.
Trademarks registered in the United States and other countries.

L

# TABLE OF CONTENTS

# INTRODUCTION

OF THE EFFECTS OF TERROR, ACTUAL REAL-LIFE TERROR, ON the human being, physiologists, psychologists and medical men know a great deal. They know that it is, to say the least, an unhealthy experience. Even you and I have experienced the unpleasant effects of fright, though we never, I trust, have suffered extremes of it. The narrow escape from an auto accident, the nightmare, the fear of being found out in some peccadillo, the haunting fear while walking through a lonely wood or a strange city street in the dark of night—these are not uncommon experiences for any of us. And we do not like them.

Then why do we like to *read* about terrifying things? Why do we enjoy a thrill in experiencing at second hand what would, at first hand, upset us? Why does the carefully built up mood of horror, the sinister atmosphere, the frightful event, make for us merely a titillating kind of "relaxation reading?" I am not sure that psychologists can give scientific answers to that question, and I know I cannot. It is part of that enormous and almost indecipherable complex that constitutes human personality. But if we knew all the answers to all the questions about ourselves, life would not hold nearly as much excitement for us as it does. Let's just admit that we like tales of terror. And to satisfy that fondness, here is a book full of them for you.

The interesting thing about this particular collection of terror stories is that it consists of a type that has been developed to its present state of rich variety only during the past few decades. Terror tales as such are as old as the art of story telling and older than the written word. Old women and minstrels, medicine men and gossips of both sexes have told tales of creepy unknown things, of ghosts and werewolves, of sinister magics and flights from the Awful, ever since mankind became conscious of the frightening mysteries in the world around him.

Down through the centuries there has been a constant rich accretion to the literature of horror. In England alone, for example, it appears with the very beginnings of written lore. Later, when English literature came to full flower, some of its richest imaginings were devoted to the fearful; "Macbeth," for example, is a masterpiece of horror. Defoe was a great teller of ghost stories. In the 18th century Horace Walpole founded the school of the Gothic novel, full of weird and fearful wonders. And ever since, the great masters of English and American literature have tried their hands at tales intended to arouse terror, from Dickens and Wilkie Collins to "Saki" and Geoffrey Household, from Poe and Hawthorne to John Collier and Will Jenkins.

In the past 25 years, however, since science fiction began exploring untrod regions of space, time and the human mind, new and different conceptions of terror themes developed that had never been possible before the modern age of advanced science and technology. So recent, indeed, are these concepts of new horrors that this is the first collection of its kind ever prepared. Science fiction itself is so "new" that it was not until the present that enough good stories, depending primarily upon fear for their effects, had been published to make possible an anthology with real variety and adequate change of pace.

Of course, there have been literally hundreds of science fiction tales that work the changes upon the human emotion of fear; but, at least in the earlier days, they tended to do so with all the literary acuity of the comics. Mad scientists invented terrifying machines or loosed horrid entities that did awful things to people. From other planets or dimensions came BEMs (otherwise known as Bug-Eyed Monsters) who frightened space corsairs, intrepid explorers, or simple "Terrans" like you and me, out of their wits. Unmentionable horrors from little-known regions of the planet, or from within the depths of the sea or the bowels of the earth, "descended" upon civilization like wolves on the fold—all done up in the most ill-favored prose imaginable.

It is worth noting, in this connection, that the oldest story in the present collection was written in 1936, and only six of the tales came out in the 'Forties. One reason for this, of course, is that many of the high-quality older stories have been anthologized to death, and so are not included here; but a more important cause is the fact that only in recent years have most science fiction writers learned how to *understate* terror. The modern reader is bored with "sound and fury." For him, stories that brashly set out to achieve their effects with all panoply of horrid adjectives, bloody verbs and arrant over-writing, miss the point by a mile. Only too often these older stories cause embarrassed laughter rather than genuine chills.

You will find, I think, none of this type of story from the childhood of science fiction in the present book. Our stories here are all deftly and quietly calculated to make you squirm, one way or another, but not with laughter. In this they join the great tradition of terror tales in the world's literature, tales like Stephen Crane's "The Upturned Face," or Ambrose Bierce's "The Boarded Window," or Thomas Hardy's "The Three Strangers," and many others of the same unforgettable quality.

There really is no need in this introduction to draw diagrams indicating the various and sundry species and sub-species of science fiction terror tales. Wherever science fiction goes exploring, there also terror may travel along. In the present book alone you will find examples from such categories as interplanetary flight, life on other worlds, aliens from deep space invading earth, travel in time or in other dimensions, imaginings of our own world in the future, dangerous inventions, and unknown "natural" horrors on (or in) our own planet of today. There is even one, as you will see, that evades any classification at all.

In short, we have here a handsome variety of goosepimple-raising tales, a variety almost as great as the subject matter of science fiction itself.

One final note of explanation. It has been my usual practice in my earlier collections to include no stories previously anthologized, or at least only one or two. I have deviated from this policy somewhat in the present book by including four tales that have appeared in other anthologies, and two that have been included in collections of the authors' own stories. The reason for this is that in a mood book such as this, balance and high quality are to be preferred to uniqueness. The copyright notices indicate the six stories that have had previous book publication. And even if you have read them before, I am sure that you will find them just as productive of cold perspiration as you did the first time—particularly since in this book they are set in the framework in which they belong—"in terrors clad, to claim an unresisting prey," i.e., you.

GROFF CONKLIN

**Ray Bradbury**

# PUNISHMENT WITHOUT CRIME

*The ethics of "machines," whether they are made of metal or of what seems to be flesh and blood, is dependent entirely on the human beings who use them. They have none of their own. This is something that George Hill forgot, in this chilling independent sequel to Bradbury's well-known "Marionettes, Inc." And—even more important—murder is murder, even if the person you kill actually continues to "exist."*

THE SIGN ON THE DOOR SAID: MARIONETTES, INC.

"You wish to kill your wife?" said the dark man at the desk.

"Yes. No . . . not exactly. I mean . . ."

"Name?"

"Hers or mine?"

"Yours."

"George Hill."

"Address?"

"11 South St. James, Glenview."

The man wrote this down, emotionlessly. "Your wife's name?"

"Katherine."

"Age?"

Ray Bradbury, PUNISHMENT WITHOUT CRIME. Copyright 1950 by Clark Publishing Company. Reprinted by permission of Harold Matson from *Other Worlds*, March 1950.

"Thirty-one."

Then came a swift series of questions. Color of hair, eyes, skin, favorite perfume, texture and size index. "Have you a dimensional photo of her? And her lipstick . . . ?"

An hour later, George Hill was perspiring.

"That's all." The dark man arose and scowled. "You still want to go through with it."

"Yes."

"Sign here."

He signed.

"You know this is illegal?"

"Yes."

"And that we're in no way responsible for what happens to you as a result of your request?"

"For God's sake!" cried George. "You've kept me long enough. Let's get on!"

The man smiled faintly. "It'll take three hours to prepare the marionette of your wife. Sleep awhile, it'll help your nerves. The third mirror room on your left is unoccupied."

George moved in a slow numbness to the mirror room. He lay on the blue velvet cot, his body pressure causing the mirrors in the ceiling to whirl. A soft voice sang, "Sleep . . . sleep . . . sleep . . ."

George murmured. "Katherine, I didn't want to come here. You forced me into it. You made me do it. God, I wish I wasn't here. I wish I could go back. I don't want to kill you."

The mirrors glittered as they rotated softly.

He slept.

He dreamed he was forty-one again, he and Katie running on a green hill somewhere with a picnic lunch, their helicopter beside them. The wind blew Katie's hair in golden strands and she was laughing. They kissed and held hands, not eating. They read poems; it seemed they were always reading poems.

Other scenes. Quick changes of color, in flight. He and Katie flying over Greece and Italy and Switzerland, in that clear, long autumn of 1997! Flying and never stopping!

And then—nightmare. Katie and Leonard Phelps. George cried out in his sleep. How had it happened? Where had Phelps sprung from? Why had he interfered? Why couldn't life be simple and good? Was it the difference in age? George touching fifty, and Katie so young, not yet twenty-eight? Why, why?

The scene was unforgettably vivid. Leonard Phelps and Katherine in a green park beyond the city. George himself appearing on a path only in time to see the kissing of their mouths.

The rage. The struggle. The attempt to kill Leonard Phelps.

More days, more nightmares.

George Hill awoke, weeping.

"Mr. Hill, we're ready for you now."

Hill arose clumsily. He saw himself in the high and now silent mirrors, and he looked all fifty of his years. It had been a wretched error. Better men than he had taken young wives only to have them dissolve away in their hands like sugar crystals under water. He eyed himself, monstrously. A little too much stomach. A little too much chin. Somewhat too much pepper in the hair and not enough in the limbs. . . .

The dark man led him to a room.

George Hill gasped. "This is *Katie's* room!"

"We try to have everything perfect."

"It *is*, to the last detail!"

George Hill drew forth a signed check for ten thousand dollars. The man departed with it.

The room was silent and warm.

George sat and felt for the gun in his pocket. A lot of money. But rich men can afford the luxury of cathartic murder. The violent unviolence. The death without death. The murder without murdering. He felt better. He was suddenly calm. He watched the door. This was a thing he had anticipated for six months and now it was to be ended. In a moment the beautiful robot, the stringless marionette would appear, and . . .

"Hello, George."

"Katie!"

He whirled.

"Katie." He let his breath out.

She stood in the doorway behind him. She was dressed in a feather-soft green gown. On her feet were woven gold-twine sandals. Her hair was bright about her throat and her eyes were blue and clear.

He did not speak for a long while. "You're beautiful," he said at last, shocked.

"How else could I be?"

His voice was slow and unreal. "Let me look at you."

He put out his vague hands like a sleepwalker. His heart pounded sluggishly. He moved forward as if walking under a deep pressure of water. He walked around and around her, touching her.

"Haven't you seen enough of me in all these years?"

"Never enough," he said, and his eyes were filled with tears.

"What did you want to talk to me about?"

"Give me time, please, a little time." He sat down weakly and put his trembling hands to his chest. He blinked. "It's incredible. Another nightmare. How did they *make* you?"

"We're not allowed to talk of that; it spoils the illusion."

"It's magic!"

"Science."

Her touch was warm. Her fingernails were perfect as seashells. There was no seam, no flaw. He looked upon her. He remembered again the words they had read so often in the good days. *Thou art fair, my love. Behold, thou art fair; Thou hast dove's eyes within thy locks. Thy lips are like a spread of scarlet. And thy speech is comely. Thy two breasts are like two young roes that are twins, which feed among the lilies. There is no spot in thee.*

"George?"

"What?" His eyes were cold glass.

He wanted to kiss her lips.

*Honey and milk are under thy tongue.*

*And the smell of thy garments is like the smell of Lebanon.*
"George."

A vast humming. The room began to whirl.

"Yes, yes, a moment, a moment." He shook his humming head.

*How beautiful are thy feet with shoes, O prince's daughter! The joints of thy thighs are like jewels, the work of the hands of a cunning workman . . .*

"How did they do it?" he cried. In so short a time. Three hours, while he slept. Had they melted gold, fixed delicate watchsprings, diamonds, glitter, confetti, rich rubies, liquid silver, copper thread? Had metal insects spun her hair? Had they poured yellow fire in moulds and set it to freeze?

"No," she said. "If you talk that way, I'll go."

"Don't!"

"Come to business, then," she said, coldly. "You want to talk to me about Leonard."

"Give me time, I'll get to it."

"Now," she insisted.

He knew no anger. It had washed out of him at her appearance. He felt childishly dirty.

"Why did you come to see me?" She was not smiling.

"Please."

"I insist. Wasn't it about Leonard? You know I love him, don't you?"

"Stop it!" He put his hands to his ears.

She kept at him. "You know, I spend all of my time with him now. Where you and I used to go, now Leonard and I stay. Remember the picnic green on Mount Verde? We were there last week. We flew to Athens a month ago, with a case of champagne."

He licked his lips. "You're not guilty, you're *not*." He rose and held her wrists. "You're fresh, you're not *her*. She's guilty, not you. You're different!"

"On the contrary," said the woman. "I *am* her. I can act only as she acts. No part of me is alien to her. For all intents and purposes we are one."

"But you did not do what she has done!"

"I did all those things. I kissed him."

"You can't have, you're just born!"

"Out of her past and from your mind."

"Look," he pleaded, shaking her to gain her attention. "Isn't there some way, can't I—pay more money? Take you away with me? We'll go to Paris or Stockholm or any place you like!"

She laughed. "The marionettes only rent. They never sell."

"But I've money!"

"It was tried, long ago. It leads to insanity. It's not possible. Even this much is illegal, you *know* that. We exist only through governmental sufferance."

"All I want is to live with you, Katie."

"That can never be, because I am Katie, every bit of me is her. We do not want competition. Marionettes can't leave the premises; dissection might reveal our secrets. Enough of this. I warned you, we mustn't speak of these things. You'll spoil the illusion. You'll feel frustrated when you leave. You paid your money, now do what you came to do."

"I don't want to kill you."

"One part of you does. You're walling it in, you're trying not to let it out."

He took the gun from his pocket. "I'm an old fool, I should never have come. You're so beautiful."

"I'm going to see Leonard tonight."

"Don't talk."

"We're flying to Paris in the morning."

"You heard what I said!"

"And then to Stockholm." She laughed sweetly and caressed his chin. "My little fat man."

Something began to stir in him. His face grew pale. He knew what was happening. The hidden anger and revulsion and hatred in him was sending out faint pulses of thoughts. And the delicate telepathic web in her wondrous head was receiving the death thoughts. The marionette. The invisible strings. He himself manipulating her body.

"Plump, odd little man, who once was so fair."

"Don't," he said.

"Old while I am only thirty-one, ah, George, you were blind, working years to give me time to fall in love again. Don't you think Leonard is lovely?"

He raised the gun blindly.

"Katie."

*"His head is as the most fine gold—"* she whispered.

"Katie, don't!" he screamed.

*"His locks are bushy and black as a raven, his hands are as gold rings set with the beryl!"*

How could she speak that song! It was in *his* mind, how could *she* mouth it!

"Katie, don't make me do this!"

*"His cheeks are as a bed of spices,"* she murmured, eyes closed, moving about the room softly. *"His belly is as bright ivory overlaid with sapphires; his legs are as pillars of marble—"*

"Katie!" he shrieked.

*"His mouth is most sweet—"*

One shot.

*"—this is my beloved—"*

Another shot.

She fell.

"Katie, Katie, Katie!"

Four more times he pumped bullets into her body.

She lay shuddering. Her senseless mouth clicked wide and some insanely warped mechanism had her repeat again and again, "beloved, beloved, beloved, beloved, beloved . . ."

George Hill fainted.

He awakened to a cool cloth on his brow.

"It's all over," said the dark man.

"Over?" George Hill whispered.

The dark man nodded.

George Hill looked weakly down at his hands. They had been covered with blood. When he fainted he had dropped to the floor. The last thing he remembered was the feeling of the real blood pouring upon his hands in a freshet.

His hands were now clean washed.

"I've got to leave," said George Hill.

"If you feel capable."

"I'm all right." He got up. "I'll go to Paris now, start over. I'm not to try to phone Katie or anything, am I?"

"Katie is dead."

"Yes. I killed her, didn't I? God, the blood, it was *real!*"

"We are proud of that touch."

He went down in the elevator to the street. It was raining and he wanted to walk for hours. The anger and destruction were purged away. The memory was so terrible that he would never wish to kill again. Even if the real Katie were to appear before him now, he would only thank God, and fall senselessly to his knees. She was dead now. He had had his way. He had broken the law and no one would know.

The rain fell cool on his face. He must leave immediately, while the purge was in effect. After all, what was the use of such purges if one took up the old threads? The marionettes' function was primarily to prevent *actual* crime. If you wanted to kill, hit or torture someone, you took it out on one of those unstringed automatons. It wouldn't do to return to the apartment now. Katie might be there. He wanted only to think of her as dead, a thing attended to in deserving fashion.

He stopped at the curb and watched the traffic flash by. He took deep breaths of the good air and began to relax.

"Mr. Hill?" said a voice at his elbow.

"Yes?"

A manacle was snapped to Hill's wrist. "You're under arrest."

"But—"

"Come along. Smith, take the other men upstairs, make the arrests!"

"You can't do this to me," said George Hill.

"For murder, yes, we can."

Thunder sounded in the sky.

It was eight-fifteen at night. It had been raining for ten days. It rained now on the prison walls. He put his hands out to feel the drops gather in pools on his trembling palms.

A door clanged and he did not move but stood with his hands in the rain. His lawyer looked up at him on his chair and said, "It's all over. You'll be executed tonight."

George Hill listened to the rain.

"She wasn't real. I didn't kill her."

"It's the law, anyhow. You remember. The others are sentenced, too. The president of Marionettes, Incorporated, will die at midnight. His three assistants will die at one. You'll go about one-thirty."

"Thanks," said George. "You did all you could. I guess it was murder, no matter how you look at it, image or not. The idea was there, the plot and the plan was there. It lacked only the real Katie herself."

"It's a matter of timing, too," said the lawyer. "Ten years ago you wouldn't have got the death penalty. Ten years from now you wouldn't, either. But they had to have an object case, a whipping boy. The use of marionettes has grown so in the last year it's fantastic. The public must be scared out of it, and scared badly. God knows where it would all wind up if it went on. There's the spiritual side of it, too, where does life begin or end, are the robots alive or dead? More than one church has been split up the seams on the question. If they aren't alive, they're the next thing to it, they react, they even think; you know the 'live robot' law that was passed two months ago; you come under that. Just bad timing, is all, bad timing."

"The government's right. I see that now," said George Hill.

"I'm glad you understand the attitude of the law."

"Yes. After all, they can't let murder be legal. Even if it's done with machines and telepathy and wax. They'd be hypocrites to let me get away with my crime. For it *was* a crime. I've felt guilty about it ever since. I've felt the need of punishment. Isn't that odd? That's how society gets to you. It makes you feel guilty even when you see no reason to be . . ."

"I have to go now. Is there anything you want?"

"Nothing, thanks."

"Goodbye then, Mr. Hill."

The door shut.

George Hill stood up on the chair, his hands twisting together, wet, outside the window bars. A red light burned in the wall suddenly. A voice came over the audio: "Mr. Hill, your wife is here to see you."

He gripped the bars.

"She's dead," he thought.

"Mr. Hill?" asked the voice.

"She's dead. I killed her."

"Your wife is waiting in the anteroom, will you see her?"

"I saw her fall, I shot her, I saw her fall dead!"

"Mr. Hill, do you hear me?"

"Yes!" he shouted, pounding at the wall with his fists. "I hear you. I hear you! She's dead, she's dead, can't she let me be! I killed her, I won't see her, she's dead!"

A pause. "Very well, Mr. Hill," murmured the voice.

The red light winked off.

Lightning flashed through the sky and lit his face. He pressed his hot cheeks to the cold bars and waited, while the rain fell. After a long time, a door opened somewhere onto the street and he saw two caped figures emerge from the prison office below. They paused under an arc light and glanced up.

It was Katie. And beside her, Leonard Phelps.

"Katie!"

Her face turned away. The man took her arm. They hurried across the avenue in the black rain and got into a low car.

"Katie!" He wrenched at the bars. He screamed and beat and pulled at the concrete ledge. "She's alive! Guard! Guard! I saw her! She's not dead, I didn't kill her, now you can let me out! I didn't murder anyone, it's all a joke, a mistake, I saw her, I saw her! Katie, come back, tell them, Katie, say you're alive! Katie!"

The guards came running.

"You can't kill me! I didn't do anything! Katie's alive, I saw her!"

"We saw her, too, sir."

"But let me free, then! Let me free!" It was insane. He choked and almost fell.

"We've been through all that, sir, at the trial."

"It's not fair!" He leaped up and clawed at the window, bellowing.

The car drove away, Katie and Leonard inside it. Drove away to Paris and Athens and Venice and London next spring and Stockholm next summer and Vienna in the fall.

"Katie, come back, you can't *do* this to me!"

The red tail-light of the car dwindled in the cold rain. Behind him, the guards moved forward to take hold of him while he screamed.

## Fredric Brown

# A R E N A

*In the old days disputes were settled among clans, tribes, or nations by means of duels, or jousts, between selected heroes. It was, at least, a less bloody way of conducting war.*

*In this story Mr. Brown imagines a time in the future when something approximating a joust takes place, between a Man and an Outsider. Who arranged the event? The story does not say. This was a duel against the unknown, much more fearful for the human being than any fight against a known opponent. And the victory was much more decisive than it used to be—in the old days.*

CARSON OPENED HIS EYES, AND FOUND HIMSELF LOOKING upward into a flickering blue dimness.

It was hot, and he was lying on sand, and a sharp rock embedded in the sand was hurting his back. He rolled over to his side, off the rock, and then pushed himself up to a sitting position.

"I'm crazy," he thought. "Crazy—or dead—or something." The sand was blue, bright blue. And there wasn't any such thing as bright blue sand on Earth or any of the planets. *Blue sand.*

Blue sand under a blue dome that wasn't the sky nor yet a room, but a circumscribed area—somehow he knew it was circumscribed and finite even though he couldn't see to the top of it.

He picked up some of the sand in his hand and let it run through his fingers. It trickled down onto his bare leg. *Bare?*

Naked. He was stark naked, and already his body was dripping perspiration from the enervating heat, coated blue with sand wherever sand had touched it.

But elsewhere his body was white.

He thought: Then this sand is really blue. If it seemed blue only because of the blue light, then I'd be blue also. But I'm white, so the sand *is* blue. *Blue sand.* There isn't any blue sand. There isn't any place like this place I'm in.

Sweat was running down in his eyes.

It was hot, hotter than hell. Only hell—the hell of the ancients—was supposed to be red and not blue.

But if this place wasn't hell, what was it? Only Mercury, among the planets, had heat like this and this wasn't Mercury. And Mercury was some four billion miles from—

It came back to him then, where he'd been. In the little one-man scouter, outside the orbit of Pluto, scouting a scant million miles to one side of the Earth Armada drawn up in battle array there to intercept the Outsiders.

That sudden strident nerve-shattering ringing of the alarm bell when the rival scouter—the Outsider ship—had come within range of his detectors—

No one knew who the Outsiders were, what they looked like, from what far galaxy they came, other than that it was in the general direction of the Pleiades.

First, sporadic raids on Earth colonies and outposts. Isolated battles between Earth patrols and small groups of Outsider spaceships; battles sometimes won and sometimes lost, but never to date resulting in the capture of an alien vessel. Nor had any member of a raided colony ever survived to describe the Outsiders who had left the ships, if indeed they had left them.

Not a too-serious menace, at first, for the raids had not been too numerous or destructive. And individually, the ships had proved slightly inferior in armament to the best of Earth's fighters, although somewhat superior in speed and maneuverability. A sufficient edge in speed, in fact, to give the Outsiders their choice of running or fighting, unless surrounded.

Nevertheless, Earth had prepared for serious trouble, for a showdown, building the mightiest armada of all time. It had been waiting now, that armada, for a long time. But now the showdown was coming.

Scouts twenty billion miles out had detected the approach of a mighty fleet—a showdown fleet—of the Outsiders. Those scouts had never come back, but their radiotronic messages had. And now Earth's armada, all ten thousand ships and half-million fighting spacemen, was out there, outside Pluto's orbit, waiting to intercept and battle to the death.

And an even battle it was going to be, judging by the advance reports of the men of the far picket line who had given their lives to report—before they had died—on the size and strength of the alien fleet.

Anybody's battle, with the mastery of the solar system hanging in the balance, on an even chance. A last and *only* chance, for Earth and all her colonies lay at the utter mercy of the Outsiders if they ran that gauntlet—

Oh yes. Bob Carson remembered now.

Not that it explained blue sand and flickering blueness. But that strident alarming of the bell and his leap for the control panel. His frenzied fumbling as he strapped himself into the seat. The dot in the visiplate that grew larger.

The dryness of his mouth. The awful knowledge that this was *it*. For him, at least, although the main fleets were still out of range of one another.

This, his first taste of battle. Within three seconds or less he'd be victorious, or a charred cinder. Dead.

Three seconds—that's how long a space-battle lasted. Time enough to count to three, slowly, and then you'd won or you were dead. One hit completely took care of a lightly armed and armored little one-man craft like a scouter.

Frantically—as, unconsciously, his dry lips shaped the word "One"—he worked at the controls to keep that growing dot centered on the crossed spiderwebs of the visiplate. His hands doing that, while his right foot hovered over the pedal that would fire the bolt. The single bolt of concentrated hell that had to hit—or else. There wouldn't be time for any second shot.

"Two." He didn't know he'd said that, either. The dot in the visiplate wasn't a dot now. Only a few thousand miles away, it showed up in the magnification of the plate as though it were only a few hundred yards off. It was a sleek, fast little scouter, about the size of his.

And an alien ship, all right.

"Thr—" His foot touched the bolt-release pedal—

And then the Outsider had swerved suddenly and was off the crosshairs. Carson punched keys frantically, to follow.

For a tenth of a second, it was out of the visiplate entirely, and then as the nose of his scouter swung after it, he saw it again, diving straight toward the ground.

*The ground?*

It was an optical illusion of some sort. It *had* to be, that planet—or whatever it was—that now covered the visiplate. Whatever it was, it couldn't be there. Couldn't possibly. There *wasn't* any planet nearer than Neptune three billion miles away—with Pluto around on the opposite side of the distant pinpoint sun.

His *detectors! They* hadn't shown any object of planetary dimensions, even of asteroid dimensions. They still didn't.

So it couldn't be there, that whatever-it-was he was diving into, only a few hundred miles below him.

And in his sudden anxiety to keep from crashing, he forgot even the Outsider ship. He fired the front braking rockets, and even as the sudden change of speed slammed him forward against the seat straps, he fired full right for an emergency turn. Pushed them down and *held* them down, knowing that he needed everything the ship had to keep from crashing and that a turn that sudden would black him out for a moment.

It did black him out.

And that was all. Now he was sitting in hot blue sand, stark naked but otherwise unhurt. No sign of his spaceship and—for that matter—no sign of *space*. That curve overhead wasn't a sky, whatever else it was.

He scrambled to his feet.

Gravity seemed a little more than Earth-normal. Not much more.

Flat sand stretching away, a few scrawny bushes in clumps here and there. The bushes were blue, too, but in varying shades, some lighter than the blue of the sand, some darker.

Out from under the nearest bush ran a little thing that was like a lizard, except that it had more than four legs. It was blue, too. Bright blue. It saw him and ran back again under the bush.

He looked up again, trying to decide what was overhead. It wasn't exactly a roof, but it was dome-shaped. It flickered and was hard to look at. But definitely, it curved down to the ground, to the blue sand, all around him.

He wasn't far from being under the center of the dome. At a guess, it was a hundred yards to the nearest wall, if it was a wall. It was as though a blue hemisphere of *something*, about two hundred and fifty yards in circumference, was inverted over the flat expanse of the sand.

And everything blue, except one object. Over near a far curving wall there was a red object. Roughly spherical, it seemed to be about a yard in diameter. Too far for him to see clearly through the flickering blueness. But, unaccountably, he shuddered.

He wiped sweat from his forehead, or tried to, with the back of his hand.

Was this a dream, a nightmare? This heat, this sand, that vague feeling of horror he felt when he looked toward the red thing?

A dream? No, one didn't go to sleep and dream in the midst of a battle in space.

Death? No, never. If there were immortality, it wouldn't be a senseless thing like this, a thing of blue heat and blue sand and a red horror.

Then he heard the voice—

Inside his head he heard it, not with his ears. It came from nowhere or everywhere.

"*Through spaces and dimensions wandering,*" rang the words in his mind, "*and in this space and this time I find two people about to wage a war that would exterminate one and so weaken the other that it would retrogress and never fulfill its destiny, but decay and return to mindless dust whence it came. And I say this must not happen.*"

"Who . . . what are you?" Carson didn't say it aloud, but the question formed itself in his brain.

"*You would not understand completely. I am—*" There was a pause as though the voice sought—in Carson's brain—for a word that wasn't there, a word he didn't know. "*I am the end of evolution of a race so old the time can not be expressed in words that have meaning to your mind. A race fused into a single entity, eternal—*

"*An entity such as your primitive race might become*"— again the groping for a word—"*time from now. So might the race you call, in your mind, the Outsiders. So I intervene in the battle to come, the battle between fleets so evenly matched that destruction of both races will result. One must survive. One must progress and evolve.*"

"One?" thought Carson. "Mine, or—?"

"*It is in my power to stop the war, to send the Outsiders back to their galaxy. But they would return, or your race would sooner or later follow them there. Only by remaining in this space and time to intervene constantly could I prevent them from destroying one another, and I cannot remain.*

"*So I shall intervene now. I shall destroy one fleet completely without loss to the other. One civilization shall thus survive.*"

Nightmare. This had to be nightmare, Carson thought. But he knew it wasn't.

It was too mad, too impossible, to be anything but real.

He didn't dare ask *the* question—*which?* But his thoughts asked it for him.

*"The stronger shall survive,"* said the voice. *"That I can not —and would not—change. I merely intervene to make it a complete victory, not"*—groping again—*"not Pyrrhic victory to a broken race.*

*"From the outskirts of the not-yet battle I plucked two individuals, you and an Outsider. I see from your mind that in your early history of nationalisms battles between champions, to decide issues between races, were not unknown.*

*"You and your opponent are here pitted against one another, naked and unarmed, under conditions equally unfamiliar to you both, equally unpleasant to you both. There is no time limit, for here there is no time. The survivor is the champion of his race. That race survives."*

"But—" Carson's protest was too inarticulate for expression, but the voice answered it.

*"It is fair. The conditions are such that the accident of physical strength will not completely decide the issue. There is a barrier. You will understand. Brain-power and courage will be more important than strength. Most especially courage, which is the will to survive."*

"But while this goes on, the fleets will—"

*"No, you are in another space, another time. For as long as you are here, time stands still in the universe you know. I see you wonder whether this place is real. It is, and it is not. As I —to your limited understanding—am and am not real. My existence is mental and not physical. You saw me as a planet; it could have been as a dustmote or a sun.*

*"But to you this place is now real. What you suffer here will be real. And if you die here, your death will be real. If you die, your failure will be the end of your race. That is enough for you to know."*

And then the voice was gone.

And he was alone, but not alone. For as Carson looked up, he saw that the red thing, the red sphere of horror which he now knew was the Outsider, was rolling toward him.

Rolling.

It seemed to have no legs or arms that he could see, no features. It rolled across the blue sand with the fluid quickness
of a drop of mercury. And before it, in some manner he could
not understand, came a paralyzing wave of nauseating, retch-
ing, horrid hatred.

Carson looked about him frantically. A stone, lying in the
sand a few feet away, was the nearest thing to a weapon. It
wasn't large, but it had sharp edges, like a slab of flint. It
looked a bit like blue flint.

He picked it up, and crouched to receive the attack. It was
coming fast, faster than he could run.

No time to think out how he was going to fight it, and how
anyway could he plan to battle a creature whose strength,
whose characteristics, whose method of fighting he did not
know? Rolling so fast, it looked more than ever like a perfect
sphere.

Ten yards away. Five. And then it stopped.

Rather, it *was stopped*. Abruptly the near side of it flattened as though it had run up against an invisible wall. It
bounced, actually bounced back.

Then it rolled forward again, but more slowly, more cautiously. It stopped again, at the same place. It tried again, a
few yards to one side.

There was a barrier there of some sort. It clicked, then, in
Carson's mind. That thought projected into his mind by the
Entity who had brought them there: "—accident of physical
strength will not completely decide the issue. There is a barrier."

A force-field, of course. Not the Netzian Field, known to
Earth science, for that glowed and emitted a crackling sound.
This one was invisible, silent.

It was a wall that ran from side to side of the inverted
hemisphere; Carson didn't have to verify that himself. The
Roller was doing that; rolling sideways along the barrier, seeking a break in it that wasn't there.

Carson took half a dozen steps forward, his left hand groping out before him, and then his hand touched the barrier. It
felt smooth, yielding, like a sheet of rubber rather than like

glass. Warm to his touch, but no warmer than the sand under-
foot. And it was completely invisible, even at close range.

He dropped the stone and put both hands against it, pushing. It seemed to yield, just a trifle. But no farther than that
trifle, even when he pushed with all his weight. It felt like a
sheet of rubber backed up by steel. Limited resiliency, and
then firm strength.

He stood on tiptoe and reached as high as he could and the
barrier was still there.

He saw the Roller coming back, having reached one side of
the arena. That feeling of nausea hit Carson again, and he
stepped back from the barrier as it went by. It didn't stop.

But did the barrier stop at ground level? Carson knelt down
and burrowed in the sand. It was soft, light, easy to dig in. At
two feet down the barrier was still there.

The Roller was coming back again. Obviously, it couldn't
find a way through at either side.

There must be a way through, Carson thought. *Some* way
we can get at each other, else this duel is meaningless.

But no hurry now, in finding that out. There was something
to try first. The Roller was back now, and it stopped just
across the barrier, only six feet away. It seemed to be studying him, although for the life of him, Carson couldn't find external evidence of sense organs on the thing. Nothing that
looked like eyes or ears, or even a mouth. There was though,
he saw now, a series of grooves—perhaps a dozen of them
altogether, and he saw two tentacles suddenly push out from
two of the grooves and dip into the sand as though testing its
consistency. Tentacles about an inch in diameter and perhaps
a foot and a half long.

But the tentacles were retractable into the grooves and
were kept there except when in use. They were retracted
when the thing rolled and seemed to have nothing to do with
its method of locomotion. That, as far as Carson could judge,
seemed to be accomplished by some shifting—just *how* he
couldn't even imagine—of its center of gravity.

He shuddered as he looked at the thing. It was alien, utterly
alien, horribly different from anything on Earth or any of the

life forms found on the other solar planets. Instinctively,
somehow, he knew its mind was as alien as its body.

But he had to try. If it had no telepathic powers at all, the
attempt was foredoomed to failure, yet he thought it had
such powers. There had, at any rate, been a projection of
something that was not physical at the time a few minutes
ago when it had first started for him. An almost tangible wave
of hatred.

If it could project that, perhaps it could read his mind as
well, sufficiently for his purpose.

Deliberately, Carson picked up the rock that had been his
only weapon, then tossed it down again in a gesture of relin-
quishment and raised his empty hands, palms up, before him.

He spoke aloud, knowing that although the words would
be meaningless to the creature before him, speaking them
would focus his own thoughts more completely upon the message.

"Can we not have peace between us?" he said, his voice
sounding strange in the utter stillness. "The Entity who
brought us here has told us what must happen if our races
fight—extinction of one and weakening and retrogression of
the other. The battle between them, said the Entity, depends
upon what we do here. Why can not we agree to an external
peace—your race to its galaxy, we to ours?"

Carson blanked out his mind to receive a reply.

It came, and it staggered him back, physically. He actually
recoiled several steps in sheer horror at the depth and intensity of the hatred and lust-to-kill of the red images that had
been projected at him. Not as articulate words—as had come
to him the thoughts of the Entity—but as wave upon wave of
fierce emotion.

For a moment that seemed an eternity he had to struggle
against the mental impact of that hatred. fight to clear his
mind of it and drive out the alien thoughts to which he had
given admittance by blanking out his own thoughts. He
wanted to retch.

Slowly his mind cleared as, slowly, the mind of a man wak-
ening from nightmare clears away the fear-fabric of which

the dream was woven. He was breathing hard and he felt weaker, but he could think.

He stood studying the Roller. It had been motionless during the mental duel it had so nearly won. Now it rolled a few feet to one side, to the nearest of the blue bushes. Three tentacles whipped out of their grooves and began to investigate the bush.

"O. K.," Carson said, "so it's war then." He managed a wry grin. "If I got your answer straight, peace doesn't appeal to you." And, because he was, after all, a quiet young man and couldn't resist the impulse to be dramatic, he added. "To the death!"

But his voice, in that utter silence, sounded very silly, even to himself. It came to him, then, that this *was* to the death. Not only his own death or that of the red spherical thing which he now thought of as the Roller, but death to the entire race of one or the other of them. The end of the human race, if he failed.

It made him suddenly very humble and very afraid to think that. More than to think it, to *know* it. Somehow, with a knowledge that was above even faith, he knew that the Entity who had arranged this duel had told the truth about its intentions and its powers. It wasn't kidding.

The future of humanity depended upon *him*. It was an awful thing to realize, and he wrenched his mind away from it. He had to concentrate on the situation at hand.

There had to be some way of getting through the barrier, or of killing through the barrier.

Mentally? He hoped that wasn't all, for the Roller obviously had stronger telepathic powers than the primitive, undeveloped ones of the human race. Or did it?

He had been able to drive the thoughts of the Roller out of his own mind; could it drive out his? If its ability to project were stronger, might not its receptivity mechanism be more vulnerable?

He stared at it and endeavored to concentrate and focus all his thoughts upon it.

*"Die,"* he thought. *"You are going to die. You are dying. You are—"*

He tried variations on it, and mental pictures. Sweat stood out on his forehead and he found himself trembling with the intensity of the effort. But the Roller went ahead with its investigation of the bush, as utterly unaffected as though Carson had been reciting the multiplication table.

So *that* was no good.

He felt a bit weak and dizzy from the heat and his strenuous effort at concentration. He sat down on the blue sand to rest and gave his full attention to watching and studying the Roller. By close study, perhaps, he could judge its strength and detect its weaknesses, learn things that would be valuable to know when and if they should come to grips.

It was breaking off twigs. Carson watched carefully, trying to judge just how hard it worked to do that. Later, he thought, he could find a similar bush on his own side, break off twigs of equal thickness himself, and gain a comparison of physical strength between his own arms and hands and those tentacles.

The twigs broke off hard; the Roller was having to struggle with each one, he saw. Each tentacle, he saw, bifurcated at the tip into two fingers, each tipped by a nail or claw. The claws didn't seem to be particularly long or dangerous. No more so than his own fingernails, if they were let to grow a bit.

No, on the whole, it didn't look too tough to handle physically. Unless, of course, that bush was made of pretty tough stuff. Carson looked around him and, yes, right within reach was another bush of identical type.

He reached over and snapped off a twig. It was brittle, easy to break. Of course, the Roller might have been faking deliberately but he didn't think so.

On the other hand, where was it vulnerable? Just how would he go about killing it, if he got the chance? He went back to studying it. The outer hide looked pretty tough. He'd need a sharp weapon of some sort. He picked up the piece of rock again. It was about twelve inches long, narrow, and fairly sharp on one end. If it chipped like flint, he could make a serviceable knife out of it.

The Roller was continuing its investigations of the bushes. It rolled again, to the nearest one of another type. A little blue lizard, many-legged like the one Carson had seen on his side of the barrier, darted out from under the bush.

A tentacle of the Roller lashed out and caught it, picked it up. Another tentacle whipped over and began to pull legs off the lizard, as coldly and calmly as it had pulled twigs off the bush. The creature struggled frantically and emitted a shrill squealing sound that was the first sound Carson had heard here other than the sound of his own voice.

Carson shuddered and wanted to turn his eyes away. But he made himself continue to watch; anything he could learn about his opponent might prove valuable. Even this knowledge of its unnecessary cruelty. Particularly, he thought with a sudden vicious surge of emotion, this knowledge of its unnecessary cruelty. It would make it a pleasure to kill the thing, if and when the chance came.

He steeled himself to watch the dismembering of the lizard, for that very reason.

But he felt glad when, with half its legs gone, the lizard quit squealing and struggling and lay limp and dead in the Roller's grasp.

It didn't continue with the rest of the legs. Contemptuously it tossed the dead lizard away from it, in Carson's direction. It arced through the air between them and landed at his feet.

It had come through the barrier! The barrier wasn't there any more!

Carson was on his feet in a flash, the knife gripped tightly in his hand, and leaped forward. He'd settle this thing here and now! With the barrier gone—

But it wasn't gone. He found that out the hard way, running head on into it and nearly knocking himself silly. He bounced back, and fell.

And as he sat up, shaking his head to clear it, he saw something coming through the air toward him, and to duck it, he threw himself flat again on the sand, and to one side. He got his body out of the way, but there was a sudden sharp pain in the calf of his left leg.

He rolled backward, ignoring the pain, and scrambled to his feet. It was a rock, he saw now, that had struck him. And the Roller was picking up another one now, swinging it back gripped between two tentacles, getting ready to throw again.

It sailed through the air toward him, but he was easily able to step out of its way. The Roller, apparently, could throw straight, but not hard nor far. The first rock had struck him only because he had been sitting down and had not seen it coming until it was almost upon him.

Even as he stepped aside from that weak second throw, Carson drew back his right arm and let fly with the rock that was still in his hand. If missiles, he thought with sudden elation, can cross the barrier, then two can play at the game of throwing them. And the good right arm of an Earthman—

He couldn't miss a three-foot sphere at only four-yard range, and he didn't miss. The rock whizzed straight, and with a speed several times that of the missiles the Roller had thrown. It hit dead center, but it hit flat, unfortunately, instead of point first.

But it hit with a resounding thump, and obviously it hurt. The Roller had been reaching for another rock, but it changed its mind and got out of there instead. By the time Carson could pick up and throw another rock, the Roller was forty yards back from the barrier and going strong.

His second throw missed by feet, and his third throw was short. The Roller was back out of range—at least out of range of a missile heavy enough to be damaging.

Carson grinned. That round had been his. Except—

He quit grinning as he bent over to examine the calf of his leg. A jagged edge of the stone had made a pretty deep cut, several inches long. It was bleeding pretty freely, but he didn't think it had gone deep enough to hit an artery. If it stopped bleeding of its own accord, well and good. If not, he was in for trouble.

Finding out one thing, though, took precedence over that cut. The nature of the barrier.

He went forward to it again, this time groping with his hands before him. He found it; then holding one hand against it, he tossed a handful of sand at it with the other hand. The sand went right through. His hand didn't.

Organic matter versus inorganic? No, because the dead lizard had gone through it, and a lizard, alive or dead, was certainly organic. Plant life? He broke off a twig and poked it at the barrier. The twig went through, with no resistance, but when his fingers gripping the twig came to the barrier, they were stopped.

*He* couldn't get through it, nor could the Roller. But rocks and sand and a dead lizard—

How about a live lizard? He went hunting, under bushes, until he found one, and caught it. He tossed it gently against the barrier and it bounced back and scurried away across the blue sand.

That gave him the answer, in so far as he could determine it now. The screen was a barrier to living things. Dead or inorganic matter could cross it.

That off his mind, Carson looked at his injured leg again. The bleeding was lessening, which meant he wouldn't need to worry about making a tourniquet. But he should find some water, if any was available, to clean the wound.

Water—the thought of it made him realize that he was getting awfully thirsty. He'd *have* to find water, in case this contest turned out to be a protracted one.

Limping slightly now, he started off to make a full circuit of his half of the arena. Guiding himself with one hand along the barrier, he walked to his right until he came to the curving sidewall. It was visible, a dull blue-gray at close range, and the surface of it felt just like the central barrier.

He experimented by tossing a handful of sand at it, and the sand reached the wall and disappeared as it went through. The hemispherical shell was a force-field, too. But an opaque one, instead of transparent like the barrier.

He followed it around until he came back to the barrier, and walked back along the barrier to the point from which he'd started.

No sign of water.

Worried now, he started a series of zigzags back and forth between the barrier and the wall, covering the intervening space thoroughly.

No water. Blue sand, blue bushes, and intolerable heat. Nothing else.

It must be his imagination, he told himself angrily, that he was suffering *that* much from thirst. How long had he been here? Of course, no time at all, according to his own space-time frame. The Entity had told him time stood still out there, while he was here. But his body processes went on here, just the same. And according to his body's reckoning, how long had he been here? Three or four hours, perhaps. Certainly not long enough to be suffering seriously from thirst.

But he was suffering from it; his throat dry and parched. Probably the intense heat was the cause. It was *hot!* A hundred and thirty Fahrenheit, at a guess. A dry, still heat without the slightest movement of air.

He was limping rather badly, and utterly fagged out when he'd finished the futile exploration of his domain.

He stared across at the motionless Roller and hoped it was as miserable as he was. And quite possibly it wasn't enjoying this, either. The Entity had said the conditions here were equally unfamiliar and equally uncomfortable for both of them. Maybe the Roller came from a planet where two-hundred degree heat was the norm. Maybe it was freezing while he was roasting.

Maybe the air was as much too thick for it as it was too thin for him. For the exertion of his explorations had left him panting. The atmosphere here, he realized now, was not much thicker than that on Mars.

No water.

That meant a deadline, for him at any rate. Unless he could find a way to cross that barrier or to kill his enemy from this side of it, thirst would kill him, eventually.

It gave him a feeling of desperate urgency. He *must* hurry. But he made himself sit down a moment to rest, to think. What was there to do? Nothing, and yet so many things.

The several varieties of bushes, for example. They didn't look promising, but he'd have to examine them for possibilities. And his leg—he'd have to do something about that, even without water to clean it. Gather ammunition in the form of rocks. Find a rock that would make a good knife.

His leg hurt rather badly now, and he decided that came first. One type of bush had leaves—or things rather similar to leaves. He pulled off a handful of them and decided, after examination, to take a chance on them. He used them to clean off the sand and dirt and caked blood, then made a pad of fresh leaves and tied it over the wound with tendrils from the same bush.

The tendrils proved unexpectedly tough and strong. They were slender, and soft and pliable, yet he couldn't break them at all. He had to saw them off the bush with the sharp edge of a piece of the blue flint. Some of the thicker ones were over a foot long, and he filed away in his memory, for future reference, the fact that a bunch of the thick ones, tied together, would make a pretty serviceable rope. Maybe he'd be able to think of a use for rope.

Next he made himself a knife. The blue flint *did* chip. From a foot-long splinter of it, he fashioned himself a crude but lethal weapon. And of tendrils from the bush, he made himself a rope-belt through which he could thrust the flint knife, to keep it with him all the time and yet have his hands free.

He went back to studying the bushes. There were three other types. One was leafless, dry, brittle, rather like a dried tumbleweed. Another was of soft, crumbly wood, almost like punk. It looked and felt as though it would make excellent tinder for a fire. The third type was the most nearly wood-like. It had fragile leaves that wilted at a touch, but the stalks, although short, were straight and strong.

It was horribly, unbearably hot.

He limped up to the barrier, felt to make sure that it was still there. It was.

He stood watching the Roller for a while. It was keeping a safe distance back from the barrier, out of effective stone-throwing range. It was moving around back there, doing something. He couldn't tell what it was doing.

Once it stopped moving, came a little closer, and seemed to concentrate its attention on him. Again Carson had to fight off a wave of nausea. He threw a stone at it and the Roller retreated and went back to whatever it had been doing before.

At least he could make it keep its distance.

And, he thought bitterly, a devil of a lot of good *that* did him. Just the same, he spent the next hour or two gathering stones of suitable size for throwing, and making several neat piles of them, near his side of the barrier.

His throat burned now. It was difficult for him to think about anything except water.

But he *had* to think about other things. About getting through that barrier, under or over it, getting *at* that red sphere and killing it before this place of heat and thirst killed him first.

The barrier went to the wall upon either side, but how high and how far under the sand?

For just a moment, Carson's mind was too fuzzy to think out how he could find out either of those things. Idly, sitting there in the hot sand—and he didn't remember sitting down—he watched a blue lizard crawl from the shelter of one bush to the shelter of another.

From under the second bush, it looked out at him.

Carson grinned at it. Maybe he was getting a bit punch-drunk, because he remembered suddenly the old story of the desert-colonists on Mars, taken from an older desert story of Earth— "Pretty soon you get so lonesome you find yourself talking to the lizards, and then not so long after that you find the lizards talking back to you—"

He should have been concentrating, of course, on how to kill the Roller, but instead he grinned at the lizard and said, "Hello, there."

The lizard took a few steps toward him. "Hello," it said.

Carson was stunned for a moment, and then he put back

his head and roared with laughter. It didn't hurt his throat to do so, either; he hadn't been *that* thirsty.

Why not? Why should the Entity who thought up this nightmare of a place not have a sense of humor, along with the other powers he had? Talking lizards, equipped to talk back in my own language, if I talk to them— It's a nice touch.

He grinned at the lizard and said, "Come on over." But the lizard turned and ran away, scurrying from bush to bush until it was out of sight.

He was thirsty again.

And he had to *do* something. He couldn't win this contest by sitting here sweating and feeling miserable. He had to *do* something. But what?

Get through the barrier. But he couldn't get through it, or over it. But was he certain he couldn't get under it? And come to think of it, didn't one sometimes find water by digging? Two birds with one stone—

Painfully now, Carson limped up to the barrier and started digging, scooping up sand a double handful at a time. It was slow, hard work because the sand ran in at the edges and the deeper he got the bigger in diameter the hole had to be. How many hours it took him, he didn't know, but he hit bedrock four feet down. Dry bedrock; no sign of water.

And the force-field of the barrier went down clear to the bedrock. No dice. No water. Nothing.

He crawled out of the hole and lay there panting, and then raised his head to look across and see what the Roller was doing. It must be doing something back there.

It was. It was making something out of wood from the bushes, tied together with tendrils. A queerly shaped framework about four feet high and roughly square. To see it better, Carson climbed up onto the mound of sand he had excavated from the hole, and stood there staring.

There were two long levers sticking out of the back of it, one with a cup-shaped affair on the end of it. Seemed to be some sort of a catapult, Carson thought.

Sure enough, the Roller was lifting a sizable rock into the cup-shaped outfit. One of his tentacles moved the other lever up and down for awhile, and then he turned the machine slightly as though aiming it and the lever with the stone flew up and forward.

The stone arced several yards over Carson's head, so far away that he didn't have to duck, but he judged the distance it had traveled, and whistled softly. He couldn't throw a rock that weight more than half that distance. And even retreating to the rear of his domain wouldn't put him out of range of that machine, if the Roller shoved it forward almost to the barrier.

Another rock whizzed over. Not quite so far away this time.

That thing could be dangerous, he decided. Maybe he'd better do something about it.

Moving from side to side along the barrier, so the catapult couldn't bracket him, he whaled a dozen rocks at it. But that wasn't going to be any good, he saw. They had to be light rocks, or he couldn't throw them that far. If they hit the framework, they bounced off harmlessly. And the Roller had no difficulty, at that distance, in moving aside from those that came near it.

Besides, his arm was tiring badly. He ached all over from sheer weariness. If he could only rest awhile without having to duck rocks from that catapult at regular intervals of maybe thirty seconds each—

He stumbled back to the rear of the arena. Then he saw even that wasn't any good. The rocks reached back there, too, only there were longer intervals between them, as though it took longer to wind up the mechanism, whatever it was, of the catapult.

Wearily he dragged himself back to the barrier again. Several times he fell and could barely rise to his feet to go on. He was, he knew, near the limit of his endurance. Yet he didn't dare stop moving now, until and unless he could put that catapult out of action. If he fell asleep, he'd never wake up.

One of the stones from it gave him the first glimmer of an idea. It struck upon one of the piles of stones he'd gathered together near the barrier to use as ammunition, and it struck sparks.

Sparks. Fire. Primitive man had made fire by striking sparks, and with some of those dry crumbly bushes as tinder—

Luckily, a bush of that type was near him. He broke it off, took it over to the pile of stones, then patiently hit one stone against another until a spark touched the punklike wood of the bush. It went up in flames so fast that it singed his eyebrows and was burned to an ash within seconds.

But he had the idea now, and within minutes he had a little fire going in the lee of the mound of sand he'd made digging the hole an hour or two ago. Tinder bushes had started it, and other bushes which burned, but more slowly, kept it a steady flame.

The tough wirelike tendrils didn't burn readily; that made the firebombs easy to make and throw. A bundle of faggots tied about a small stone to give it weight and a loop of the tendril to swing it by.

He made half a dozen of them before he lighted and threw the first. It went wide, and the Roller started a quick retreat, pulling the catapult after him. But Carson had the others ready and threw them in rapid succession. The fourth wedged in the catapult's framework, and did the trick. The Roller tried desperately to put out the spreading blaze by throwing sand, but its clawed tentacles would take only a spoonful at a time and his efforts were ineffectual. The catapult burned.

The Roller moved safely away from the fire and seemed to concentrate its attention on Carson and again he felt that wave of hatred and nausea. But more weakly; either the Roller itself was weakening or Carson had learned how to protect himself against the mental attack.

He thumbed his nose at it and then sent it scuttling back to safety by throwing a stone. The Roller went clear to the back of its half of the arena and started pulling up bushes again. Probably it was going to make another catapult.

Carson verified—for the hundredth time—that the barrier was still operating, and then found himself sitting in the sand beside it because he was suddenly too weak to stand up.

His leg throbbed steadily now and the pangs of thirst were

severe. But those things paled beside the utter physical exhaustion that gripped his entire body.

And the heat.

Hell must be like this, he thought. The hell that the ancients had believed in. He fought to stay awake, and yet staying awake seemed futile, for there was nothing he could do. Nothing, while the barrier remained impregnable and the Roller stayed back out of range.

But there must be *something*. He tried to remember things he had read in books of archaeology about the methods of fighting used back in the days before metal and plastic. The stone missile, that had come first, he thought. Well, that he already had.

The only improvement on it would be a catapult, such as the Roller had made. But he'd never be able to make one, with the tiny bits of wood available from the bushes—no single piece longer than a foot or so. Certainly he could figure out a mechanism for one, but he didn't have the endurance left for a task that would take days.

Days? But the Roller had made one. Had they been here days already? Then he remembered that the Roller had many tentacles to work with and undoubtedly could do such work faster than he.

And besides, a catapult wouldn't decide the issue. He had to do better than that.

Bow and arrow? No; he had tried archery once and knew his own ineptness with a bow. Even with a modern sportsman's durasteel weapon, made for accuracy. With such a crude, pieced-together outfit as he could make here, he doubted if he could shoot as far as he could throw a rock, and knew he couldn't shoot as straight.

Spear? Well, he *could* make that. It would be useless as a throwing weapon at any distance, but would be a handy thing at close range, if he ever got to close range.

And making one would give him something to do. Help keep his mind from wandering, as it was beginning to do. Sometimes now, he had to concentrate awhile before he could remember why he was here, why he had to kill the Roller.

Luckily he was still beside one of the piles of stones. He sorted through it until he found one shaped roughly like a spearhead. With a smaller stone he began to chip it into shape, fashioning sharp shoulders on the sides so that if it penetrated it would not pull out again.

Like a harpoon? There was something in that idea, he thought. A harpoon was better than a spear, maybe, for this crazy contest. If he could once get it into the Roller, and had a rope on it, he could pull the Roller up against the barrier and the stone blade of his knife would reach through that barrier, even if his hands wouldn't.

The shaft was harder to make than the head. But by splitting and joining the main stems of four of the bushes, and wrapping the joints with the tough but thin tendrils, he got a strong shaft about four feet long, and tied the stone head in a notch cut in the end.

It was crude, but strong.

And the rope. With the thin tough tendrils he made himself twenty feet of line. It was light and didn't look strong, but he knew it would hold his weight and to spare. He tied one end of it to the shaft of the harpoon and the other end about his right wrist. At least, if he threw his harpoon across the barrier, he'd be able to pull it back if he missed.

Then when he had tied the last knot and there was nothing more he could do, the heat and the weariness and the pain in his leg and the dreadful thirst were suddenly a thousand times worse than they had been before.

He tried to stand up, to see what the Roller was doing now, and found he couldn't get to his feet. On the third try, he got as far as his knees and then fell flat again.

"I've got to sleep," he thought. "If a showdown came now, I'd be helpless. He could come up here and kill me, if he knew. I've got to regain some strength."

Slowly, painfully, he crawled back away from the barrier. Ten yards, twenty—

The jar of something thudding against the sand near him waked him from a confused and horrible dream to a more confused and more horrible reality, and he opened his eyes again to blue radiance over blue sand.

How long had he slept? A minute? A day?

Another stone thudded nearer and threw sand on him. He got his arms under him and sat up. He turned around and saw the Roller twenty yards away, at the barrier.

It rolled away hastily as he sat up, not stopping until it was as far away as it could get.

He'd fallen asleep too soon, he realized, while he was still in range of the Roller's throwing ability. Seeing him lying motionless, it had dared come up to the barrier to throw at him. Luckily, it didn't realize how weak he was, or it could have stayed there and kept on throwing stones.

Had he slept long? He didn't think so, because he felt just as he had before. Not rested at all, no thirstier, no different. Probably he'd been there only a few minutes.

He started crawling again, this time forcing himself to keep going until he was as far as he could go, until the colorless, opaque wall of the arena's outer shell was only a yard away.

Then things slipped away again—

When he awoke, nothing about him was changed, but this time he knew that he had slept a long time.

The first thing he became aware of was the inside of his mouth; it was dry, caked. His tongue was swollen.

Something was wrong, he knew, as he returned slowly to full awareness. He felt less tired, the stage of utter exhaustion had passed. The sleep had taken care of that.

But there was pain, agonizing pain. It wasn't until he tried to move that he knew that it came from his leg.

He raised his head and looked down at it. It was swollen terribly below the knee and the swelling showed even halfway up his thigh. The plant tendrils he had used to tie on the protective pad of leaves now cut deeply into the swollen flesh.

To get his knife under that imbedded lashing would have been impossible. Fortunately, the final knot was over the shin bone, in front, where the vine cut in less deeply than elsewhere. He was able, after an agonizing effort, to untie the knot.

A look under the pad of leaves told him the worst. Infection and blood poisoning, both pretty bad and getting worse.

And without drugs, without cloth, without even *water*, there wasn't a thing he could do about it.

Not a thing, except *die*, when the poison had spread through his system.

He knew it was hopeless, then, and that he'd lost.

And with him, humanity. When he died here, out there in the universe he knew, all his friends, everybody, would die too. And Earth and the colonized planets would be the home of the red, rolling, alien Outsiders. Creatures out of nightmare, things without a human attribute, who picked lizards apart for the fun of it.

It was the thought of that which gave him courage to start crawling, almost blindly in pain, toward the barrier again. Not crawling on hands and knees this time, but pulling himself along only by his arms and hands.

A chance in a million, that maybe he'd have strength left, when he got there, to throw his harpoon-spear just *once*, and with deadly effect, if—on another chance in a million—the Roller would come up to the barrier. Or if the barrier was gone, now.

It took him years, it seemed, to get there.

The barrier wasn't gone. It was as impassable as when he'd first felt it.

And the Roller wasn't at the barrier. By raising up on his elbows, he could see it at the back of its part of the arena, working on a wooden framework that was a half-completed duplicate of the catapult he'd destroyed.

It was moving slowly now. Undoubtedly it had weakened, too.

But Carson doubted that it would ever need that second catapult. He'd be dead, he thought, before it was finished.

If he could attract it to the barrier, now, while he was still alive—He waved an arm and tried to shout, but his parched throat would make no sound.

Or if he could get through the barrier—

His mind must have slipped for a moment, for he found himself beating his fists against the barrier in futile rage, and made himself stop.

He closed his eyes, tried to make himself calm.

"Hello," said the voice.

It was a small, thin voice. It sounded like—

He opened his eyes and turned his head. It *was* a lizard.

"Go away," Carson wanted to say. "Go away, you're not really there, or you're there but not really talking. I'm imagining things again."

But he couldn't talk; his throat and tongue were past all speech with the dryness. He closed his eyes again.

"Hurt," said the voice. "Kill. Hurt—kill. Come."

He opened his eyes again. The blue ten-legged lizard was still there. It ran a little way along the barrier, came back, started off again, and came back.

"Hurt," it said. "Kill. Come."

Again it started off, and came back. Obviously it wanted Carson to follow it along the barrier.

He closed his eyes again. The voice kept on. The same three meaningless words. Each time he opened his eyes, it ran off and came back.

"Hurt. Kill. Come."

Carson groaned. There would be no peace unless he followed the blasted thing. Like it wanted him to.

He followed it, crawling. Another sound, a high-pitched squealing, came to his ears and grew louder.

There was something lying in the sand, writhing, squealing. Something small, blue, that looked like a lizard and yet didn't—

Then he saw what it was—the lizard whose legs the Roller had pulled off, so long ago. But it wasn't dead; it had come back to life and was wriggling and screaming in agony.

"Hurt," said the other lizard. "Hurt. Kill. Kill."

Carson understood. He took the flint knife from his belt and killed the tortured creature. The live lizard scurried off quickly.

Carson turned back to the barrier. He leaned his hands and head against it and watched the Roller, far back, working on the new catapult.

"I could get that far," he thought, "if I could get through. If I could get through, I might win yet. It looks weak, too. I might—"

And then there was another reaction of black hopelessness, when pain snapped his will and he wished that he were dead. He envied the lizard he'd just killed. It didn't have to live on and suffer. And he did. It would be hours, it might be days, before the blood poisoning killed him.

If only he could use that knife on himself—

But he knew he wouldn't. As long as he was alive, there was the millionth chance—

He was straining, pushing on the barrier with the flat of his hands, and he noticed his arms, how thin and scrawny they were now. He must really have been here a long time, for days, to get as thin as that.

How much longer now, before he died? How much more heat and thirst and pain could flesh stand?

For a little while he was almost hysterical again, and then came a time of deep calm, and a thought that was startling.

The lizard he had just killed. *It had crossed the barrier, still alive.* It had come from the Roller's side; the Roller had pulled off its legs and then tossed it contemptuously at him and it had come through the barrier. He'd thought, because the lizard was dead.

But it hadn't been dead; it had been unconscious.

A live lizard couldn't go through the barrier, but an unconscious one could. The barrier was not a barrier, then, to living flesh, but to conscious flesh. It was a *mental* projection, a *mental* hazard.

And with that thought, Carson started crawling along the barrier to make his last desperate gamble. A hope so forlorn that only a dying man would have dared try it.

No use weighing the odds of success. Not when, if he didn't try it, those odds were infinitely to zero.

He crawled along the barrier to the dune of sand, about

four feet high, which he'd scooped out in trying—how many days ago?—to dig under the barrier or to reach water.

That mound was right at the barrier, its farther slope half on one side of the barrier, half on the other.

Taking with him a rock from the pile nearby, he climbed up to the top of the dune and over the top, and lay there against the barrier, his weight leaning against it so that if the barrier were taken away he'd roll on down the short slope, into the enemy territory.

He checked to be sure that the knife was safely in his rope belt, that the harpoon was in the crook of his left arm and that the twenty-foot rope was fastened to it and to his wrist.

Then with his right hand he raised the rock with which he would hit himself on the head. Luck would have to be with him on that blow; it would have to be hard enough to knock him out, but not hard enough to knock him out for long.

He had a hunch that the Roller was watching him, and would see him roll down through the barrier, and come to investigate. It would think he was dead, he hoped—he thought it had probably drawn the same deduction about the nature of the barrier that he had drawn. But it would come cautiously. He would have a little time—

He struck.

Pain brought him back to consciousness. A sudden, sharp pain in his hip that was different from the throbbing pain in his head and the throbbing pain in his leg.

But he had, thinking things out before he had struck himself, anticipated that very pain, even hoped for it, and had steeled himself against awakening with a sudden movement.

He lay still, but opened his eyes just a slit, and saw that he had guessed rightly. The Roller was coming closer. It was twenty feet away and the pain that had awakened him was the stone it had tossed to see whether he was alive or dead.

He lay still. It came closer, fifteen feet away, and stopped again. Carson scarcely breathed.

As nearly as possible, he was keeping his mind a blank, lest its telepathic ability detect consciousness in him. And with his mind blanked out that way, the impact of its thoughts upon his mind was nearly soul-shattering.

He felt sheer horror at the utter *alienness*, the *differentness* of those thoughts. Things that he felt but could not understand and could never express, because no terrestrial language had words, no terrestrial mind had images to fit them. The mind of a spider, he thought, or the mind of a praying mantis or a Martian sand-serpent, raised to intelligence and put in telepathic rapport with human minds, would be a homely familiar thing, compared to this.

He understood now that the Entity had been right: Man or Roller, and the universe was not a place that could hold them both. Farther apart than god and devil, there could never be even a balance between them.

Closer. Carson waited until it was only feet away, until its clawed tentacles reached out—

Oblivious to agony now, he sat up, raised and flung the harpoon with all the strength that remained to him. Or he thought it was all; sudden final strength flooded through him, along with a sudden forgetfulness of pain as definite as a nerve block.

As the Roller, deeply stabbed by the harpoon, rolled away, Carson tried to get to his feet to run after it. He couldn't do that; he fell, but kept crawling.

It reached the end of the rope, and he was jerked forward by the pull of his wrist. It dragged him a few feet and then stopped. Carson kept on going, pulling himself toward it hand over hand along the rope.

It stopped there, writhing tentacles trying in vain to pull out the harpoon. It seemed to shudder and quiver, and then it must have realized that it couldn't get away, for it rolled back toward him, clawed tentacles reaching out.

Stone knife in hand, he met it. He stabbed, again and again, while those horrid claws ripped skin and flesh and muscle from his body.

He stabbed and slashed, and at last it was still.

A bell was ringing, and it took him a while after he'd opened his eyes to tell where he was and what it was. He was strapped into the seat of his scouter, and the visiplate before him showed only empty space. No Outsider ship and no impossible planet.

The bell was the communications plate signal; someone wanted him to switch power into the receiver. Purely reflex action enabled him to reach forward and throw the lever.

The face of Brander, captain of the *Magellan*, mother-ship of his group of scouters, flashed into the screen. His face was pale and his black eyes glowed with excitement.

"*Magellan* to Carson," he snapped. "Come on in. The fight's over. We've won!"

The screen went blank; Brander would be signaling the other scouters of his command.

Slowly, Carson set the controls for the return. Slowly, unbelievingly, he unstrapped himself from the seat and went back to get a drink at the cold-water tank. For some reason, he was unbelievably thirsty. He drank six glasses.

He leaned there against the wall, trying to think.

*Had* it happened? He was in good health, sound, uninjured. His thirst had been mental rather than physical; his throat hadn't been dry. His leg—

He pulled up his trouser leg and looked at the calf. There was a long white scar there, but a perfectly healed scar. It hadn't been there before. He zipped open the front of his shirt and saw that his chest and abdomen was criss-crossed with tiny, almost unnoticeable, perfectly healed scars.

It *had* happened.

The scouter, under automatic control, was already entering the hatch of the mother-ship. The grapples pulled it into its individual lock, and a moment later a buzzer indicated that the lock was air-filled. Carson opened the hatch and stepped outside, went through the double door of the lock.

He went right to Brander's office, went in, and saluted.

Brander still looked dizzily dazed. "Hi, Carson," he said. "What you missed! What a show!"

"What happened, sir?"

"Don't know, exactly. We fired one salvo, and their whole fleet went up in dust! Whatever it was jumped from ship to ship in a flash, even the ones we hadn't aimed at and that were out of range! The whole fleet disintegrated before our eyes, and we didn't get the paint of a single ship scratched!

"We can't even claim credit for it. Must have been some unstable component in the metal they used, and our sighting shot just set it off. Man, oh man, too bad you missed all the excitement."

Carson managed to grin. It was a sickly ghost of a grin, for it would be days before he'd be over the mental impact of his experience, but the captain wasn't watching, and didn't notice.

"Yes, sir," he said. Common sense, more than modesty, told him he'd be branded forever as the worst liar in space if he ever said any more than that. "Yes, sir, too bad I missed all the excitement."

**Robert Sheckley**

# THE LEECH

*Interstellar space is still a great question mark. What it may contain of wonders, mysteries, horrors, man does not yet know. The following nightmare of what one sort of space-being might do to Earth is not, we hope, typical of the discoveries that will be made when man finally learns how to cross between the stars.*

*And let us also hope that such a monstrous entity does not discover us, here on earth, at least not before we learn how to cope with it . . .*

*This story was originally published under a pseudonym, "Phillips Barbee." It is at Mr. Sheckley's request that his real name is now appended to it.*

---

THE LEECH WAS WAITING FOR FOOD. FOR MILLENNIA IT HAD been drifting across the vast emptiness of space. Without consciousness, it had spent the countless centuries in the void between the stars. It was unaware when it finally reached a sun. Life-giving radiation flared around the hard, dry spore. Gravitation tugged at it.

A planet claimed it, with other stellar debris, and the leech fell, still dead-seeming within its tough spore case.

---

One speck of dust among many, the winds blew it around the Earth, played with it, and let it fall.

On the ground, it began to stir. Nourishment soaked in, permeating the spore case. It grew— and fed.

Frank Conners came up on the porch and coughed twice. "Say, pardon me, Professor," he said.

The long, pale man didn't stir from the sagging couch. His horn-rimmed glasses were perched on his forehead, and he was snoring very gently.

"I'm awful sorry to disturb you," Conners said, pushing back his battered felt hat. "I know it's your restin' week and all, but there's something damned funny in the ditch."

The pale man's left eyebrow twitched, but he showed no other sign of having heard.

Frank Conners coughed again, holding his spade in one purple-veined hand. "Didja hear me, Professor?"

"Of course I heard you," Micheals said in a muffled voice, his eyes still closed. "You found a pixie."

"A what?" Conners asked, squinting at Micheals.

"A little man in a green suit. Feed him milk, Conners."

"No, sir. I think it's a rock."

Micheals opened one eye and focused it in Conners' general direction.

"I'm awfully sorry about it," Conners said. Professor Micheals' resting week was a ten-year-old custom, and his only eccentricity. All winter Micheals taught anthropology, worked on half a dozen committees, dabbled in physics and chemistry, and still found time to write a book a year. When summer came, he was tired.

Arriving at his worked-out New York State farm, it was his invariable rule to do absolutely nothing for a week. He hired Frank Conners to cook for that week and generally make himself useful, while Professor Micheals slept.

During the second week, Micheals would wander around, look at the trees and fish. By the third week he would be getting a tan, reading, repairing the sheds and climbing mountains. At the end of four weeks, he could hardly wait to get back to the city.

But the resting week was sacred.

"I really wouldn't bother you for anything small," Conners said apologetically. "But that damned rock melted two inches off my spade."

Micheals opened both eyes and sat up. Conners held out the spade. The rounded end was sheared cleanly off. Micheals swung himself off the couch and slipped his feet into battered moccasins.

"Let's see this wonder," he said.

The object was lying in the ditch at the end of the front lawn, three feet from the main road. It was round, about the size of a truck tire, and solid throughout. It was about an inch thick, as far as he could tell, grayish black and intricately veined.

"Don't touch it," Conners warned.

"I'm not going to. Let me have your spade." Micheals took the spade and prodded the object experimentally. It was completely unyielding. He held the spade to the surface for a moment, then withdrew it. Another inch was gone.

Micheals frowned, and pushed his glasses tighter against his nose. He held the spade against the rock with one hand, the other held close to the surface. More of the spade disappeared.

"Doesn't seem to be generating heat," he said to Conners. "Did you notice any the first time?"

Conners shook his head.

Micheals picked up a clod of dirt and tossed it on the object. The dirt dissolved quickly, leaving no trace on the gray-black surface. A large stone followed the dirt, and disappeared in the same way.

"Isn't that just about the damnedest thing you ever saw, Professor?" Conners asked.

"Yes," Micheals agreed, standing up again. "It just about is."

He hefted the spade and brought it down smartly on the

object. When it hit, he almost dropped the spade. He had been gripping the handle rigidly, braced for a recoil. But the spade struck that unyielding surface and *stayed*. There was no perceptible give, but absolutely no recoil.

"Whatcha think it is?" Conners asked.

"It's no stone," Micheals said. He stepped back. "A leech drinks blood. This thing seems to be drinking dirt. And spades." He struck it a few more times, experimentally. The two men looked at each other. On the road, half a dozen Army trucks rolled past.

"I'm going to phone the college and ask a physics man about it," Micheals said. "Or a biologist. I'd like to get rid of that thing before it spoils my lawn."

They walked back to the house.

Everything fed the leech. The wind added its modicum of kinetic energy, ruffling across the gray-black surface. Rain fell, and the force of each individual drop added to its store. The water was sucked in by the all-absorbing surface.

The sunlight above it was absorbed, and converted into mass for its body. Beneath it, the soil was consumed, dirt, stones and branches broken down by the leech's complex cells and changed into energy. Energy was converted back into mass, and the leech grew.

Slowly, the first flickers of consciousness began to return. Its first realization was of the impossible smallness of its body.

It grew.

When Micheals looked the next day, the leech was eight feet across, sticking out into the road and up the side of the lawn. The following day it was almost eighteen feet in diameter, shaped to fit the contour of the ditch, and covering most of the road. That day the sheriff drove up in his model A, followed by half the town.

"Is that your leech thing, Professor Micheals?" Sheriff Flynn asked.

"That's it," Micheals said. He had spent the past days looking unsuccessfully for an acid that would dissolve the leech.

"We gotta get it out of the road," Flynn said, walking truculently up to the leech. "Something like this, you can't let it block the road, Professor. The Army's gotta use this road."

"I'm terribly sorry," Micheals said with a straight face. "Go right ahead, Sheriff. But be careful. It's hot." The leech wasn't hot, but it seemed the simplest explanation under the circumstances.

Micheals watched with interest as the sheriff tried to shove a crowbar under it. He smiled to himself when it was removed with half a foot of its length gone.

The sheriff wasn't so easily discouraged. He had come prepared for a stubborn piece of rock. He went to the rumble seat of his car and took out a blowtorch and a sledgehammer, ignited the torch and focused it on one edge of the leech.

After five minutes, there was no change. The gray didn't turn red or even seem to heat up. Sheriff Flynn continued to bake it for fifteen minutes, then called to one of the men.

"Hit that spot with the sledge, Jerry."

Jerry picked up the sledgehammer, motioned the sheriff back, and swung it over his head. He let out a howl as the hammer struck unyieldingly. There wasn't a fraction of recoil.

In the distance they heard the roar of an Army convoy.

"Now we'll get some action," Flynn said.

Micheals wasn't so sure. He walked around the periphery of the leech, asking himself what kind of substance would react that way. The answer was easy—no substance. No *known* substance.

The driver in the lead jeep held up his hand, and the long convoy ground to a halt. A hard, efficient-looking officer stepped out of the jeep. From the star on either shoulder, Micheals knew he was a brigadier general.

"You can't block this road," the general said. He was a tall, spare man in suntans, with a sunburned face and cold eyes. "Please clear that thing away."

"We can't move it," Micheals said. He told the general what had happened in the past few days.

"It must be moved," the general said. "This convoy must

go through." He walked closer and looked at the leech. "You
say it can't be jacked up by a crowbar? A torch won't burn
it?"

"That's right," Micheals said, smiling faintly.

"Driver," the general said over his shoulder. "Ride over it."

Micheals started to protest, but stopped himself. The military mind would have to find out in its own way.

The driver put his jeep in gear and shot forward, jump-
ing the leech's four-inch edge. The jeep got to the center of
the leech and stopped.

"I didn't tell you to stop!" the general bellowed.

"I didn't, sir!" the driver protested.

The jeep had been yanked to a stop and had stalled. The
driver started it again, shifted to four-wheel drive, and tried
to ram forward. The jeep was fixed immovably as though
set in concrete.

"Pardon me," Micheals said. "If you look, you can see
that the tires are melting down."

The general stared, his hand creeping automatically toward his pistol belt. Then he shouted, "Jump, driver! Don't
touch that gray stuff."

White-faced, the driver climbed to the hood of his
jeep, looked around him, and jumped clear.

There was complete silence as everyone watched the jeep.
First its tires melted down, and then the rims. The body, resting on the gray surface, melted, too.

The aerial was the last to go.

The general began to swear softly under his breath. He
turned to the driver. "Go back and have some men bring up
hand grenades and dynamite."

The driver ran back to the convoy.

"I don't know what you've got here," the general said.
"But it's not going to stop a U.S. Army convoy."

Micheals wasn't so sure.

The leech was nearly awake now, and its body was calling
for more and more food. It dissolved the soil under it at a
furious rate, filling it in with its own body, flowing outward.

A large object landed on it, and that became food also. Then suddenly—

A burst of energy against its surface, and then another, and another. It consumed them gratefully, converting them into mass. Little metal pellets struck it, and their kinetic energy was absorbed, their mass converted. More explosions took place, helping to fill the starving cells.

It began to sense things—controlled combustion around it, vibrations of wind, mass movements.

There was another, greater explosion, a taste of *real* food! Greedily it ate, growing faster. It waited anxiously for more explosions, while its cells screamed for food.

But no more came. It continued to feed on the soil and on the Sun's energy. Night came, noticeable for its lesser energy possibilities, and then more days and nights. Vibrating objects continued to move around it.

It ate and grew and flowed.

Micheals stood on a little hill, watching the dissolution of his house. The leech was several hundred yards across now, lapping at his front porch.

Good-by, home, Micheals thought, remembering the ten summers he had spent there.

The porch collapsed into the body of the leech. Bit by bit, the house crumpled.

The leech looked like a field of lava now, a blasted spot on the green Earth.

"Pardon me, sir," a soldier said, coming up behind him. "General O'Donnell would like to see you."

"Right," Micheals said, and took his last look at the house.

He followed the soldier through the barbed wire that had been set up in a half-mile circle around the leech. A company of soldiers was on guard around it, keeping back the reporters and the hundreds of curious people who had flocked to the scene. Micheals wondered why he was still allowed inside. Probably, he decided, because most of this was taking place on his land.

The soldier brought him to a tent. Micheals stooped and went in. General O'Donnell, still in suntans, was seated at a small desk. He motioned Micheals to a chair.

"I've been put in charge of getting rid of this leech," he said to Micheals.

Micheals nodded, not commenting on the advisability of giving a soldier a scientist's job.

"You're a professor, aren't you?"

"Yes. Anthropology."

"Good. Smoke?" The general lighted Micheals' cigarette. "I'd like you to stay around here in an advisory capacity. You were one of the first to see this leech. I'd appreciate your observations on—" he smiled—"the enemy."

"I'd be glad to," Micheals said. "However, I think this is more in the line of a physicist or a biochemist."

"I don't want this place cluttered with scientists," General O'Donnell said, frowning at the tip of his cigarette. "Don't get me wrong. I have the greatest appreciation for science. I am, if I do say so, a scientific soldier. I'm always interested in the latest weapons. You can't fight any kind of a war any more without science."

O'Donnell's sunburned face grew firm. "But I can't have a team of longhairs poking around this thing for the next month, holding me up. My job is to destroy it, by any means in my power, and at once. I am going to do just that."

"I don't think you'll find it that easy," Micheals said.

"That's what I want you for," O'Donnell said. "Tell me why and I'll figure out a way of doing it."

"Well, as far as I can figure out, the leech is an organic mass-energy converter, and a frighteningly efficient one. I would guess that it has a double cycle. First, it converts mass into energy, then back into mass for its body. Second, energy is converted directly into the body mass. How this takes place, I do not know. The leech is not protoplasmic. It may not even be cellular—"

"So we need something big against it," O'Donnell interrupted. "Well, that's all right. I've got some big stuff here."

"I don't think you understand me," Micheals said. "Perhaps I'm not phrasing this very well. *The leech eats energy.* It can consume the strength of any energy weapon you use against it."

"What happens," O'Donnell asked, "if it keeps on eating?"

"I have no idea what its growth-limits are," Micheals said. "Its growth may be limited only by its food source."

"You mean it could continue to grow probably forever?"

"It could possibly grow as long as it had something to feed on."

"This is really a challenge," O'Donnell said. "That leech can't be totally impervious to force."

"It seems to be. I suggest you get some physicists in here. Some biologists also. Have them figure out a way of nullifying it."

The general put out his cigarette. "Professor, I cannot wait while scientists wrangle. There is an axiom of mine which I am going to tell you." He paused impressively. "Nothing is impervious to force. Muster enough force and anything will give. *Anything.*

"Professor," the general continued, in a friendlier tone, "you shouldn't sell short the science you represent. We have, massed under North Hill, the greatest accumulation of energy and radioactive weapons ever assembled in one spot. Do you think your leech can stand the full force of them?"

"I suppose it's possible to overload the thing," Micheals said doubtfully. He realized now why the general wanted him around. He supplied the trappings of science, without the authority to override O'Donnell.

"Come with me," General O'Donnell said cheerfully, getting up and holding back a flap of the tent. "We're going to crack that leech in half."

After a long wait, rich food started to come again, piped into one side of it. First there was only a little, and then more and more. Radiations, vibrations, explosions, solids, liquids—an amazing variety of edibles. It accepted them all. But the food was coming too slowly for the starving cells, for new cells were constantly adding their demands to the rest.

The ever-hungry body screamed for more food, faster!

Now that it had reached a fairly efficient size, it was fully awake. It puzzled over the energy-impressions around it, locating the source of the new food massed in one spot.

Effortlessly it pushed itself into the air, flew a little way and dropped on the food. Its super-efficient cells eagerly gulped the rich radioactive substances. But it did not ignore the lesser potentials of metal and clumps of carbohydrates.

"The damned fools," General O'Donnell said. "Why did they have to panic? You'd think they'd never been trained." He paced the ground outside his tent, now in a new location three miles back.

The leech had grown to two miles in diameter. Three farming communities had been evacuated.

Micheals, standing beside the general, was still stupefied by the memory. The leech had accepted the massed power of the weapons for a while, and then its entire bulk had lifted in the air. The Sun had been blotted out as it flew leisurely over North Hill, and dropped. There should have been time for evacuation, but the frightened soldiers had been blind with fear.

Sixty-seven men were lost in Operation Leech, and General O'Donnell asked permission to use atomic bombs. Washington sent a group of scientists to investigate the situation.

"Haven't those experts decided yet?" O'Donnell asked, halting angrily in front of the tent. "They've been talking long enough."

"It's a hard decision," Micheals said. Since he wasn't an official member of the investigating team, he had given his information and left. "The physicists consider it a biological matter, and the biologists seem to think the chemists should have the answer. No one's an expert on this, because it's never happened before. We just don't have the data."

"It's a military problem," O'Donnell said harshly. "I'm not interested in what the thing is—I want to know what can destroy it. They'd better give me permission to use the bomb."

Micheals had made his own calculations on that. It was impossible to say for sure, but taking a flying guess at the leech's mass-energy absorption rate, figuring in its size and apparent capacity for growth, an atomic bomb *might* overload it—if used soon enough.

He estimated three days as the limit of usefulness. The leech was growing at a geometric rate. It could cover the United States in a few months.

"For a week I've been asking permission to use the bomb," O'Donnell grumbled. "And I'll get it, but not until after those jackasses end their damned talking." He stopped pacing and turned to Micheals. "I am going to destroy the leech. I am going to smash it, if that's the last thing I do. It's more than a matter of security now. It's personal pride."

That attitude might make great generals, Micheals thought, but it wasn't the way to consider this problem. It was anthropomorphic of O'Donnell to see the leech as an enemy. Even the identification, "leech," was a humanizing factor. O'Donnell was dealing with it as he would any physical obstacle, as though the leech were the simple equivalent of a large army.

But the leech was not human, not even of this planet, perhaps. It should be dealt with in its own terms.

"Here come the bright boys now," O'Donnell said.

From a nearby tent a group of weary men emerged, led by Allenson, a government biologist.

"Well," the general asked, "have you figured out what it is?"

"Just a minute, I'll hack off a sample," Allenson said, glaring through red-rimmed eyes.

"Have you figured out some *scientific* way of killing it?"

"Oh, that wasn't too difficult," Moriarty, an atomic physicist, said wryly. "Wrap it in a perfect vacuum. That'll do the trick. Or blow it off the Earth with antigravity."

"But failing that," Allenson said, "we suggest you use your atomic bombs, and use them fast."

"Is that the opinion of your entire group?" O'Donnell asked, his eyes glittering.

"Yes."

The general hurried away. Micheals joined the scientists. "He should have called us in at the very first," Allenson complained. "There's no time to consider anything but force now."

"Have you come to any conclusions about the nature of the leech?" Micheals asked.

"Only general ones," Moriarty said, "and they're about the same as yours. The leech is probably extraterrestrial in origin. It seems to have been in a spore-stage until it landed on Earth." He paused to light a pipe. "Incidentally, we should be damned glad it didn't drop in an ocean. We'd have had the Earth eaten out from under us before we knew what we were looking for."

They walked in silence for a few minutes.

"As you mentioned, it's a perfect converter—it can transform mass into energy, and any energy into mass." Moriarty grinned. "Naturally that's impossible and I have figures to prove it."

"I'm going to get a drink," Allenson said. "Anyone coming?"

"Best idea of the week," Micheals said. "I wonder how long it'll take O'Donnell to get permission to use the bomb."

"If I know politics," Moriarty said, "too long."

The findings of the government scientists were checked by other government scientists. That took a few days. Then Washington wanted to know if there wasn't some alternative to exploding an atomic bomb in the middle of New York State. It took a little time to convince them of the necessity. After that, people had to be evacuated, which took more time.

Then orders were made out, and five atomic bombs were checked out of a cache. A patrol rocket was assigned, given orders, and put under General O'Donnell's command. This took a day more.

Finally, the stubby scout rocket was winging its way over

New York. From the air, the grayish-black spot was easy to find. Like a festered wound, it stretched between Lake Placid and Elizabethtown, covering Keene and Keene Valley, and lapping at the edges of Jay.

The first bomb was released.

It had been a long wait after the first rich food. The greater radiation of day was followed by the lesser energy of night many times, as the leech ate away the Earth beneath it, absorbed the air around it, and grew. Then one day—

An amazing burst of energy!

Everything was food for the leech, but there was always the possibility of choking. The energy poured over it, drenched it, battered it, and the leech grew frantically, trying to contain the titanic dose. Still small, it quickly reached its overload limit. The strained cells, filled to satiation, were given more and more food. The strangling body built new cells at lightning speed. And—

It held. The energy was controlled, stimulating further growth. More cells took over the load, sucking in the food.

The next doses were wonderfully palatable, easily handled. The leech overflowed its bounds, growing, eating, and growing.

That was a taste of real food! The leech was as near ecstasy as it had ever been. It waited hopefully for more, but no more came.

It went back to feeding on the Earth. The energy, used to produce more cells, was soon dissipated. Soon it was hungry again.

It would always be hungry.

O'Donnell retreated with his demoralized men. They camped ten miles from the leech's southern edge, in the evacuated town of Schroon Lake. The leech was over sixty miles in diameter now and still growing fast. It lay sprawled over the Adirondack Mountains, completely blanketing everything from Saranac Lake to Port Henry, with one edge of it over Westport, in Lake Champlain.

Everyone within two hundred miles of the leech was evacuated.

General O'Donnell was given permission to use hydrogen bombs, contingent on the approval of his scientists.

"What have the bright boys decided?" O'Donnell wanted to know.

He and Micheals were in the living room of an evacuated Schroon Lake house. O'Donnell had made it his new command post.

"Why are they hedging?" O'Donnell demanded impatiently. "The leech has to be blown up quick. What are they fooling around for?"

"They're afraid of a chain reaction," Micheals told him. "A concentration of hydrogen bombs might set one up in the Earth's crust or in the atmosphere. It might do any of half a dozen things."

"Perhaps they'd like me to order a bayonet attack," O'Donnell said contemptuously.

Micheals sighed and sat down in an armchair. He was convinced that the whole method was wrong. The government scientists were being rushed into a single line of inquiry. The pressure on them was so great that they didn't have a chance to consider any other approach but force—and the leech thrived on that.

Micheals was certain that there were times when fighting fire with fire was not applicable.

Fire. Loki, god of fire. And of trickery. No, there was no answer there. But Micheals' mind was in mythology now, retreating from the unbearable present.

Allenson came in, followed by six other men.

"Well," Allenson said, "there's a damned good chance of splitting the Earth wide open if you use the number of bombs our figures show you need."

"You have to take chances in war," O'Donnell replied bluntly. "Shall I go ahead?"

Micheals saw, suddenly, that O'Donnell didn't care if he did crack the Earth. The red-faced general only knew that he was going to set off the greatest explosion ever produced by the hand of Man.

"Not so fast," Allenson said. "I'll let the others speak for themselves."

The general contained himself with difficulty. "Remember," he said, "according to your own figures, the leech is growing at the rate of twenty feet an hour."

"And speeding up," Allenson added. "But this isn't a decision to be made in haste."

Micheals found his mind wandering again, to the lightning bolts of Zeus. That was what they needed. Or the strength of Hercules.

Or—

He sat up suddenly. "Gentlemen, I believe I can offer you a possible alternative, although it's a very dim one."

They stared at him.

"Have you ever heard of Antaeus?" he asked.

The more the leech ate, the faster it grew and the hungrier it became. Although its birth was forgotten, it did remember a long way back. It had eaten a planet in that ancient past. Grown tremendous, ravenous, it had made the journey to a nearby star and eaten that, replenishing the cells converted into energy for the trip. But then there was no more food, and the next star was an enormous distance away.

It set out on the journey, but long before it reached the food, its energy ran out. Mass, converted back to energy to make the trip, was used up. It shrank.

Finally, all the energy was gone. It was a spore, drifting aimlessly, lifelessly, in space.

That was the first time. Or was it? It thought it could remember back to a distant, misty time when the Universe was evenly covered with stars. It had eaten through them, cutting away whole sections, growing, swelling. And the stars had swung off in terror, forming galaxies and constellations.

Or was that a dream?

Methodically, it fed on the Earth, wondering where the

rich food was. And then it was back again, but this time above the leech.

It waited, but the tantalizing food remained out of reach. It was able to sense how rich and pure the food was.

Why didn't it fall?

For a long time the leech waited, but the food stayed out of reach. At last, it lifted and followed.

The food retreated, up, up from the surface of the planet. The leech went after as quickly as its bulk would allow.

The rich food fled out, into space, and the leech followed. Beyond, it could sense an even richer source.

The hot, wonderful food of a sun!

O'Donnell served champagne for the scientists in the control room. Official dinners would follow, but this was the victory celebration.

"A toast," the general said, standing. The men raised their glasses. The only man not drinking was a lieutenant, sitting in front of the control board that guided the drone spaceship.

"To Micheals, for thinking of—what was it again, Micheals?"

"Antaeus." Micheals had been drinking champagne steadily, but he didn't feel elated. Antaeus, born of Ge, the Earth, and Poseidon, the Sea. The invincible wrestler. Each time Hercules threw him to the ground, he arose refreshed.

Until Hercules held him in the air.

Moriarty was muttering to himself, figuring with slide rule, pencil and paper. Allenson was drinking, but he didn't look too happy about it.

"Come on, you birds of evil omen," O'Donnell said, pouring more champagne. "Figure it out later. Right now, drink." He turned to the operator. "How's it going?"

Micheals' analogy had been applied to a spaceship. The ship, operated by remote control, was filled with pure radioactives. It hovered over the leech until, rising to the bait, it had followed. Antaeus had left his mother, the Earth, and was losing his strength in the air. The operator was allowing the spaceship to run fast enough to keep out of the leech's grasp, but close enough to keep it coming.

The spaceship and the leech were on a collision course with the Sun.

"Fine, sir," the operator said. "It's inside the orbit of Mercury now."

"Men," the general said, "I swore to destroy that thing. This isn't exactly the way I wanted to do it. I figured on a more personal way. But the important thing is the destruction. You will all witness it. Destruction is at times a sacred mission. This is such a time. Men, I feel wonderful."

"Turn the spaceship!" It was Moriarty who had spoken. His face was white. "Turn the damned thing!"

He shoved his figures at them.

They were easy to read. The growth-rate of the leech. The energy-consumption rate, estimated. Its speed in space, a constant. The energy it would receive from the Sun as it approached, an exponential curve. Its energy-absorption rate, figured in terms of growth, expressed as a hyped-up discontinuous progression.

The result—

"It'll consume the Sun," Moriarty said, very quietly.

The control room turned into a bedlam. Six of them tried to explain it to O'Donnell at the same time. Then Moriarty tried, and finally Allenson.

"Its rate of growth is so great and its speed so slow—and it will get so much energy—that the leech will be able to consume the Sun by the time it gets there. Or, at least, to live off it until it can consume it."

O'Donnell didn't bother to understand. He turned to the operator.

"Turn it," he said.

They all hovered over the radar screen, waiting.

The food turned out of the leech's path and streaked away. Ahead was a tremendous source, but still a long way off. The leech hesitated.

Its cells, recklessly expending energy, shouted for a decision. The food slowed, tantalizingly near.

The closer source or the greater?

The leech's body wanted food *now*.

It started after it, away from the Sun.

The Sun would come next.


"Pull it out at right angles to the plane of the Solar System," Allenson said.

The operator touched the controls. On the radar screen, they saw a blob pursuing a dot. It had turned.

Relief washed over them. It had been close!

"In what portion of the sky would the leech be?" O'Donnell asked, his face expressionless.

"Come outside; I believe I can show you," an astronomer said. They walked to the door. "Somewhere in that section," the astronomer said, pointing.

"Fine. All right, Soldier," O'Donnell told the operator. "Carry out your orders."

The scientists gasped in unison. The operator manipulated the controls and the blob began to overtake the dot. Micheals started across the room.

"Stop," the general said, and his strong, commanding voice stopped Micheals. "I know what I'm doing. I had that ship especially built."

The blot overtook the dot on the radar screen.

"I told you this was a personal matter," O'Donnell said. "I swore to destroy that leech. We can never have any security while it lives." He smiled. "Shall we look at the sky?"

The general strolled to the door, followed by the scientists.

"Push the button, Soldier!"

The operator did. For a moment, nothing happened. Then the sky lit up!

A bright star hung in space. Its brilliance filled the night, grew, and started to fade.

"What did you do?" Micheals gasped.

"That rocket was built around a hydrogen bomb," O'Donnell said, his strong face triumphant. "I set it off at the contact moment." He called to the operator again. "Is there anything showing on the radar?"

"Not a speck, sir."

"Men," the general said, "I have met the enemy and he is mine. Let's have some more champagne."

But Micheals found that he was suddenly ill.

It had been shrinking from the expenditure of energy, when the great explosion came. No thought of containing it. The leech's cells held for the barest fraction of a second, and then spontaneously overloaded.

The leech was smashed, broken up, destroyed. It was split into a thousand particles, and the particles were split a million times more.

The particles were thrown out on the wave front, of the explosion, and they split further, spontaneously.

Into spores.

The spores closed into dry, hard, seemingly lifeless specks of dust, billions of them, scattered, drifting. Unconscious, they floated in the emptiness of space.

Billions of them, waiting to be fed.

Richard Matheson

# THROUGH CHANNELS

---

*This little interrogation, by one of the modern masters of horror in science fantasy, needs no more introduction than this: Maybe television is not such a good idea after all . . .*

---

*Click*
  *Swish swish swish*
  All set, Sergeant?
  Set.
  OK. This recording made on January fifteenth, nineteen fifty five, twenty third precinct police . . .
  *Swish*
  . . . in the presence of Detective James Taylor and, uh, Sergeant Louis Ferazzio.
  *Swish swish*
  Name, please.
  Huh?
  What's your name, son?
  My name?
  Come on, son, we're trying to help you.
  *Swish*

---

L-Leo.

Last name.

I d-don't . . . Leo.

What's your last name, son?

Vo . . . Vo . . .

All right, son. Take it easy.

V-Vogel.

Leo Vogel. That it?

Yeah.

Address?

T-twenty two thirty, avena J.

Age?

I'm . . . almost. Where's . . . my ma?

*swish swish*

Turn it off a minute, Sergeant.

Right.

*click*

*click*

*swish*

All right, son. OK now?

Y-yeah. But where . . .

You're how old?

Fi-fifteen.

Now, uh, where were you last night from six o'clock till you went home?

I was . . . at . . . at the show. Ma give . . . give me the dough.

How come you didn't stay home to watch television with your parents?

'Cause. Because . . .

Yes?

The Le-Lenottis was comin' over to watch it with them.

They came often?

N-no. It was the first time they'd . . . ever come.

Uh-huh. So your mother sent you to the movies?

Y-yeah.

Sergeant, give the kid some of that coffee. And see if you can find him a blanket.

Right away, chief.

Now, uh, son. What time did you get out of the movies?

Time? I . . . don't know what time.

About nine thirty, would you say?

I guess. I don't know . . . wh-what time. All I . . .

Yes?

Nothin'.

Well, you saw the show only once, didn't you?

*swish*

Huh?

You only saw it once. You didn't see any picture twice, did you?

No. No, I only seen it once.

OK. That would make it, ahh . . .

*swish*

. . . roughly about nine thirty, then, that you got of the movies. You went home right away?

Yeah . . . I mean no.

Where did you stop?

I had a coke at the . . . at the drugstore.

I see. Then you went home.

Ye—

*swish*

. . . yeah, then I went home.

The house was dark?

Yeah. But . . . they never used no lights when they watched TV.

Uh-huh. You went in?

Y-yeah.

Take a sip of that coffee, son, before it gets cold. Take it easy, take it easy. Don't choke on it. There. OK?

Yeah.

All right then. Now . . . Oh, good. Put it over his shoulders, Sergeant. There we go. Better?

Mmmm.

OK. Let's get on with it. And believe me, son, this is no more fun for us than it is for you. We saw it too.

I want mama. I want her. Please, can I . . .

Oh. What did . . . well, shut it off, Sergeant. Here, kid. You don't have a handkerchief, do you? Here. Did you shut it off, Sergeant?

Oh. Right away.

*swish click*


*click*

When you went in, was there anything . . . peculiar?

What?

You told us last night you smelled something.

Yeah. It . . . it . . . There was a funny smell.

Anything you know?

Huh?

Did it smell like anything you ever smelled before?

No. It wasn't much. Not in the . . . hall.

All right. So you went in the living room?

No. No. I went . . . Ma. Can I . . .

*swish swish*

Come on, son, snap out of it. We know you've had a bad time. But we're trying to help.

*swish swish swish*

You, uh, didn't go in the living room. Didn't you think you should mention that smell?

I . . . h-heard the set on and . . .

Set?

The TV set. I thought—I figured they was still watchin'.

Yeah.

And ma didn't like me to . . . b-bust in on them. So I went up to my room so's I wouldn't . . . you know.

Bother them.

Y-yeah.

OK. How long were you up there?

I was . . . I don't know how long. Maybe an hour.

And?

There . . . wasn't no sounds downstairs.

Nothing at all?

No. There wasn't nothing at all.

Didn't that make you suspicious?

Yeah. Well, I figured . . . they'd . . . laugh at somethin' or talk loud or . . .

Dead quiet.

Yeah. Dead quiet.

Did you go down then?

L-later I went. I was goin' to bed. I figured I . . .

You wanted to say goodnight.

Yeah. I . . .

*swish*

You went down and opened the livingroom door?

Yeah, I—Yeah.

What did you see?

I . . . I . . . Oh, can't ya . . . I want my ma. Lemme alone. I want her!

Kid! Hold him, Sergeant. Take it easy!

*swish swish*

I'm sorry, kid. Did it hurt? I had to calm you. I know . . . how you feel, Leo. We saw it too. We feel sick and . . . awful too.

*swish*

Just a few more questions and we'll take you to your aunt's. Now first. The television set. Was it on?

Yeah. It was on.

And you . . . smelled something?

Yeah. Like in the hall. Only worse. Only lots worse.

That smell.

That smell. Dead. A dead stink. Like a pile o' dead . . . dead . . . I don't know. Garbage. Piles of it.

No one was talking?

No, there was nothin'. 'Cept the TV.

What was on it?

I already told ya.

I know, I know. Tell us again. For the record.

It was—like I said—just them letters. Great big letters.

What were they?

F . . . uh . . . F-E-E-D.

F-E-E-D?

Y-yeah. Big crooked-like letters.

You'd seen them before?

Yeah, I told ya. They was on our set all the time . . . Not all the time. Plenty though.

Your parents never wondered about it?

No. They said . . . they figured it was a sort of commercial. You know.

But the things you saw?

I don't know. Ma said . . . it was for kids. Some, I mean.

What did you see?

*swish swish swish*

Sort of . . . mouths. Big ones. Wide. Open, all open. They wasn't p-people.

*swish*

What did it look like? I mean, couldn't you tell what it was?

No. I mean— They was like . . . bugs, maybe. Or maybe . . . w-worms. Big ones. All mouths. Wide open.

All right.

*swish*

You, uh, said the letters flashed on, then off, and you saw the . . . the mouths, and then the letters again?

Yeah. Like that.

This happen every night?

Yeah.

Same time?

No. Different times.

Between programs?

No. Any time.

Was it always the same channel?

No. All different ones. No matter which one we had . . . we seen them.

And . . .

I wanna go. Can't I . . . Ma! Where is she? I want her. I want her.

*swish click*

*click*

A few more questions, Leo, and that's it. Now, you said your parents never had the set checked?

No, I told you. They thought it was—

All right.

*swish*

You went in the livingroom. You said something about slipping, didn't you?

Yeah. On that stuff.

What stuff?

I don't know. Greasy stuff. Like hot grease. It stunk awful.

And then you . . . you found . . .

*swish*

I found them. Ma. And pa. And the Lenottis. They was . . . Ohhhh, I wanna . . .

Leo! What about the set, Leo? What about it?

Huh, what?

The picture on the set. You said something about it.

I, yeah, I . . .

It was the letters, wasn't it, Leo?

Yeah, yeah. Them letters. Them big crooked letters. They was up there. On the set. I seen them. And . . . and . . .

What?

One of the E's. It kinda . . . faded. It went away. And . . . and . . .

What, Leo?

The other letters. They come together. So . . . so there was only three. And . . . and it was a word.

*swish swish swish*

Take him to his aunt, Sergeant.

And the tube went black . . .

All right, Leo. The sergeant'll take you ho—to your aunt's.

I turned on the lights.

All right, Leo.

I turned on the lights! Ma! *MAMA!*

*click*

## Peter Phillips

# LOST MEMORY

*One of the common underlying components of fear
is incomprehension. One fears what one cannot
understand. However, in this unforgettable tale of
the far future it is the opposite that terrifies: the
blood-curdling realization of what actually is going
on. Here the more one grasps the reality, the more
one is terrified.*

COLLAPSED JOINTS AND HUNG UP TO TALK WITH DAK-
whirr. He blinked his eyes in some discomfort.

"What do you want, Palil?" he asked complainingly.

"As if you didn't know."

"I can't give you permission to examine it. The thing is
being saved for inspection by the board. What guarantee do
I have that you won't spoil it for them?"

I thrust confidentially at one of his body-plates. "You owe
me a favor," I said. "Remember?"

"That was a long time in the past."

"Only two thousand revolutions and a reassembly ago. If
it wasn't for me, you'd be eroding in a pit. All I want is a
quick look at its thinking part. I'll vrull the consciousness
without laying a single pair of pliers on it."

He went into a feedback twitch, an indication of the conflict between his debt to me and his self-conceived duty.

Finally he said, "Very well, but keep tuned to me. If I warn that a board member is coming, remove yourself quickly. Anyway how do you know it has consciousness? It may be mere primal metal."

"In that form? Don't be foolish. It's obviously a manufacture. And I'm not conceited enough to believe that we are the only form of intelligent manufacture in the Universe."

"Tautologous phrasing, Palil," Dak-whirr said pedantically. "There could not conceivably be 'unintelligent manufacture.' There can be no consciousness without manufacture, and no manufacture without intelligence. Therefore there can be no consciousness without intelligence. Now if you should wish to dispute—"

I turned off his frequency abruptly and hurried away. Dak-whirr is a fool and a bore. Everyone knows there's a fault in his logic circuit, but he refuses to have it traced down and repaired. Very unintelligent of him.

The thing had been taken into one of the museum sheds by the carriers. I gazed at it in admiration for some moments. It was quite beautiful, having suffered only slight exterior damage, and it was obviously no mere conglomeration of sky metal.

In fact, I immediately thought of it as "he" and endowed it with the attributes of self-knowing, although, of course, his consciousness could not be functioning or he would have attempted communication with us.

I fervently hoped that the board, after his careful disassembly and study, could restore his awareness so that he could tell us himself which solar system he came from.

Imagine it! He had achieved our dream of many thousands of revolutions—space flight—only to be fused, or worse, in his moment of triumph.

I felt a surge of sympathy for the lonely traveler as he lay there, still, silent, non-emitting. Anyway, I mused, even if we couldn't restore him to self-knowing, an analysis of his construction might give us the secret of the power he had used to achieve the velocity to escape his planet's gravity.

In shape and size he was not unlike Swen—or Swen Two, as he called himself after his conversion—who failed so disastrously to reach our satellite, using chemical fuels. But where Swen Two had placed his tubes, the stranger had a curious helical construction studded at irregular intervals with small crystals.

He was thirty-five feet tall, a gracefully tapering cylinder. Standing at his head, I could find no sign of exterior vision cells, so I assumed he had some kind of vrulling sense. There seemed to be no exterior markings at all, except the long, shallow grooves dented in his skin by scraping to a stop along the hard surface of our planet.

I am a reporter with warm current in my wires, not a cold-thinking scientist, so I hesitated before using my own vrulling sense. Even though the stranger was non-aware—per...ps permanently—I felt it would be a presumption, an invasion of privacy. There was nothing else I could do, though, of course.

I started to vrull, gently at first, then harder, until I was positively glowing with effort. It was incredible; his skin seemed absolutely impermeable.

The sudden realization that metal could be so alien nearly fused something inside me. I found myself backing away in horror, my self-preservation relay working overtime.

Imagine watching one of the beautiful cone-rod-and-cylinder assemblies performing the Dance of the Seven Spanners, as he's conditioned to do, and then suddenly refusing to do anything except stump around unattractively, or even becoming obstinately motionless, unresponsive. That might give you an idea of how I felt in that dreadful moment.

Then I remembered Dak-whirr's words—there could be no such thing as an "unintelligent manufacture." And a product so beautiful could surely not be evil. I overcame my repugnance and approached again.

I halted as an open transmission came from someone near at hand.

"Who gave that squeaking reporter permission to snoop around here?"

I had forgotten the museum board. Five of them were standing in the doorway of the shed, radiating anger. I recognized Chirik, the chairman, and addressed myself to him. I explained that I'd interfered with nothing and pleaded for permission on behalf of my subscribers to watch their investigation of the stranger. After some argument, they allowed me to stay.

I watched in silence and some amusement as one by one they tried to vrull the silent being from space. Each showed the same reaction as myself when they failed to penetrate the skin.

Chirik, who is wheeled—and inordinately vain about his suspension system—flung himself back on his supports and pretended to be thinking.

"Fetch Fiff-fiff," he said at last. "The creature may still be aware, but unable to communicate on our standard frequencies."

Fiff-fiff can detect anything in any spectrum. Fortunately he was at work in the museum that day and soon arrived in answer to the call. He stood silently near the stranger for some moments, testing and adjusting himself, then slid up the electromagnetic band.

"He's emitting," he said.

"Why can't we get him?" asked Chirik.

"It's a curious signal on an unusual band."

"Well, what does he say?"

"Sounds like utter nonsense to me. Wait, I'll relay and convert it to standard."

I made a direct recording naturally, like any good reporter.

"— after planetfall," the stranger was saying. "Last dribble of power. If you don't pick this up, my name is Entropy. Other instruments knocked to hell, airlock jammed and I'm too weak to open it manually. Becoming delirious, too. I guess. Getting strong undirectional ultra-wave reception in Inglish, craziest stuff you ever heard, like goblins muttering, and I know we were the only ship in this sector. If you pick this up, but can't get a fix in time, give my love to the boys in the mess. Signing off for another couple of hours, but keeping this channel open and hoping . . ."

"The fall must have deranged him," said Chirik, gazing at the stranger. "Can't he see us or hear us?"

"He couldn't hear you properly before, but he can now, through me," Fiff-fiff pointed out. "Say something to him, Chirik."

"Hello," said Chirik doubtfully. "Er—welcome to our planet. We are sorry you were hurt by your fall. We offer you the hospitality of our assembly shops. You will feel better when you are repaired and repowered. If you will indicate how we can assist you—"

"What the hell! What ship is that? Where are you?"

"We're here," said Chirik. "Can't you see us or vrull us? Your vision circuit is impaired, perhaps? Or do you depend entirely on vrulling? We can't find your eyes and assumed either that you protected them in some way during flight, or dispensed with vision cells altogether in your conversion."

Chirik hesitated, continued apologetically: "But we cannot understand how you vrull, either. While we thought that you were unaware, or even completely fused, we tried to vrull you. Your skin is quite impervious to us, however."

The stranger said: "I don't know if you're batty or I am. What distance are you from me?"

Chirik measured quickly. "One meter, two-point-five centimeters from my eyes to your nearest point. Within touching distance, in fact." Chirik tentatively put out his hand. "Can you not feel me, or has your contact sense also been affected?"

It became obvious that the stranger had been pitifully deranged. I reproduce his words phonetically from my record, although some of them make little sense. Emphasis, punctuative pauses and spelling of unknown terms are mere guesswork, of course.

He said: "For godsakemann stop talking nonsense, whoever you are. If you're outside, can't you see the airlock is jammed? Can't shift it myself. I'm badly hurt. Get me out of here, please."

"Get you out of where?" Chirik looked around, puzzled. "We brought you into an open shed near our museum for a preliminary examination. Now that we know you're intelligent, we shall immediately take you to our assembly shops for healing and recuperation. Rest assured that you'll have the best possible attention."

There was a lengthy pause before the stranger spoke again, and his words were slow and deliberate. His bewilderment is understandable, I believe, if we remember that he could not see, vrull or feel.

He asked: "What manner of creature are you? Describe yourself."

Chirik turned to us and made a significant gesture toward his thinking part, indicating gently that the injured stranger had to be humored.

"Certainly," he replied. "I am an unspecialized bipedal manufacture of standard proportions, lately self-converted to wheeled traction, with a hydraulic suspension system of my own devising which I'm sure will interest you when we restore your sense circuits."

There was an even longer silence.

"You are robots," the stranger said at last. "Crise knows how you got here or why you speak Inglish, but you must try to understand me. I am mann. I am a friend of your master, your maker. You must fetch him to me at once."

"You are not well," said Chirik firmly. "Your speech is incoherent and without meaning. Your fall has obviously caused several serious feedbacks of a very serious nature. Please lower your voltage. We are taking you to our shops immediately. Reserve your strength to assist our specialists as best you can in diagnosing your troubles."

"Wait. You must understand. You are—ogodno that's no good. Have you no memory of mann? The words you use—what meaning have they for you? *Manufacture*—made by hand hand hand damyou. *Healing.* Metal is not healed. *Skin.*

Skin is not metal. *Eyes.* Eyes are not scanning cells. Eyes grow. Eyes are soft. My eyes are soft. Mine eyes have seen the glory—steady on, sun. Get a grip. Take it easy. You out there listen."

"Out where?" asked Prrr-chuk, deputy chairman of the museum board.

I shook my head sorrowfully. This was nonsense, but, like any good reporter, I kept my recorder running.

The mad words flowed on. "You call me he. Why? You have no seks. You are knewter. You are *it it it!* I am he, he who made you, sprung from shee, born of wumman. What is wumman, who is silv-ya what is shee that all her swains commend her ogod the bluds flowing again. Remember. Think back, you out there. These words were made by mann, for mann. Hurt, healing, hospitality, horror, deth by loss of blud. *Deth. Blud.* Do you understand these words? Do you remember the soft things that made you? Soft little mann who konkurred the Galaxy and made sentient slaves of his machines and saw the wonders of a million worlds, only this miserable representative has to die in lonely desperation on a far planet, hearing goblin voices in the darkness."

Here my recorder reproduces a most curious sound, as though the stranger were using an ancient type of vibratory molecular vocalizer in a gaseous medium to reproduce his words before transmission, and the insulation on his diaphragm had come adrift.

It was a jerky, high-pitched, strangely disturbing sound; but in a moment the fault was corrected and the stranger resumed transmission.

"Does blud mean anything to you?"

"No," Chirik replied simply.

"Or deth?"

"No."

"Or wor?"

"Quite meaningless."

"What is your origin? How did you come into being?"

"There are several theories," Chirik said. "The most popular one—which is no more than a grossly unscientific legend, in my opinion—is that our manufacturer fell from the skies, imbedded in a mass of primal metal on which He drew to erect the first assembly shop. How He came into being is left to conjecture. My own theory, however—"

"Does legend mention the shape of this primal metal?"

"In vague terms, yes. It was cylindrical, of vast dimensions."

"An interstellar vessel," said the stranger.

"That is my view also," said Chirik complacently. "And—"

"What was the supposed appearance of your—manufacturer?"

"He is said to have been of magnificent proportions, based harmoniously on a cubical plan, static in Himself, but equipped with a vast array of senses."

"An automatic computer," said the stranger.

He made more curious noises, less jerky and at a lower pitch than the previous sounds.

He corrected the fault and went on: "God that's funny. A ship falls, menn are no more, and an automatic computer has pupps. Oh, yes, it fits in. A self-setting computer and navigator, operating on verbal orders. It learns to listen for itself and know itself for what it is, and to absorb knowledge. It comes to hate menn—or at least their bad qualities—so it deliberately crashes the ship and pulps their puny bodies with a calculated nicety of shock. Then it propagates and does a dam fine job of selective erasure on whatever it gave its pupps to use for a memory. It passes on only the good it found in menn, and purges the memory of him completely. Even purges all of his vocabulary except scientific terminology. Oil is thicker than blud. So may they live without the burden of knowing that they are—ogod they must know, they must understand. You outside, what happened to this manufacturer?"

Chirik, despite his professed disbelief in the supernormal aspects of the ancient story, automatically made a visual sign of sorrow.

"Legend has it," he said, "that after completing His task, He fused himself beyond possibility of healing."

Abrupt, low-pitched noises came again from the stranger. "Yes. He would. Just in case any of His pupps should give themselves forbidden knowledge and an infeeryorrity komplecks by probing his mnemonic circuits. The perfect self-sacrificing muther. What sort of environment did He give you? Describe your planet."

Chirik looked around at us again in bewilderment, but he replied courteously, giving the stranger a description of our world.

"Of course," said the stranger. "Of course. Sterile rock and metal suitable only for you. But there must be some way . . ."

He was silent for a while.

"Do you know what growth means?" he asked finally. "Do you have anything that grows?"

"Certainly," Chirik said helpfully. "If we should suspend a crystal of some substance in a saturated solution of the same element or compound—"

"No, no," the stranger interrupted. "Have you nothing that grows of itself, that fruktiffies and gives increase without your intervention?"

"How could such a thing be?"

"Criseallmytee I should have guessed. If you had one blade of gras, just one tiny blade of growing gras, you could extrapolate from that to me. Green things, things that feed on the rich brest of erth, cells that divide and multiply, a cool grove of treez in a hot summer, with tiny warm-bludded burds preening their fethers among the leeves; a feeld of spring weet with newbawn mise timidly threading the dangerous jungul of storks; a stream of living water where silver fish dart and pry and feed and procreate; a farm yard where things grunt and cluck and greet the new day with the stirring pulse of life, with a surge of blud. Blud—"

For some inexplicable reason, although the strength of his carrier wave remained almost constant, the stranger's transmission seemed to be growing fainter. "His circuits are failing," Chirik said. "Call the carriers. We must take him to an assembly shop immediately. I wish he would reserve his power."

My presence with the museum board was accepted without question now. I hurried along with them as the stranger was carried to the nearest shop.

I now noticed a circular marking in that part of his skin on which he had been resting, and guessed that it was some kind of orifice through which he would have extended his planetary traction mechanism if he had not been injured.

He was gently placed on a disassembly cradle. The doctor in charge that day was Chur-chur, an old friend of mine. He had been listening to the two-way transmissions and was already acquainted with the case.

Chur-chur walked thoughtfully around the stranger.

"We shall have to cut," he said. "It won't pain him, since his intra-molecular pressure and contact senses have failed. But since we can't vrull him, it'll be necessary for him to tell us where his main brain is housed, or we might damage it."

Fiff-fiff was still relaying, but no amount of power boost would make the stranger's voice any clearer. It was quite faint now, and there are places on my recorder tape from which I cannot make even the roughest phonetic transliteration.

" . . . strength going. Can't get into my zoot . . . done for if they bust through lock, done for if they don't . . . must tell them I need oxygen . . ."

"He's in bad shape, desirous of extinction," I remarked to Chur-chur, who was adjusting his arc-cutter. "He wants to poison himself with oxidation now."

I shuddered at the thought of that vile, corrosive gas he had mentioned, which causes that almost unmentionable condition we all fear—rust.

Chirik spoke firmly through Fiff-fiff. "Where is your thinking part, stranger? Your central brain?"

"In my head," the stranger replied. "In my head ogod my head . . . eyes blurring everything going dim . . . luv to mairee . . . kids . . . a carry me home to the lone paryee . . . get this bluddy airlock open then they'll see me die . . . but they'll see me . . . some kind of atmosphere with this gravity . . . see me die . . extrapolate from body what I was . . . what they are

damthem damthem damthem . . . mann . . . master . . . I AM
YOUR MAKER!"

For a few seconds the voice rose strong and clear, then
faded away again and dwindled into a combination of those
two curious noises I mentioned earlier. For some reason that
I cannot explain, I found the combined sound very disturbing despite its faintness. It may be that it induced some kind
of sympathetic oscillation.

Then came words, largely incoherent and punctuated by
a kind of surge like the sonic vibrations produced by variations of pressure in a leaking gas-filled vessel.

" . . . done it . . . . crawling into chamber, closing inner . . .
must be mad . . . they'd find me anyway . . . but finished
. . . want see them before I die . . . want see them see me
. . . liv few seconds, watch them . . . get outer one open . . ."

Chur-chur had adjusted his arc to a broad, clean, blue-white
glare. I trembled a little as he brought it near the edge of
the circular marking in the stranger's skin. I could almost feel
the disruption of the intra-molecular sense currents in my
own skin.

"Don't be squeamish, Palil," Chur-chur said kindly. "He
can't feel it now that his contact sense has gone. And you
heard him say that his central brain is in his head." He brought
the cutter firmly up to the skin. "I should have guessed that.
He's the same shape as Swen Two, and Swen very logically
concentrated his main thinking part as far away from his explosion chambers as possible."

Rivulets of metal ran down into a tray which a calm assistant had placed on the ground for that purpose. I averted my
eyes quickly. I could never steel myself enough to be a sur-
gical engineer or assembly technician.

But I had to look again, fascinated. The whole area circumscribed by the marking was beginning to glow.

Abruptly the stranger's voice returned, quite strongly, each
word clipped, emphasized, high-pitched.

"Ar no no no . . . god my hands . . . they're burning through
the lock and I can't get back I can't get away . . . stop it you

feens stop it can't you hear . . . I'll be burned to deth I'm
here in the airlock . . . the air's getting hot you're burning me
alive . . ."

Although the words made little sense, I could guess what
had happened and I was horrified.

"Stop, Chur-chur," I pleaded. "The heat has somehow
brought back his skin currents. It's hurting him."

Chur-chur said reassuringly: "Sorry, Palil. It occasionally
happens during an operation—probably a local thermo-elec-
tric effect. But even if his contact senses have started working again and he can't switch them off, he won't have to bear
this very long."

Chirik shared my unease, however. He put out his hand
and awkwardly patted the stranger's skin.

"Easy there," he said. "Cut out your senses if you can. If
you can't well, the operation is nearly finished. Then we'll re-
power you, and you'll soon be fit and happy again, healed and
fitted and reassembled."

I decided that I liked Chirik very much just then. He ex-
hibited almost as much self-induced empathy as any reporter;
he might even come to like my favorite blue stars, despite his
cold scientific exactitude in most respects.

My recorder tape shows, in its reproduction of certain
sounds, how I was torn away from that strained reverie.

During the one-and-a-half seconds since I had recorded the
distinct vocables "burning me alive," the stranger's words had
become quite blurred, running together and rising even higher
in pitch until they reached a sustained note—around E-flat in
the standard sonic scale.

It was not like a voice at all.

This high, whining noise was suddenly modulated by apparent words, but without changing its pitch. Transcribing
what seem to be words is almost impossible, as you can see
for yourself—this is the closest I can come phonetically:

"Eeee ahahmbeeeeing baked aliiive in an uvennn ahdeeer-
jeeesussunmuuutherrr!"

The note swooped higher and higher until it must have

neared supersonic range, almost beyond either my direct or recorded hearing.

Then it stopped as quickly as a contact break.

And although the soft hiss of the stranger's carrier wave carried on without perceptible diminution, indicating that some degree of awareness still existed, I experienced at that moment one of those quirks of intuition given only to reporters:

I felt that I would never greet the beautiful stranger from the sky in his full senses.

Chur-chur was muttering to himself about the extreme toughness and thickness of the stranger's skin. He had to make four complete cutting revolutions before the circular mass of nearly white-hot metal could be pulled away by a magnetic grapple.

A billow of smoke puffed out of the orifice. Despite my repugnance, I thought of my duty as a reporter and forced myself to look over Chur-chur's shoulder.

The fumes came from a soft, charred, curiously shaped mass of something which lay just inside the opening.

"Undoubtedly a kind of insulating material," Chur-chur explained.

He drew out the crumpled blackish heap and placed it carefully on a tray. A small portion broke away, showing a red, viscid substance.

"It looks complex," Chur-chur said, "but I expect the stranger will be able to tell us how to reconstitute it or make a substitute."

His assistant gently cleaned the wound of the remainder of the material, which he placed with the rest, and Chur-chur resumed his inspection of the orifice.

You can, if you want, read the technical accounts of Chur-chur's discovery of the stranger's double skin at the point where the cut was made; of the incredible complexity of his driving mechanism, involving principles which are still not understood to this day; of the museum's failure to analyze the exact nature and function of the insulating material found in only that one portion of his body; and of the other scientific mysteries connected with him.

But this is my personal, non-scientific account. I shall never forget hearing about the greatest mystery of all, for which not even the most tentative explanation has been advanced, nor the utter bewilderment with which Chur-chur announced his initial findings that day.

He had hurriedly converted himself to a convenient size to permit actual entry into the stranger's body.

When he emerged, he stood in silence for several minutes. Then, very slowly, he said:

"I have examined the 'central brain' in the forepart of his body. It is no more than a simple auxiliary computer mechanism. It does not possess the slightest trace of consciousness. And there is no other conceivable center of intelligence in the remainder of his body."

There is something I wish I could forget. I can't explain why it should upset me so much. But I always stop the tape before it reaches the point where the voice of the stranger rises in pitch, going higher and higher until it cuts out.

There's a quality about that noise that makes me tremble and think of rust.

# Theodore Sturgeon

# MEMORIAL

*Most of Theodore Sturgeon's masterpieces of horror fall into the categories of the weird and the supernatural. Those who have read his "Bianca's Hands" or his "It", to name only two of his many superb tales of this type, will agree that in this medium there are few to equal him.*

*Only rarely has he used straight science fiction— and sociological science fiction at that—to terrify. And in the present story he terrifies by logic, by reason, by the use of serious scientific extrapolation, rather than by importing some nightmarish concepts from the creepy "other side" of the mind. And perhaps that is just what makes this tale so ominous: it* really could happen.

The Pit, in A.D. 5000, had changed little over the centuries. Still it was an angry memorial to the misuse of great power; and because of it, organized warfare was a forgotten thing. Because of it, the world was free of the wasteful smoke and dirt of industry. The scream and crash of bombs and the

Theodore Sturgeon, MEMORIAL. Copyright 1946 in the United States and Great Britain by Street and Smith Publications, Inc.; copyright 1948 by Prime Press, Inc., for *Without Sorcery*, by Theodore Sturgeon. Reprinted by permission of the author from *Astounding Science Fiction*, April 1946.

*soporific beat of marching feet were never heard, and at long
last the earth was at peace.*

*To go near The Pit was slow, certain death, and it was re-
spected and feared, and would be for centuries more. It
winked and blinked redly at night, and was surrounded by a
bald and broken tract stretching out and away over the horizon; and around it flickered a ghostly blue glow. Nothing
lived there. Nothing could.*

*With such a war memorial, there could only be peace. The
earth could never forget the horror that could be loosed by
war.*

*That was Grenfell's dream.*

Grenfell handed the typewritten sheet back. "That's it,
Jack. My idea, and—I wish I could express it like that." He
leaned back against the littered workbench, his strangely
asymmetrical face quizzical. "Why is it that it takes a useless
person to adequately express an abstract?"

Jack Roway grinned as he took back the paper and tucked
it into his breast pocket. "Interestin' question, Grenfell, because this *is* your expression, the words *are* yours. Practically
verbatim. I left out the 'er's' and 'Ah's' that you play conversa-
tional hopscotch with, and strung together all the effects ye
mentioned without mentioning any of the technologic
causes. Net result: you think I did it, when you did. You
think it's good writing, and I don't."

"You don't?"

Jack spread his bony length out on the hard little cot. His
relaxation was a noticeable act, like the unbuttoning of a shirt
collar. His body seemed to unjoint itself a little. He laughed.

"Of course I don't. Much too emotional for my taste. I'm
just a fumbling aesthete—useless, did you say? Mm-m-m—
yeah. I suppose so." He paused reflectively. "You see, you
cold-blooded characters, you scientists, are the true vision-
aries. Seems to me the essential difference between a scientist
and an artist is that the scientist can mix his hope with pa-
tience. "The scientist visualizes his ultimate goal, but pays little attention to it. He is all caught up with the achievement of

the next step upward. The artist looks so far ahead that more often than not he can't see what's under his feet; so he falls flat on his face and gets called useless by scientists. But if you strip all of the intermediate steps away from the scientist's thinking, you have an artistic concept to which the scientist responds distantly and with surprise, giving some artist credit for being deeply perspicacious purely because the artist repeated something the scientist said."

"You amaze me," Grenfell said candidly. "You wouldn't be what you are if you weren't lazy and superficial. And yet you come out with things like that. I don't know that I understand what you just said. I'll have to think—but I do believe that you show all the signs of clear thinking. With a mind like yours, I can't understand why you don't use it to build something instead of wasting it in these casual interpretations of yours."

Jack Roway stretched luxuriously. "What's the use? There's more waste involved in the destruction of something which is already built than in dispersing the energy it would take to start building something. Anyway, the world is filled with builders—and destroyers. I'd just as soon sit by and watch, and feel things. I like my environment, Grenfell. I want to feel all I can of it, while it lasts. It won't last much longer. I want to touch all of it I can reach, taste of it. hear it, while there's time. What is around me, here and now, is what is important to me. The acceleration of human progress, and the increase of its mass—to use your own terms—are taking humanity straight to Limbo. You, with your work, think you are fighting humanity's inertia. Well, you are. But it's the kind of inertia called momentum. You command no force great enough to stop it, or even to change its course appreciably."

"I have sub-atomic power."

Roway shook his head, smiling. "That's not enough. No power is enough. It's just too late."

"That kind of pessimism does not affect me," said Grenfell. "You can gnaw all you like at my foundations, Jack, and achieve nothing more than the loss of your front teeth. I think you know that."

"Certainly I know that. I'm not trying to. I have nothing to sell, no one to change. I am even more impotent than you and your atomic power; and you are completely helpless. Uh—I quarrel with your use of the term 'pessimist', though. I am nothing of the kind. Since I have resolved for myself the fact that humanity, as we know it, is finished, I'm quite resigned to it. Pessimism from me, under the circumstances, would be the pessimism of a photophobiac predicting that the sun would rise tomorrow."

Grenfell grinned. "I'll have to think about that, too. You're such a mass of paradoxes that turn out to be chains of reasoning. Apparently you live in a world in which scientists are poets and the grasshopper has it all over the ant."

"I always did think that ant was a stinker."

"Why do you keep coming here, Jack? What do you get out of it? Don't you realize I'm a criminal?"

Roway's eyes narrowed. "Sometimes I think you wish you were a criminal. The law says you are, and the chances are very strong that you'll be caught and treated accordingly. Ethically, you know you're not. It sort of takes the spice out of being one of the hunted."

"Maybe you're right," Grenfell said thoughtfully. He sighed. "It's so completely silly. During the war years, the skills I had were snatched up and the government flogged me into the Manhattan Project, expecting, and getting, miracles. I have never stopped working along the same lines. And now the government has changed the laws, and pulled legality from under me."

"Hardly surprising. The government deals rather severely with soldiers who go on killing other soldiers after the war is over." He held up a hand to quell Grenfell's interruption. "I know you're not killing anyone, and are working for the opposite result. I was only pointing out that it's the same switcheroo. We the people," he said didactically, "have, in our sovereign might, determined that no atomic research be done except in government laboratories. We have then permitted our politicians to allow so little for maintenance of those laboratories—unlike our overseas friends—that no really exhaustive research can be done in them. We have further made it a major offense to operate such a bootleg lab as yours." He shrugged. "Comes the end of mankind. We'll get walloped first. If we put more money and effort into nuclear research than any other country, some other country would get walloped first. If we last another hundred years—which seems doubtful—some poor, spavined, underpaid government researcher will stumble on the aluminum-isotope space-heating system you have already perfected."

"That was a little rough," said Grenfell bitterly. "Driving me underground just in time to make it impossible for me to announce it. What a waste of time and energy it is to heat homes and buildings the way they do now! Space heating—the biggest single use for heat-energy—and I have the answer to it over there." He nodded toward a compact cube of lead-alloys in the corner of the shop. "Build it into a foundation, and you have controllable heat for the life of the building, with not a cent for additional fuel and practically nothing for maintenance." His jaw knotted. "Well, I'm glad it happened that way."

"Because it got you started on your war memorial— The Pit? Yeah. Well, all I can say is, I hope you're right. It hasn't been possible to scare humanity yet. The invention of gunpowder was going to stop war, and didn't. Likewise the submarine, the torpedo, the airplane, that two-by-four bomb they pitched at Hiroshima, and the H-bomb."

"None of that applies to The Pit," said Grenfell. "You're right; humanity hasn't been scared off war yet; but the H-bomb rocked 'em back on their heels. My little memorial is the real stuff. I'm not depending on a fission or fusion effect, you know, with a release of one-tenth of one percent of the energy of the atom. I'm going to transmute it completely, and get all the energy there is in it, and in all matter the fireball touches. And it'll be *more* than a thousand times as powerful as the Hiroshima bomb, because I'm going to use twelve times as much explosive; and it's going off on the ground, not a hundred and fifty feet above it." Grenfell's brow, over suddenly hot eyes, began to shine with sweat. "And then—The Pit," he said softly. "The war memorial to end war, and all other war memorials. A vast pit, alive with bubbling lava, radiating death for ten thousand years. A living reminder of the devastation mankind has prepared for itself. Out here on the desert, where there are no cities, where the land has always been useless, will be the scene of the most useful thing in the history of the race—a never-ending sermon, a warning, an example of the dreadful antithesis of peace." His voice shook to a whisper, and faded.

"Sometimes," said Roway, "you frighten me, Grenfell. It occurs to me that I am such a studied sensualist, tasting everything I can, because I am afraid to feel any one thing that much." He shook himself, or shuddered. "You're a fanatic, Grenfell. Hyperemotional. A monomaniac. I hope you can do it."

"I can do it," said Grenfell.

Two months passed, and in those two months Grenfell's absorption in his work had been forced aside by the increasing pressure of current events. Watching a band of vigilantes riding over the waste to the south of his little buildings one afternoon, he thought grimly of what Roway had said. "Sometimes I think you wish you were a criminal." Roway, the sensualist, would say that. Roway would appreciate the taste of danger, in the same way that he appreciated all the other emotions. As it intensified, he would wait to savor it, no matter how bad it got.

Twice Grenfell shut off the instigating power of the boron-aluminum pile he had built, as he saw government helicopters hovering on the craggy skyline. He knew of hard-radiation detectors; he had developed two different types of them during the war; and he wanted no questions asked. His utter frustration at being unable to announce the success of his space-heating device, for fear that he would be punished as a criminal and his device impounded and forgotten—that frustration had been indescribable. It had canalized his mind, and intensified the devoted effort he had put forth for the things he believed in during the war. Every case of neural shock he encountered in men who had been hurt by war and despised it made him work harder on his monument—on The Pit. For if humans could be frightened by war, humanity could be frightened by The Pit.

And those he met who had been hurt by war and who still hated the late enemy—those who would have been happy to go back and kill some more, reckoning vital risk well worth it —those he considered mad, and forgot them.

So he could not stand another frustration. He was the center of his own universe, and he realized it dreadfully, and he had to justify his position there. He was a humanitarian, a philanthropist in the word's truest sense. He was probably as mad as any other man who has, through his own efforts, moved the world.

For the first time, then, he was grateful when Jack Roway arrived in his battered old convertible, although he was deliriously frightened at the roar of the motor outside his laboratory window. His usual reaction to Jack's advent was a mixture of annoyance and gratification, for it was a great deal of trouble to get out to his place. His annoyance was not because of the interruption, for Jack was certainly no trouble to have around. Grenfell suspected that Jack came out to see him partly to get the taste of the city out of his mouth, and partly to be able to feel superior to somebody he considered of worth.

But the increasing fear of discovery, and his race to complete his work before it was taken from him by a hysterical public, had had the unusual effect of making him lonely. For such a man as Grenfell to be lonely bordered on the extraordinary; for in his daily life there were simply too many things to be done. There had never been enough hours in a day nor days in a week to suit him, and he deeply resented the encroachments of sleep, which he considered a criminal waste.

"Roway!" he blurted, as he flung the door open, his tone so warm that Roway's eyebrows went up in surprise. "What dragged you out here?"

"Nothing in particular," said the writer, as they shook

hands. "Nothing more than usual, which is a great deal. How goes it?"

"I'm about finished." They went inside, and as the door closed, Grenfell turned to face Jack. "I've been finished for so long I'm ashamed of myself," he said intently.

"Ha! Ardent confession so early in the day! What are you talking about?"

"Oh, there have been things to do," said Grenfell restlessly. "But I could go ahead with the . . . with the big thing at almost any time."

"You hate to be finished. You've never visualized what it would be like to have the job done." His teeth flashed. "You know, I've never heard a word from you as to what your plans are after the big noise. You going into hiding?"

"I . . . haven't thought much about it. I used to have a vague idea of broadcasting a warning and an explanation before I let go with the disruptive explosion. I've decided against it, though. In the first place, I'd be stopped within minutes, no matter how cautious I was with the transmitter. In the second place—well, this is going to be so big that it won't need any explanation."

"No one will know who did it, or why it was done."

"Is that necessary?" asked Grenfell quietly.

Jack's mobile face stilled as he visualized The Pit, spewing its ten-thousand-year hell. "Perhaps not," he said. "Isn't it necessary, though, to you?"

"To me?" asked Grenfell, surprised. "You mean, do I care if the world knows I did this thing, or not? No; of course I don't. A chain of circumstance is occurring, and it has been working through me. It goes directly to The Pit; The Pit will do all that is necessary from then on. I will no longer have any part in it."

Jack moved, clinking and splashing, around the sink in the corner of the laboratory. "Where's all your coffee? Oh—here. Uh . . . I have been curious about how much personal motive you had for your work. I think that answers it pretty well. I think, too, that you believe what you are saying. Do you know that people who do things for impersonal motives are as rare as fur on a fish?"

"I hadn't thought about it."

"I believe that, too. Sugar? And milk. I remember. And have you been listening to the radio?"

"Yes. I'm . . . a little upset, Jack," said Grenfell, taking the cup. "I don't know where to time this thing. I'm a technician, not a Machiavelli."

"Visionary, like I said. You don't know if you'll throw this gadget of yours into world history too soon or too late — is that it?"

"Exactly. Jack, the whole world seems to be going crazy. Even fusion bombs are too big for humanity to handle."

"What else can you expect," said Jack grimly, "with our dear friends across the water sitting over their push buttons waiting for an excuse to punch them?"

"And we have our own set of buttons, of course."

Jack Roway said: "We've got to defend ourselves."

"Are you kidding?"

Roway glanced at him, his dark brows plotting a V. "Not about this. I seldom kid about anything, but particularly not about this." And he—shuddered.

Grenfell stared amazedly at him and then began to chuckle. "Now," he said, "I've seen everything. My iconoclastic friend Jack Roway, of all people, caught up by a . . . a fashion. A national pastime, fostered by uncertainty and fed by yellow journalism—fear of the enemy."

"This country is not at war."

"You mean, we have no enemy? Are you saying that the gentlemen over the water, with their itching fingertips hovering about the push buttons, are not our enemies?"

"Well—"

Grenfell came across the room to his friend, and put a hand on his shoulder. "Jack—what's the matter? You can't be so troubled by the news—not you!"

Roway stared out at the brazen sun, and shook his head slowly. "International balance is too delicate," he said softly; and if a voice could glaze like eyes, his did. "I see the nations of the world as masses balanced each on its own mathematical point, each with its center of gravity directly above. But the masses are fluid, shifting violently away from the center lines. The opposing trends aren't equal; they can't cancel each other; the phasing is too slow. One or the other is going to topple, and then the whole works is going to go."

"But you've known that for a long time. You've known that ever since Hiroshima. Possibly before. Why should it frighten you now?"

"I didn't think it would happen so soon."

"Oh-ho! So that's it! You have suddenly realized that the explosion is going to come in your lifetime. Hm-m-m? And you can't take that. You're capable of all of your satisfying aesthetic rationalizations as long as you can keep the actualities at arm's length!"

"*Whew!*" said Roway, his irrepressible humor passing close enough to nod to him. "Keep it clean, Grenfell! Keep your . . . your sesquipedalian polysyllabics, for a scientific report."

"*Touché!*" Grenfell smiled. "Y'know, Jack, you remind me powerfully of some erstwhile friends of mine who write science-fiction. They had been living very close to atomic power for a long time—years before the man on the street—or the average politician, for that matter—knew an atom from Adam. Atomic power was handy to these specialized word-merchants because it gave them a limitless source of power for background to a limitless source of story material. In the heyday of the Manhattan Project, most of them suspected what was going on, some of them knew—some even worked on it. All of them were quite aware of the terrible potentialities of nuclear energy. Practically all of them were scared silly of the whole idea. They were afraid for humanity, but they themselves were not really afraid, except in a delicious drawing room sort of way, because they couldn't conceive of this Buck Rogers event happening to anything but posterity. But it happened, right smack in the middle of their own sacrosanct lifetimes.

"And I will be dog-goned if you're not doing the same thing. You've gotten quite a bang out of figuring out the doom humanity faces in an atomic war. You've consciously risen above it by calling it inevitable, and in the meantime leave us gather rosebuds before it rains. You thought you'd be safe home—dead—before the first drops fell. Now social progress has rolled up a thunderhead and you find yourself a mile from home with a crease in your pants and no umbrella. And you're scared!"

Roway looked at the floor and said, "It's so soon. It's so soon." He looked up at Grenfell, and his cheekbones seemed too large. He took a deep breath. "You . . . we can stop it, Grenfell."

"Stop what?"

"The war . . . the . . . this thing that's happening to us. The explosion that will come when the strains get too great in the international situation. And it's *got* to be stopped!"

"That's what The Pit is for."

"The Pit!" Roway said scornfully. "I've called you a visionary before. Grenfell, you've got to be more practical! Humanity is not going to learn anything by example. It's got to be kicked and carved. Surgery."

Grenfell's eyes narrowed. "Surgery? What you said a minute ago about my stopping it . . . do you mean what I think you mean?"

"Don't you see it?" said Jack urgently. "What you have here—the total conversion of mass to energy—the peak of atomic power. One or two wallops with this, in the right place, and we can stop anybody."

"This isn't a weapon. I didn't make this to be a weapon."

"The first rock ever thrown by a prehistoric man wasn't made to be a weapon, either. But it was handy and it was effective, and it was certainly used because it had to be used." He suddenly threw up his hands in a despairing gesture. "You don't understand. Don't you realize that this country is likely to be attacked at any second—that diplomacy is now hopeless and helpless, and the whole world is just waiting for the thing to start? It's probably too late even now—but it's the least we can do."

"What, specifically, is the least thing we can do?"

"Turn your work over to the Defense Department. In a few hours the government can put it where it will do the most good." He drew his finger across his throat. "Anywhere we want to, over the ocean."

There was a taut silence. Roway looked at his watch and licked his lips. Finally Grenfell said, "Turn it over to the government. Use it for a weapon—and what for? To stop war?"

"Of course!" blurted Roway. "To show the rest of the world that our way of life . . . to scare the daylights out of . . . to—"

"*Stop it!*" Grenfell roared. "Nothing of the kind. You think —you hope anyway—that the use of total disruption as a weapon will stall off the inevitable—at least in your lifetime. Don't you?"

"No. I—"

"Don't you?"

"Well, I—"

"You have some more doggerel to write," said Grenfell scathingly. "You have some more blondes to chase. You want to go limp over a few more Bach fugues."

Jack Roway said: "No one knows where the first bomb might hit. It might be anywhere. There's nowhere I . . . we . . . can go to be safe." He was trembling.

"Are the people in the city quivering like that?" asked Grenfell.

"Riots," breathed Roway, his eyes bright with panic. "The radio won't announce anything about the riots."

"Is that what you came out here for today—to try to get me to give disruptive power to *any* government?"

Jack looked at him guiltily. "It was the only thing to do. I don't know if your bomb will turn the trick, but it has to be tried. It's the only thing left. We've got to be prepared to hit first, and hit harder than anyone else."

"No." Grenfell's one syllable was absolutely unshakable.

"Grenfell—I thought I could argue you into it. Don't make it tough for yourself. You've got to do it. Please do it on your own. Please, Grenfell." He stood up slowly.

"Do it on my own—or what? *Keep away from me!*"

"No . . . I—" Roway stiffened suddenly, listening. From far above and to the north came the whir of rotary wings. Roway's fear-slackened lips tightened into a grin, and with two incredibly swift strides he was across to Grenfell. He swept in a handful of the smaller man's shirt front and held him half off the floor.

"Don't try a thing," he gritted. There was not a sound then except their harsh breathing, until Grenfell said wearily: "There was somebody called Judas—"

"You can't insult me," said Roway, with a shade of his old cockiness, "And you're flattering yourself."

A helicopter sank into its own roaring dust-cloud outside the building. Men pounded out of it and burst in the door. There were three of them. They were not in uniform.

"Dr. Grenfell," said Jack Roway, keeping his grip, "I want you to meet—"

"Never mind that," said the taller of the three in a brisk voice. "You're Roway? Hm-m-m. Dr. Grenfell, I understand you have a nuclear energy device on the premises."

"Why did you come by yourself?" Grenfell asked Roway softly. "Why not just send these stooges?"

"For you, strangely enough. I hoped I could argue you into giving the thing freely. You know what will happen if you resist?"

"I know." Grenfell pursed his lips for a moment, and then turned to the tall man. "Yes. I have some such thing here. Total atomic disruption. Is that what you were looking for?"

"Where is it?"

"Here, in the laboratory, and then there's the pile in the other building. You'll find—" He hesitated. "You'll find two samples of the concentrate. One's over there—" he pointed to a lead case on a shelf behind one of the benches. "And there's another like it in a similar case in the shed back of the pile building."

Roway sighed and released Grenfell. "Good boy. I knew you'd come through."

"Yes," said Grenfell. "Yes—"

"Go get it," said the tall man. One of the others broke away.

"It will take two men to carry it," said Grenfell in a shaken voice. His lips were white.

The tall man pulled out a gun and held it idly. He nodded to the second man. "Go get it. Bring it here and we'll strap the two together and haul 'em to the plane. Snap it up."

The two men went out toward the shed.

"Jack?"

"Yes, Doc."

"You really think humanity can be scared?"

"It will be—now. This thing will be used right."

"I hope so. Oh, I hope so," Grenfell whispered.

The men came back. "Up on the bench," said the leader, nodding toward the case the men carried between them.

As they climbed up on the bench and laid hands on the second case, to swing it down from the shelf, Jack Roway saw Grenfell's face spurt sweat, and a sudden horror swept over him.

"Grenfell!" he said hoarsely. "It's—"

"Of course," Grenfell whispered. "Critical mass."

When the two leaden cases came together, it let go.

It was like Hiroshima, but much bigger. And yet, that explosion did not create The Pit. It was the pile that did—the boron-aluminum lattice which Grenfell had so arduously pieced together from parts bootlegged over the years. Right there at the heart of the fission explosion, total disruption took place in the pile, for that was its function. This was slower. It took more than an hour for its hellish activity to reach a peak, and in that time a huge crater had been gouged out of the earth, a seething, spewing mass of volatilized elements, raw radiation, and incandescent gases. It was—The Pit. Its activity curve was plotted abruptly—up to peak in an hour and eight minutes, and then a gradual subsidence as it tried to feed further afield with less and less fueling effect, and as it consumed its own flaming wastes in an effort to reach inactivity. Rain would help to blanket it, through energy lost in volatilizing the drops; and each of the many elements involved went through its respective secondary radioactivity, and passed away its successive half-lives. The subsidence of The Pit would take between eight and nine thousand years.

And like Hiroshima, this explosion had effects which reached into history and into men's hearts in places far separated in time from the cataclysm itself.

These things happened:

The explosion could not be concealed; and there was too much hysteria afoot for anything to be confirmed. It was easier to run headlines saying WE ARE ATTACKED. There was an instantaneous and panicky demand for reprisals, and the government acceded, because such "reprisals" suited the policy of certain members who could command emergency powers. And so the First Atomic War was touched off.

And the Second.

There were no more atomic wars after that. The Mutants' War was a barbarous affair, and the mutants defeated the tattered and largely sterile remnants of humanity, because the mutants were strong. And then the mutants died out because they were unfit. For a while there was some very interesting material to be studied on the effects of radiation on heredity, but there was no one to study it.

There were some humans left. The rats got most of them, after increasing in fantastic numbers; and there were three plagues.

After that there were half-stooping, naked things whose twisted heredity could have been traced to humankind; but these could be frightened, as individuals and as a race, so therefore they could not progress. They were certainly not human.

*The Pit, in A.D. 5000, had changed little over the centuries. Still it was an angry memorial to the misuse of great power; and because of it, organized warfare was a forgotten thing. Because of it, the world was free of the wasteful smoke* and dirt of industry. The scream and crash of bombs and the soporific beat of marching feet were never heard, and at long last the earth was at peace.

To go near The Pit was slow, certain death, and it was respected and feared, and would be for centuries more. It winked and blinked redly at night, and was surrounded by a bald and broken tract stretching out and away over the horizon; and around it flickered a ghostly blue glow. Nothing lived there. Nothing could.

With such a war memorial, there could only be peace. The earth could never forget the horror that could be loosed by war.

That was Grenfell's dream.

# Margaret St. Clair

# PROTT

*It may be hard to imagine a comic terror tale; fear and fun are hard to mix. But it has been done, in this itchy little story about a new kind of space inhabitant. Of course, the Prott are much less lethal than Mr. Sheckley's leech (see page 43), but one may be permitted to wonder whether, despite that fact, they are more desirable.*

"READ IT," SAID THE SPACEMAN. "YOU'LL FIND IT INTERESTing—under the circumstances. It's not long. One of the salvage crews found it tied to a signal rocket just outside the Asteroid Belt. It'd been there quite a while.

"I thought of taking it to somebody at the university, a historian or somebody, but I don't suppose they'd be interested. They don't have any more free time than anybody else."

He handed a metal cylinder to Fox, across the table, and ordered drinks for them both. Fox sipped from his glass before he opened the tube.

"Sure you want me to read it now?" he asked. "Not much of a way to spend our free time."

"Sure, go ahead and read it. What difference does it make?"

---

Margaret St. Clair, PROTT. Copyright 1953 by Galaxy Publishing Corp. Reprinted by permission of John Schaffner from *Galaxy*, January 1953.

*So Fox spread out the emtex sheets. He began to read.*

Dating a diary in deep space offers special problems. Philosophic problems, I mean—that immense "When is now?" which, vexatious enough within a solar system or even on the surface of a planet, becomes quite insoluble in deep space except empirically or by predicating a sort of super-time, an enormous Present Moment which would extend over everything. And yet a diary entry must be dated, if only for convenience. So I will call today Tuesday and take the date of April 21st from the gauges.

Tuesday it is.

On this Tuesday, then, I am quite well and cheerful, snug and comfortable, in the *Ellis*. The *Ellis* is a model of comfort and convenience; a man who couldn't be comfortable in it couldn't be comfortable anywhere. As to where I am, I could get the precise data from the calculators, but I think, for the casual purposes of this record, it's enough to say that I am almost at the edges of the area where the prott are said to abound. And my speed is almost exactly that at which they are supposed to appear.

I said I was well and cheerful. I am. But just under my euphoria, just at the edge of consciousness, I am aware of an intense loneliness. It's a normal response to the deep space situation, I think. And I am upborne by the feeling that I stand on the threshold of unique scientific discoveries.

Thursday the 26th (my days are more than twenty-four hours long). Today my loneliness is definitely conscious. I am troubled, too, by the fear that perhaps the prott won't—aren't going to—put in an appearance. After all, their existence is none too well confirmed. And then what becomes of all my plans, of my smug confidence of a niche for myself in the hall of fame of good investigators?

It seemed like a brilliant idea when I was on Earth. I know the bursar thought so, too, when I asked for funds for the project. To investigate the life habits of a non-protoplasmic form of life, with special emphasis on its reproduction—excellent! But now?

Saturday, April 30th. Still no prott. But I am feeling better. I went over my files on them and again it seems to me that there is only one conclusion possible:

They exist.

Over an enormous sector in the depth of space, during many years, they have been sighted. For my own comfort, let's list the known facts about prott.

First, they are a non-protoplasmic form of life. (How could they be otherwise, in this lightless, heatless gulf?) Second, their bodily organization is probably electrical. Simmons, who was electrical engineer on the *Thor*, found that his batteries showed discharges when prott were around. Third, they appear only to ships which are in motion between certain rates of speed. (Whether motion at certain speeds attracts them, or whether it is only at certain frequencies that they are visible, we don't know.) Fourth, whether or not they are intelligent, they are to some extent telepathic, according to the reports. This fact, of course, is my hope of communicating with them at all. And fifth, prott have been evocatively if unscientifically described as looking like big poached eggs.

On the basis of these facts, I've aspired to be the Columbus —or, more accurately, the Dr. Kinsey—of the prott. Well, it's good to know that, lonely and rather worried as I am, I can still laugh at my own jokes.

May 3rd. I saw my first prott. More later. It's enough for now: I saw my first prott.

May 4th. The *Ellis* has all-angle viewing plates, through 360 degrees. I had set up an automatic signal, and yesterday it rang. My heart thumping with an almost painful excitement, I ran to the battery of plates.

There it was, seemingly some five yards long, a cloudy, whitish thing. There was a hint of a large yellow nucleus. Damned if the thing *didn't* look like a big poached egg!

I saw at once why everyone has assumed that prott are life-forms and not, for example, minute spaceships, robots, or machines of some sort. The thing had the irregular, illogical symmetry of life.

I stood goggling at it. It wasn't alarming, even in its enormous context. After a moment, it seemed to flirt away from the ship with the watery ease of a fish.

I waited hopefully, but it didn't come back.

May 4th. No prott. Question: Since there is so little light in deep space, how was I able to see it? It wasn't luminous.

I wish I had had more training in electronics and allied subjects. But the bursar thought it more important to send out a man trained in survey techniques.

May 5th. No prott.

May 6th. No prott. But I have been having very odd thoughts.

May 8th. As I half-implied in my last entry, the ideas I have been having (such odd ideas—they made me feel, mentally, as if some supporting membrane of my personality were being overstrained) were an indication of the proximity of prott.

I had just finished eating lunch today when the automatic signal rang. I hurried to the viewers. There, perfectly clear against their jet-black background, were three prott. Two were almost identical; one was slightly smaller in size. I had retraced over and over in my mind the glimpse of the one prott I had had before, but now that three of them were actually present in the viewers, I could only stare at them. They're not alarming, but they do have an odd effect upon the mind.

After several tense seconds, I recovered my wits. I pressed a button to set the automatic photographic records going. I'd put in plates to cover the whole spectrum of radiant energy, and it will be interesting when I go to develop my pictures to see what frequencies catch the prott best. I also—this was more difficult—began to send out the basic "Who? Who? Who?" in which all telepathic communicators are trained.

I have become reasonably good at telepathy through practice, but I have no natural talent for it. I remember McIlwrath telling me jokingly, just before I left New York, that I'd never have trouble with one of the pitfalls of natural telepaths— transmitting a desired answer into the mind of a subject by telepathy. I suppose any deficiency has some advantageous side.

I began to send out my basic "Who?" It may have been only a coincidence, but as soon as the fourth or fifth impulse had left my mind, all three prott slid out of the viewing plates. They didn't come back. It would seem that my attempts at communication alarmed them. I hope not, though.

When I was convinced that they would not return for a while, I began to develop my plates. Those in the range of visible light show the prott very much as they appear to the eye. The infra-red plates show nothing at all. But the ultra-violet-sensitive ones are really interesting.

Two of the prott appear as a network of luminous lines intricately knotted and braided. For some reason, I was reminded of the "elfish light" of Coleridge's water snakes, which "moved in tracks of shining white." The thi·· ·rott, which I assume to have been the smaller one, gave an opaque, flattened-ovoid image, definitely smaller than that of its companions, with a round dark shadow in the center. This shadow would appear to be the large yellow nucleus.

Question: Do these photographic differences correspond to organizational differences? Probably, though it might be a matter of phase.

Further question: If the difference is in fact organizational, do we have here an instance of that specialization which, among protoplasmic creatures, would correspond to sex? It is possible. But such theorizing is bound to be plain guesswork.

May 9th (I see I gave up dating by days some while ago.). No prott. I think it would be of some interest if, at this point,

I were to try to put down my impression of those "odd thoughts" which I believe the prott inspired in me.

In the first place, there is a reluctance. I didn't want to think what I was thinking. This is not because the ideas were in themselves repellent or disgusting, but because they were uncongenial to my mind. I don't mean uncongenial to my personality or my idiosyncrasies, to the sum of differences that make up "me," but uncongenial to the whole biological orientation of my thinking. The differences between protoplasmic and non-protoplasmic life must be enormous.

In the second place, there is a frustration. I said, "I didn't want to think what I was thinking," but it would be equally true to say that I *couldn't* think it. Hence, I suppose, that sensation of ineffectuality.

And in the third place, there is a great boredom. Frustration often does make one feel bored, I suppose. I couldn't apprehend my own thoughts. But whenever I finally did, I found them boring. They were so remote, so incomprehensible, that they were uninteresting.

But the thoughts themselves? What were they? I can't say.

How confused all this is! Well, nothing is more tiresome than to describe the indescribable.

Perhaps it is true that the only creature th ' could understand the thoughts of a prott would be another  rott.

May 10th. Were the "odd thoughts" the results of attempts on the protts' part to communicate with me? I don't think so. I believe they were near the ship, but out of "view-shot," so to speak, and I picked up some of their interpersonal communications accidentally.

I have been devoting a good deal of thought to the problem of communicating with them. It is too bad that there is no way of projecting a visual image of myself onto the exterior of the ship. I have Matheson's signaling devices, and next time—if there is a next—I shall certainly try them. I have little confidence in devices, however. I feel intuitively that it is going to have to be telepathy or nothing. But if they respond to the basic "who?" with flight . . . well, I must think of something else.

Suppose I were to begin the attempt at contact with a "split-question." "Splits" are hard for any telepath, almost impossible for me. But in just that difficulty, my hope of success might lie. After all, I suppose the prott flirted away from the ship at my "who?" because mental contact with me was painful to them.

Later. Four of them are here now. I tried a split and they went away, but came back. I am going to try something else.

May 11th. It worked. My "three-way split"—something I had only read about in journals, but that I would never have believed myself capable of—was astoundingly effective.

Not at first, though. At my first attempt, the prott darted right out of the viewers. I had a moment of despair. Then, with an almost human effect of hesitation, reluctance, and inclination, they came back. They clustered around the viewer. Once more I sent out my impulse; sweat was running down my back with the effort. And they stayed.

I don't know what I should have done if they hadn't. A split is exhausting because, in addition to the three normal axes of the mind, it involves a fourth one, at right angles to all the others. A telepath would know what I mean. But a three-way split is, in the old-fashioned phrase, "lifting yourself up by your bootstraps." Some experts say it's impossible. I still have trouble believing I brought it off.

I did, however. There was a sudden rush, a gush, of communication. I'd like to try to get it down now, while it's still fresh in my mind. But I'm too tired. Even the effort of using the playback is almost beyond me. I've got to rest.

Later. I've been asleep for four hours. I don't think I ever slept so soundly. Now I'm almost myself again, except that my hands shake.

I said I wanted to get the communication with the prott down while it was still fresh. Already it has begun to seem a little remote, I suppose because the subject matter was inherently alien. But the primary impression I retain of it is the gush, the suddenness. It was like pulling the cork out of a bottle of warm champagne which has been thoroughly shaken up.

In the middle, I had to try to maintain my mental balance in the flood. It was difficult; no wonder the effort left me so tired. But I did learn basic things.

One: identity. The prott are individuals, and though their designations for themselves escape me, they have individual consciousness. This is not a small matter. Some protoplasmic life-forms have only group consciousness. Each of the four prott in my viewer was thoroughly aware of itself as distinct from the others.

Two: difference. The prott were not only aware of identity, they were aware of differences of class between themselves. And I am of the opinion that these differences correspond to those shown on my photographic plates.

Three: place. The prott are quite clearly conscious that they are *here* and not somewhere else. This may seem either trivial or so basic as not to be worth bothering with. But there are whole groups of protoplasmic life-forms on Venus whose only cognizance of place is a distinction between "me" and "not-me."

Four: time. For the prott, time is as it is for us, an irreversible flowing in one direction only. I caught in their thinking a hint of a discrimination between biological (for such a life-form? That is what it seemed) time and something else, I am not sure what.

Beyond these four basic things, I am unsure. I do feel, though it is perhaps overoptimistic of me, that further communication, communication of great interest, is possible. I feel that I may be able to discover what their optimum life conditions and habitat are. I do not despair of discovering how they reproduce themselves.

I have the feeling that there is something they want very much to tell me.

May 13th. Six prott today. According to my photographic record, only one of them was of the opaque solid-nucleus kind. The others all showed the luminous light-tracked mesh.

The communication was difficult. It is exhausting to me physically. I had again that sense of psychic pressure, of urgency, in their sendings. If I only knew what they wanted to "talk" about, it would be so much easier for me.

I have the impression that they have a psychic itch they want me to help them scratch. That's silly? Yes, I know, yet that is the odd impression I have.

After they were gone, I analyzed my photographs carefully. The knotted light meshes are not identical in individuals. If the patterns are constant for individuals, it would seem that two of the light-mesh kind have been here before.

What do they want to talk about?

May 14th. Today the prott—seven of them—and I communicated about habitat. This much is fairly certain. It would appear—and I think that from now on any statement I make about them is going to have to be heavily qualified—it would appear that they are not necessarily confined to the lightless, heatless depths of space. I can't be sure about this. But I thought I got the hint of something "solid" in their thinking.

Wild speculation: do they get their energy from stars?

Behind their sendings, I got again the hint of some other more desired communication. Something which at once attracts and—repels? frightens? embarrasses?

Sometimes the humor of my situation comes to me suddenly. An embarrassed prott! But I suppose there's no reason why not.

All my visitors today were of the knotted network kind.

May 16th. No prott yesterday or today.

May 18th. At last! Three prott! From subsequent analysis of the network patterns, all had been here to interview me before. We began communication about habitat and what, with protoplasm, would be metabolic processes, but they did not seem interested. They left soon.

Why do they visit the ship, anyhow? Curiosity? That motive must not be so powerful by now. Because of something they want from me? I imagine so; it is again an awareness of some psychic itch. And that gives me a lead as to the course I should follow.

The next time they appear, I shall try to be more passive in my communications. I shall try not to lead them on to any particular subject. Not only is this good interviewing technique, it is essential in this case if I am to gain their full co-operation.

May 20. After a fruitless wait yesterday, today there was one lone prott. In accordance with my recent decision, I adopted a highly passive attitude toward it. I sent out signals of willingness and receptivity, and I waited, watching the prott.

For five or ten minutes there was "silence." The prott moved about in the viewers with an effect of restlessness, though it might have been any other emotion, of course. Suddenly, with great haste and urgency, it began to send. I had again that image of the cork blowing out of the champagne bottle.

Its sending was remarkably difficult for me to follow. At the end of the first three minutes or so, I was wringing wet with sweat. Its communications were repetitive, urgent, and, I believe, pleasurable. I simply had no terms into which to translate them. They seemed to involve many verbs.

I "listened" passively, trying to preserve my mental equilibrium. My bewilderment increased as the prott continued to send. Finally I had to recognize that I was getting to a point where intellectual frustration would interfere with my telepathy. I ventured to put a question, a simple "Please classify" to the prott.

Its sending slackened and then ceased abruptly. It disappeared.

What did I learn from the interview? That the passive approach is the correct one, and that a prott will send freely (and most confusingly, as far as I am concerned) if it is not harassed with questions or directed to a particular topic. What I didn't learn was what the prott was sending about.

Whatever it was, I have the impression that it was highly agreeable to the prott.

Later—I have been rereading the notes I made on my sessions with the prott. What has been the matter with me? I wonder at my blindness. For the topic about which the prott was sending—the pleasurable, repetitive, embarrassing topic, the one about which it could not bear to be questioned, the subject which involved so many verbs—that topic could be nothing other than its sex life.

When put this baldly, it sounds ridiculous. I make haste to qualify it. We don't, as yet—and what a triumph it is to be able to say "as yet"—know anything about the manner in which prott reproduce themselves. They may, for example, increase by a sort of fission. They may be dioecious, as so much highly organized life is. Or their reproductive cycle may involve the cooperative activity of two, three or even more different sorts of prott.

So far, I have seen only the two sorts, those with the solid nucleus, and those with the intricate network of light. That does not mean there may not be other kinds.

But what I am driving at is this: The topic about which the prott communicated with me today is one which, to the prott, has the same emotional and psychic value that sex has to protoplasmic life.

(Somehow, at this point, I am reminded of a little anecdote of my grandmother's. She used to say that there are four things in a dog's life which it is important for it to keep in mind, one for each foot. The things are food, food, sex, and *food*. She bred dachshunds and she knew. Question: Does my coming up with this recollection at this time mean that I suspect the prott's copulatory activity is also nutritive, like the way in which ameba conjugate? Their exchange of nuclei seems to have a beneficial effect on their metabolism.)

Be that as it may, I now have a thesis to test in my dealings with the prott!

May 21st. There were seven prott in the viewer when the signal rang. While I watched, more and more arrived. It was impossible to count them accurately, but I think there must have been at least fifteen.

They started communicating almost immediately. Not wanting to disturb them with directives, I attempted to "listen" passively, but the effect on me was that of being caught in a crowd of people all talking at once. After a few minutes, I was compelled to ask them to send one at a time.

From then on, the sending was entirely orderly.

Orderly, but incomprehensible. So much so that, at the end of some two hours, I was forced to break off the interview.

It is the first time I have ever done such a thing.

Why did I do it? My motives are not entirely clear even to myself. I was trying to receive passively, keeping in mind the theory I had formed about the prott's communication. (And let me say at this point that I have found nothing to contradict it. Nothing whatever.) Yet, as time passed, my bewilderment increased almost painfully. Out of the mass of chaotic, repetitive material presented to me, I was able to form *not one single clear idea.*

I would not have believed that a merely intellectual frustration could be so difficult to take.

The communication itself was less difficult than yesterday. I must think.

I have begun to lose weight.

June 12th. I have not made an entry in my diary for a long time. In the interval, I have had thirty-six interviews with prott.

What emerges from these sessions, which are so painful and frustrating to me, so highly enjoyed by the prott?

First, communication with them has become very much

easier. It has become, in fact, too easy. I continually find their thoughts intruding on me at times when I cannot welcome them—when I am eating, writing up my notes, or trying to sleep. But the strain of communication is much less and I suppose that does constitute an advance.

Second, out of the welter of material presented to me, I have at last succeeded in forming one fairly clear idea. That is that the main topic of the prott's communication is a process that could be represented verbally as —ing the—. I add at once that the blanks do not necessarily represent an obscenity. I have, in fact, no idea what they *do* represent.

(The phrases that come into my mind in this connection are "kicking the bucket" and "belling the cat." It may not be without significance that one of these phrases relates to death and the other to danger. Communication with prott is so unsatisfactory that one cannot afford to neglect any intimations that might clarify it. It is possible that —ing the— is something which is potentially dangerous to prott, but that's only a guess. I could have it all wrong, and I probably do.)

At any rate, my future course has become clear. From now on I will attempt, by every mental means at my disposal, to get the prott to specify what —ing the— is. There is no longer any fear of losing their cooperation. Even as I dictate these words to the playback, they are sending more material about —ing the— to me.

June 30th. The time has gone very quickly, and yet each individual moment has dragged. I have had fifty-two formal interviews with prott—they appear in crowds ranging from fifteen to forty or so—and countless informal ones. My photographic record shows that more than ninety per cent of those that have appeared have been of the luminous network kind.

In all this communication, what have I learned? It gives me a sort of bitter satisfaction to say: "Nothing at all."

I am too chagrined to go on.

July 1st. I don't mean that I haven't explored avenue after avenue. For instance, at one time it appeared that —ing the—

had something to do with the intersections of the luminous network in prott of that sort. When I attempted to pursue this idea, I met with a negative that seemed amused as well as indignant. They indicated that —ing the— was concerned with the whitish body surfaces, but when I picked up the theme, I got another negative signal. And so on. I must have attacked the problem from fifty different angles, but I had to give up on all of them.

—ing the—, it would appear, is electrical, non-electrical, solitary, dual, triple, communal, constant, never done at all. At one time I thought that it might apply to any pleasurable activity, but the prott signaled that I was all wrong. I broke that session off short.

Outside of their baffling communications on the subject of —ing the—, I have learned almost nothing from the prott.

(How sick I am of them and their inane, vacuous babbling! The phrases of our communication ring in my mind for hours afterward. They haunt me like a clinging odor or stubbornly lingering taste.)

During one session, a prott (solid nucleus, I think, but I am not sure) informed me that they could live under a wide variety of conditions, provided there was a source of radiant energy not too remote. Besides that scrap of information, I have an impression that they are grateful to me for listening to them. Their feelings, I think, could be expressed in the words "understanding and sympathetic."

I don't know why they think so, I'm sure. I would rather communicate with a swarm of dog-fish, which are primitively telepathic, than listen to any more prott.

I have had to punch another hole in my wristwatch strap to take up the slack. This makes the third one.

July 3rd. It is difficult for me to use the playback, the prott are sending so hard. I have scarcely a moment's rest from their communications, all concerned with the same damned subject. But I have come to a resolve: I am going home.

Yes, home. It may be that I have failed in my project, because of inner weaknesses. It may be that no man alive could have accomplished more. I don't know. But I ache to get away from them and the flabby texture of their babbling minds. If only there were some way of shutting them off, of stopping my mental ears against them temporarily, I think I could stand it. But there isn't.

I'm going home. I've started putting course data in the computors.

July 4th. They say they are going back with me. It seems they like me so much, they don't want to be without me.

I will have to decide.

July 12th. It is dreadfully hard to think, for they are sending like mad.

I am not so altruistic, so unselfish, that I would condemn myself to a lifetime of listening to prott if I could get out of it. But suppose I ignore the warnings of instinct, the dictates of conscience, and return to Earth, anyhow—what will be the result?

The prott will go with me. I will not be rid of them. And I will have loosed a wave of prott on Earth.

They want passionately to send about —ing the—. They have discovered that Earthmen are potential receptors. I have myself to blame for that. If I show them the way to Earth . . .

The dilemma is inherently comic, I suppose. It is none the less real. Oh, it is possible that there is some way of destroying prott, and that the resources of Earth intelligence might discover it. Or, failing that, we might be able to work out a way of living with them. But the danger is too great; I dare not ask my planet to face it. I will stay here.

The *Ellis* is a strong, comfortable ship. According to my calculations, there is enough air, water and food to last me the rest of my natural life. Power—since I am not going back—I have in abundance. I ought to get along all right.

Except for the prott. When I think of them, my heart contracts with despair and revulsion. And yet—a scientist must be honest—it is not all despair. I feel a little sorry for them, a little flattered at their need for me. And I am not, even now, altogether hopeless. Perhaps some day—*some day*—I shall understand the prott.

I am going to put this diary in a permaloy cylinder and jet it away from the ship with a signal rocket. I can soup up the rocket's charge with power from the fuel tanks. I have tried it on the calculators, and I think the rocket can make it to the edge of the gravitational field of the Solar System.

Good-by, Earth. I am doing it for you. Remember me.

*Fox put the last page of the manuscript down. "The poor bastard," he said.*

*"Yeah, the poor bastard. Sitting out there in deep space, year after year, listening to those things bellyaching, and thinking what a savior he was."*

*"I can't say I feel much sympathy for him, really. I suppose they followed the signal rocket back."*

*"Yeah. And then they increased. Oh, he fixed it, all right."*

*There was a depressed silence. Then Fox said, "I'd better go. Impatient."*

*"Mine, too."*

*They said good-by to each other on the curb. Fox stood waiting, still not quite hopeless. But after a moment the hateful voice within his head began:*

*"I want to tell you more about —ing the—"*

**Isaac Asimov**

# FLIES

*This story is almost impossible to introduce. For one thing, it is in a class by itself; as far as I know, nothing like it has ever been written before. For another, its exploration of muscid theology is so subtly horrible that it almost lies beyond discussion. And, finally, the tale has the curious quality of giving some people (the editor included) the cold shivers, and leaving others totally unmoved. Read it carefully, for it is simple only on the surface. Beneath there are strange undercurrents that touch on one's most primitive fears . . .*

"FLIES!" SAID KENDELL CASEY, WEARILY. HE SWUNG HIS arm. The fly circled, returned and nestled on Casey's shirt-collar.

From somewhere there sounded the buzzing of a second fly.

Dr. John Polen covered the slight uneasiness of his chin by moving his cigarette quickly to his lips.

He said, "I didn't expect to meet you, Casey. Or you, Winthrop. Or ought I call you Reverend Winthrop?"

Isaac Asimov, FLIES. Copyright 1953 by Fantasy House, Inc. Reprinted by permission of the author from *Fantasy and Science Fiction*, June 1953.

"Ought I call you Professor Polen?" said Winthrop, carefully striking the proper vein of rich-toned friendship.

They were trying to snuggle into the cast-off shell of twenty years back, each one of them. Squirming and cramming and not fitting.

Damn, thought Polen fretfully, why do people attend college reunions?

Casey's hot blue eyes were still filled with the aimless anger of the college sophomore who has discovered intellect, frustration, and the tag-ends of cynical philosophy all at once.

Casey! Bitter man of the campus!

He hadn't outgrown that. Twenty years later and it was Casey, bitter ex-man of the campus! Polen could see that in the way his finger tips moved aimlessly and in the manner of his spare body.

As for Winthrop? Well, twenty years older, softer, rounder. Skin pinker, eyes milder. Yet no nearer the quiet certainty he would never find. It was all there in the quick smile he never entirely abandoned, as though he feared there would be nothing to take its place, that its absence would turn his face into a smooth and featureless flush.

Polen was tired of reading the aimless flickering of a muscle's end; tired of usurping the place of his machines; tired of the too much they told him.

Could they read him as he read them? Could the small restlessness of his own eyes broadcast the fact that he was damp with the disgust that had bred mustily within him?

Damn, thought Polen, why didn't I stay away?

They stood there, all three, waiting for one another to say something, to flick something from across the gap and bring it, quivering, into the present.

Polen tried it. He said, "Are you still working in chemistry, Casey?"

"In my own way, yes," said Casey, gruffly. "I'm not the scientist you're considered to be. I do research on insecticides for E. J. Link at Chatham."

Winthrop said, "Are you really? You said you would work

on insecticides. Remember, Polen? And with all that, the flies dare still be after you, Casey?"

Casey said, "Can't get rid of them. I'm the best proving ground in the labs. No compound we've made keeps them away when I'm around. Someone once said it was my odor. I attract them."

Polen remembered the someone who had said that.

Winthrop said, "Or else—"

Polen felt it coming. He tensed.

"Or else," said Winthrop, "it's the curse, you know." His smile intensified to show that he was joking, that he forgave past grudges.

Damn, thought Polen, they haven't even changed the words. And the past came back.

"Flies," said Casey, swinging his arm, and slapping. "Ever see such a thing? Why don't they light on you two?"

Johnny Polen laughed at him. He laughed often then. "It's something in your body odor, Casey. You could be a boon to science. Find out the nature of the odorous chemical, concentrate it, mix it with DDT, and you've got the best fly-killer in the world."

"A fine situation. What do I smell like? A lady fly in heat? It's a shame they have to pick on me when the whole damned world's a dung heap."

Winthrop frowned and said with a faint flavor of rhetoric, "Beauty is not the only thing, Casey, in the eye of the beholder."

Casey did not deign a direct response. He said to Polen, "You know what Winthrop told me yesterday? He said those damned flies were the curse of Beelzebub."

"I was joking," said Winthrop.

"Why Beelzebub?" asked Polen.

"It amounts to a pun," said Winthrop. "The ancient Hebrews used it as one of their many terms of derision for alien gods. It comes from *Ba'al*, meaning *lord* and *zevuv*, meaning *fly*. The lord of flies."

Casey said, "Come on, Winthrop, don't say you don't be-lieve in Beelzebub."

"I believe in the existence of evil," said Winthrop, stiffly.

"I mean Beelzebub. Alive. Horns. Hooves. A sort of com-petition deity."

"Not at all." Winthrop grew stiffer. "Evil is a short-term affair. In the end it must lose—"

Polen changed the subject with a jar. He said, "I'll be doing graduate work for Venner, by the way. I talked with him day before yesterday, and he'll take me on."

"No! That's wonderful." Winthrop glowed and leaped to the subject-change instantly. He held out a hand with which to pump Polen's. He was always conscientiously eager to rejoice in another's good fortune. Casey often pointed that out.

Casey said, "Cybernetics Venner? Well, if you can stand him, I suppose he can stand you."

Winthrop went on. "What did he think of your idea? Did you tell him your idea?"

"What idea?" demanded Casey.

Polen had avoided telling Casey so far. But now Venner had considered it and had passed it with a cool, "Interesting!" How could Casey's dry laughter hurt it now?

Polen said, "It's nothing much. Essentially, it's just a notion that emotion is the common bond of life, rather than reason or intellect. It's practically a truism, I suppose. You can't tell what a baby thinks or even *if* it thinks, but it's perfectly obvi-ous that it can be angry, frightened or contented even when a week old. See?

"Same with animals. You can tell in a second if a dog is happy or if a cat is afraid. The point is that their emotions are the same as those we would have under the same circum-stances."

"So?" said Casey. "Where does it get you?"

"I don't know yet. Right now, all I can say is that emotions are universals. Now suppose we could properly analyze all the actions of men and certain familiar animals and equate them with the visible emotion. We might find a tight relation-ship. Emotion A might always involve Motion B. Then we could apply it to animals whose emotions we couldn't guess at by common sense alone. Like snakes, or lobsters."

"Or flies," said Casey, as he slapped viciously at another and flicked its remains off his wrist in furious triumph.

He went on. "Go ahead, Johnny. I'll contribute the flies and you study them. We'll establish a science of flychology and labor to make them happy by removing their neuroses. After all, we want the greatest good of the greatest number, don't we? And there are more flies than men."

"Oh, well," said Polen.

Casey said, "Say, Polen, did you ever follow up that weird idea of yours? I mean, we all know you're a shining cybernetic light, but I haven't been reading your papers. With so many ways of wasting time, something has to be neglected, you know."

"What idea?" asked Polen, woodenly.

"Come on. You know. Emotions of animals and all that sort of gug. Boy, those were the days. I used to know madmen. Now I only come across idiots."

Winthrop said, "That's right, Polen. I remember it very well. Your first year in graduate school you were working on dogs and rabbits. I believe you even tried some of Casey's flies."

Polen said, "It came to nothing in itself. It gave rise to certain new principles of computing, however, so it wasn't a total loss."

Why did they talk about it?

Emotions! What right had anyone to meddle with emotions? Words were invented to conceal emotions. It was the dreadfulness of raw emotion that had made language a basic necessity.

Polen knew. His machines had by-passed the screen of verbalization and dragged the unconscious into the sunlight. The boy and the girl, the son and the mother. For that matter, the cat and the mouse or the snake and the bird. The data rattled together in its universality and it had all poured into and through Polen until he could no longer bear the touch of life.

In the last few years he had so painstakingly schooled his thoughts in other directions. Now these two came, dabbling in his mind, stirring up its mud.

Casey batted abstractedly across the tip of his nose to dislodge a fly. "Too bad," he said. "I used to think you could get some fascinating things out of, say, rats. Well, maybe not fascinating, but then not as boring as the stuff you would get out of our somewhat-human beings. I used to think—"

Polen remembered what he used to think.

Casey said, "Damn this DDT. The flies feed on it, I think. You know, I'm going to do graduate work in chemistry and then get a job on insecticides. So help me. I'll personally get something that *will* kill the vermin."

They were in Casey's room, and it had a somewhat keroseny odor from the recently applied insecticide.

Polen shrugged and said, "A folded newspaper will always kill."

Casey detected a non-existent sneer and said instantly, "How would you summarize your first year's work, Polen? I mean aside from the true summary any scientist could state if he dared, by which I mean: 'Nothing.'"

"Nothing," said Polen. "There's your summary."

"Go on," said Casey. "You use more dogs than the physiologists do and I bet the dogs mind the physiological experiments less. I would."

"Oh, leave him alone," said Winthrop. "You sound like a piano with 87 keys eternally out of order. You're a bore.'

You couldn't say that to Casey.

He said, with sudden liveliness, looking carefully away from Winthrop, "I'll tell you what you'll probably find in animals, if you look closely enough. Religion."

"What the dickens!" said Winthrop, outraged. "That's a foolish remark."

Casey smiled. "Now, now, Winthrop. *Dickens* is just a euphemism for *devil* and you don't want to be swearing."

"Don't teach me morals. And don't be blasphemous."

"What's blasphemous about it? Why shouldn't a flea consider the dog as something to be worshipped? It's the source of warmth, food, and all that's good for a flea."

"I don't want to discuss it."

"Why not? Do you good. You could even say that to an ant, an anteater is a higher order of creation. He would be too big for them to comprehend, too mighty to dream of resisting. He would move among them like an unseen, inexplicable whirlwind, visiting them with destruction and death. But that wouldn't spoil things for the ants. They would reason that destruction was simply their just punishment for evil. And the anteater wouldn't even know he was a deity. Or care."

Winthrop had gone white. He said, "I know you're saying this only to annoy me and I am sorry to see you risking your soul for a moment's amusement. Let me tell you this," his voice trembled a little, "and let me say it very seriously. The flies that torment you are your punishment in this life. Beelzebub, like all the forces of evil, may think he does evil, but it's only the ultimate good after all. The curse of Beelzebub is on you for *your* good. Perhaps it will succeed in getting you to change your way of life before it's too late."

He ran from the room.

Casey watched him go. He said, laughing, "I told you Winthrop believed in Beelzebub. It's funny the respectable names you can give to superstition." His laughter died a little short of its natural end.

There were two flies in the room, buzzing through the vapors toward him.

Polen rose and left in heavy depression. One year had taught him little, but it was already too much, and his laughter was thinning. Only his machines could analyze the emotions of animals properly, but he was already guessing too deeply concerning the emotions of men.

He did not like to witness wild murder-yearnings where others could see only a few words of unimportant quarrel.

Casey said, suddenly, "Say, come to think of it, you did try some of my flies, the way Winthrop says. How about that?"

"Did I? After twenty years, I scarcely remember," murmured Polen.

Winthrop said, "You must. We were in your laboratory and you complained that Casey's flies followed him even there. He suggested you analyze them and you did. You recorded their motions and buzzings and wing-wiping for half an hour or more. You played with a dozen different flies."

Polen shrugged.

"Oh, well," said Casey. "It doesn't matter. It was good seeing you, old man." The hearty hand-shake, the thump on the shoulder, the broad grin—to Polen it all translated into sick disgust on Casey's part that Polen was a "success" after all.

Polen said, "Let me hear from you sometimes."

The words were dull thumps. They meant nothing. Casey knew that. Polen knew that. Everyone knew that. But words were meant to hide emotion and whe they failed, humanity loyally maintained the pretence.

Winthrop's grasp of the hand was gentler. He said, "This brought back old times, Polen. If you're ever in Cincinnati, why don't you stop in at the meeting-house? You'll always be welcome."

To Polen, it all breathed of the man's relief at Polen's obvious depression. Science, too, it seemed, was not the answer, and Winthrop's basic and ineradicable insecurity felt pleased at the company.

"I will," said Polen. It was the usual polite way of saying, I won't.

He watched them thread separately to other groups.

Winthrop would never know. Polen was sure of that. He wondered if Casey knew. It would be the supreme joke if Casey did not.

He *had* run Casey's flies, of course, not that once alone, but many times. Always the same answer! Always the same unpublishable answer.

With a cold shiver he could not quite control, Polen was suddenly conscious of a single fly loose in the room, veering aimlessly for a moment, then beating strongly and reverently in the direction Casey had taken a moment before.

Could Casey *not* know? Could it be the essence of the primal punishment that he never learn he was Beelzebub?

Casey! Lord of the Flies!

Paul Ernst

# THE MICROSCOPIC GIANTS

*One of the subjects that has fascinated imaginative
writers for over a century is the possibility of intelligent life forms existing at great depths in the earth.
Jules Verne, Bulwer-Lytton and Edgar Allan Poe,
among the oldsters, and A. Merritt, Arthur C. Clarke,
and Hal Clement among more modern writers, all
have dealt with it. But none of them, I think, ever
produced a more vivid and shocking picture of beings living under thoroughly inhuman conditions
than has Paul Ernst in this famous tale.*

IT HAPPENED TOWARD THE END OF THE GREAT WAR, WHICH
was an indirect cause. You'll find mention of it in the official
records filed at Washington. Curious reading, some of those
records! Among them are accounts of incidents so bizarre—
freak accidents and odd discoveries fringing war activities—
that the filing clerks must have raised their eyebrows skep-
tically before they buried them in steel cabinets, to remain
unread for the rest of time.

But this particular one will never be buried in oblivion for

me. Because I was on the spot when it happened, and I was
the one who sent in the report.

Copper!

A war-worn world was famished for it. The thunder of
guns, from the Arctic to the Antarctic and from the Pacific
to the Atlantic and back again, drummed for it. Equipment
behind the lines demanded it. Statesmen lied for it and national bankers ran up bills that would never be paid to get it.

Copper, copper, copper!

Every obscure mine in the world was worked to capacity.
Men risked their lives to salvage fragments from battlefields
a thousand miles long. And still not enough copper was available.

Up in the Lake Superior region we had gone down thirty-
one thousand feet for it. Then, in answer to the enormous
prices being paid for copper, we sank a shaft to forty thousand five hundred feet, where we struck a vein of almost pure
ore. And it was shortly after this that my assistant, a young
mining engineer named Belmont, came into my office, his
eyes afire with the light of discovery.

"We've uncovered the greatest archaeological find since
the days of the Rosetta Stone!" he announced bluntly. "Down
in the new low level. I want to phone the Smithsonian Institution at once. There may be a war on, but the professors will
forget all about war when they see this!"

Jim Belmont was apt to be over-enthusiastic. Under thirty,
a tall, good-looking chap with light blue eyes looking lighter
than they really were in a tanned, lean face, he sometimes
overshot his mark by leaping before he looked.

"Wait a minute!" I said. "What have you found? Prehistoric
bones? Some new kind of fossil monster?"

"Not bones," said Belmont, fidgeting toward the control
board that dialed our private number to Washington on the
radio telephone. "Footprints, Frayter. Fossil footsteps."

"You mean men's footprints?" I demanded, frowning. The
rock formation at the forty-thousand-foot level was age-old.

The Pleistocene era had not occurred when those rocks were formed. "Impossible."

"But I tell you they're down there! Footprints preserved in the solid rock. Men's footprints! They antedate anything ever thought of in the age of Man."

Belmont drew a deep breath.

"And more than that," he almost whispered. "They are prints of shod men, Frank! The men who made those prints, millions of years ago, wore shoes. We've stumbled on traces of a civilization that existed long, long before man was supposed to have evolved on this earth at all!"

His whisper reverberated like a shout, such was its great import. But I still couldn't believe it. Prints of men—at the forty-thousand-foot level—and prints of shod feet at that!

"If they're prints of feet with shoes on them," I said, "they might be simply prints of our own workmen's boots. If the Smithsonian men got up here and found that, a laugh would go up that would ruin us."

"No, no," said Belmont. "That's impossible. You see, these prints are those of *little* men. I hadn't told you before, had I? I guess I'm pretty excited. The men who made these prints were small—hardly more than two feet high, if the size of their feet can be taken as a true gauge. The prints are hardly more than three inches long."

"Where did you happen to see them?" I asked.

"Near the concrete we poured to fill in the rift we uncovered at the far end of the level."

"Some of the workmen may have been playing a trick."

"Your confounded skepticism!" Belmont cried. "Tricks! Perhaps they're prints of our own men! Didn't I tell you the prints were preserved in *solid rock?* Do you think a workman would take the trouble to carve, most artistically, a dozen footprints three inches long in solid rock? Or that—if we had any men with feet that small—their feet would sink into the rock for a half inch or more? I tell you these are fossil prints, made millions of years ago when that rock was mud and preserved when the rock hardened."

"And I tell you," I replied a little hotly, "that it's all impossible. Because I supervised the pouring of that concrete, and I would have noticed if there were prints."

"Suppose you come down and look," said Belmont. "After all, that's the one sure way of finding out if what I say is true."

I reached for my hat. Seeing for myself was the one way of finding out if Belmont had gone off half-cocked again.

It takes a long time to go down forty thousand feet. We hadn't attempted to speed up the drop too much; at such great depths there are abnormalities of pressure and temperature to which the human machine takes time to become accustomed.

By the time we'd reached the new low level I'd persuaded myself that Belmont must surely be mad. But having come this far I went through with it, of course.

Fossil prints of men who could not have been more than two feet high, shod in civilized fashion, preserved in rock at the forty-thousand-foot level! It was ridiculous.

We got near the concrete fill at the end of the tunnel, and I pushed the problem of prints out of my mind for a moment while I examined its blank face. Rearing that slanting concrete wall had presented some peculiar problems.

As we had bored in, ever farther under the thick skin of Mother Earth, we had come to a rock formation that had no right to exist there at all. It was a layer of soft, mushy stuff, with gaping cracks in it, slanting down somewhere toward the bowels of the earth. Like a soft strip of marrow in hard bone, it lay between dense, compressed masses of solid rock. And we had put ten feet of concrete over its face to avoid cave-ins.

Concrete is funny stuff. It acts differently in different pressures and temperatures. The concrete we'd poured here, where atmospheric pressure made a man gasp and the temperature was above a hundred and eighteen in spite of cooling systems, hadn't acted at all like any I'd ever seen before. It hadn't seemed to harden as well as it should, and it still rayed out perceptible, self-generated heat in the pressure surrounding it. But it seemed to be serving its purpose, all right, though it was as soft as cheese compared to the rock around it.

"Here!" said Belmont, pointing down in the bright light of the raw electric bulbs stringing along the level. "Look!"

I looked—and got a shock that I can still feel. A half inch or so deep in the rock floor of the level at the base of the concrete retaining wall, there were footprints. The oddest, tiniest things imaginable!

Jim Belmont had said they were three inches long. If anything he had overstated their size. I don't think some of them were more than two and a half inches long! And they were the prints of shod feet, undeniably. Perfect soles and heels, much like those of shoes we wear, were perceptible.

I stared at the prints with disbelief for a moment, even though my own eyes gave proof of their presence. And I felt an icy finger trace its way up my spine.

I had spent hours at this very spot while the concrete fill was made over the face of the down-slanting rift of mush rock. And I hadn't seen the little prints then. Yet here they were, a dozen of them made by feet of at least three varying sizes. How had I missed seeing them before?

"Prints made millions of years ago," Belmont whispered ecstatically. "Preserved when the mud hardened to rock—to be discovered here! Proof of a civilization on earth before man was thought to have been born . . . For Heaven's sake! Look at that concrete!"

I stared along the line of his pointing finger, and saw another queer thing. Queer? It was impossible!

The concrete retaining wall seemed slightly milky, and not quite opaque! Like a great block of frosted glass, into which the eye could see for a few inches before vision was lost.

And then, again, the icy finger touched my spine. This time so plainly that I shuddered a little in spite of the heat.

For a moment I had thought to see movement in the concrete! A vague, luminous swirl that was gone before I had fairly seen it. Or had I seen it! Was imagination, plus the presence of these eerie footprints, working overtime?

"Transparent concrete," said Belmont. "There's one for the

book. Silicon in greater than normal amounts in the sand we used? Some trick of pressure? But it doesn't matter. The prints are more important. Shall we phone the Institute, Frank?"

For a moment I didn't answer. I was observing one more odd thing:

The footprints went in only two directions. They led out from the concrete wall, and led back to it again. And I could still swear they hadn't been there up to three days before, when I had examined the concrete fill most recently.

But of course they must have been there—for a million years or more!

"Let's wait a while on it," I heard myself say. "The prints won't vanish. They're in solid rock."

"But why wait?"

I stared at Belmont, and I saw his eyes widen at something in my face.

"There's something more than peculiar about those prints!" I said. "Fossil footsteps of men two feet high are fantastic enough. But there's something more fantastic than that! See the way they point from the concrete, and then back to it again? As if whatever made them had come out of the concrete, and had looked around for a few minutes, and then had gone back into the concrete again!"

It was Belmont's turn to look at me as if suspecting a lack of sanity. Then he laughed.

"The prints were here a long, long time before the concrete was ever poured, Frank. They just happened to be pointing in the directions they do. All right, we'll wait on the Smithsonian Institution notifications." He stopped and exclaimed aloud, gaze on the rock floor.

"What's the matter?" I asked.

"An illustration of how you could have overlooked the prints when you were supervising the fill," he said, grinning. "When I was down here last, a few hours ago, I counted an even twelve prints. Now, over here where I'd have sworn there were no prints, I see four more, made by still another pair of feet back before the dawn of history. It's funny how unobservant the eye can be."

"Yes," I said slowly. "It's very—funny."

For the rest of the day the drive to get more ore out of the ground, ever more copper for the guns and war instruments, drove the thought of the prints to the back of my mind. But back there the thought persisted.

Tiny men, wearing civilized-looking boots, existing long, long ago! What could they have looked like? The prints, marvelously like those of our own shod feet, suggested that they must have been perfect little humans, like our midgets. What business could they have been about when they left those traces of their existence in mud marshes millions of years ago. . . .

Yes, of course, millions of years ago! Several times I had to rein in vague and impossible impressions with those words. But some deep instinct refused to be reined.

And then Carson, my foreman, came to me when the last of the men had emerged from the shafts.

Carson was old; all the young men save highly trained ones like Belmont and myself, who were more valuable in peace zones, were at the various war fronts. He was nearly seventy, and cool and level-headed. It was unusual to see a frown on his face such as was there when he walked up to me.

"Mr. Frayter," he said, "I'm afraid we'll have trouble with the men."

"Higher wages?" I said. "What they need is more patriotism."

"They're not kicking about wages," Carson said. "It's a lot different than that. Steve Boland, he started it."

He spat tobacco juice at a nailhead.

"Steve works on the new low level, you know. Near the concrete fill. And he's been passing crazy talk among the men. He says he can see into the concrete a little way—"

"That's right," I interrupted him. "I was down this afternoon, and for some curious reason the stuff is a little transparent. Doubtless we could investigate and find out what causes the phenomenon. But it isn't worth taking the time for."

"Maybe it would be worth it," replied Carson quietly. "If it would stop Steve's talk, it might save a shutdown."

"What is Steve saying?"

"He says he saw a man in the concrete, two hours ago. A little man."

I stared at Carson.

"I know he's crazy," the old man went on. "But he's got the rest halfway believing it. He says he saw a man about a foot and a half high, looking at him out of the concrete. The man was dressed in strips of some shiny stuff that made him look like he had a metal shell on. He looked at Steve for maybe a minute, then turned and walked back through the concrete, like it was nothing but thick air. Steve followed him for a foot or so and then was unable to see him any more."

I smiled at Carson while sweat suddenly formed under my arms and trickled down my sides.

"Send Steve to me," I said. "I'll let him tell me the story, too. Meanwhile, kill the story among the men."

Carson sighed.

"It's going to be pretty hard to kill, Mr. Frayter. You see, there's footprints down there. Little footprints that might be made by what Steve claimed he saw."

"You think a man eighteen inches high could sink into solid rock for half an inch—" I began. Then I stopped. But it was already too late.

"Oh, you've seen them too!" said Carson, with the glint of something besides worry in his eyes.

Then I told him of how and when the prints had been made.

"I'll send Steve to you," was all he said, avoiding my eyes.

Steve Boland was a hulking, powerful man of fifty. He was not one of my best men, but as far as I knew he had no record of being either unduly superstitious or a liar.

He repeated to me the story Carson had quoted him as telling. I tried to kill the fear I saw peering out of his eyes.

"You saw those prints, made long ago, and then you imagined you saw what had made them," I argued. "Use your head, man. Do you think anything could live and move around in concrete?"

"I don't think nothing about nothing, Mr. Frayter," he said doggedly. "I saw what I saw. A little man, dressed in some shiny stuff, in the concrete. And those footprints weren't made a long time ago. They were made in the last few days!"

I couldn't do anything with him. He was terrified, under his laborious show of self-control.

"I'm leaving, Mr. Frayter. Unless you let me work in an upper level. I won't go down there any more."

After he had left my office shack, I sent for Belmont.

"This may get serious," I told him, after revealing what I'd heard. "We've got to stop this story right now."

He laughed. "Of all the crazy stuff! But you're right. We ought to stop it. What would be the best way?"

"We'll pull the night shift out of there," I said, "and we'll spend the night watching the concrete. Tell all the men in advance. Then when we come up in the morning, we can see if they'll accept our word of honor that nothing happened."

Belmont grinned and nodded.

"Take a gun," I added, staring at a spot over his head.

"What on earth for?"

"Why not?" I evaded. "They don't weigh much. We might as well carry one apiece in our belts."

His laugh stung me as he went to give orders to the crew usually working at night in the forty-thousand-foot level.

We started on the long trip down, alone.

There is no day or night underground. Yet somehow, as Belmont and I crouched in the low level we could know that it was not day. We could sense that deep night held the world outside; midnight darkness in which nothing was abroad save the faint wind rattling the leaves of the trees.

We sat on the rock fragments, with our backs against the wall, staring at the concrete fill till our eyes ached in the raw electric light. We felt like fools, and said so to each other. And yet—

"Steve has some circumstantial evidence to make his insane yarn sound credible," I said. "The way we overlooked those footprints in the rock till recently makes it look as if they'd been freshly formed. You observed a few more this afternoon than you'd noticed before. And this ridiculous concrete is a shade transparent, as though some action or movement within it had changed its character slightly."

Belmont grimaced toward the concrete.

"If I'd known the report about the footprints was going to turn us all into crazy men," he grumbled, "I'd have kept my mouth shut—"

His voice cracked off abruptly. I saw the grin freeze on his lips; saw him swallow convulsively.

"Look!" he whispered, pointing toward the center of the eight-by-thirty-foot wall.

I stared, but could see nothing unusual about the wall. That is, nothing but the fact we'd observed before; you could look into the thing for a few inches before vision was lost.

"What is it?" I snapped, stirred by the expression on his face.

He sighed, and shook his head.

"Nothing, I guess. I thought for a minute I saw something in the wall. A sort of moving bright spot. But I guess it's only another example of the kind of imagination that got Steve Boland—"

Again he stopped abruptly. And this time he got unsteadily to his feet.

"No, it's not imagination! Look, Frank! If you can't see it, then I'm going crazy!"

I stared again. And this time I could swear I saw something too.

Deep in the ten-foot-thick retaining wall, a dim, luminous spot seemed to be growing. As though some phosphorescent growth were slowly mushrooming in there.

"You see it too?" he breathed.

"I see it too," I whispered.

"Thank God for that! Then I'm sane or we're both mad.

What's happening inside that stuff? It's getting brighter, and larger—" His fingers clamped over my arm. "Look! Look!"

But there was no need for him to tell me to look. I was staring already with starting eyes, while my heart began to hammer in my chest like a sledge.

As the faint, luminous spot in the concrete grew larger it also took recognizable form. And the form that appeared in the depths of the stuff was that of a human!

Human? Well, yes, if you can think of a thing no bigger than an eighteen-inch doll as being human.

A mannikin a foot and a half high, embedded in the concrete! But not embedded—for it was moving! Toward us!

In astounded silence, Belmont and I stared. It didn't occur to us then to be afraid. Nothing occurred to us save indescribable wonder at the impossible vision we saw.

I can close my eyes and see the thing now: a manlike little figure walking toward us through solid concrete. It bent forward as though shouldering a way against a sluggish tide, or a heavy wind; it moved as a deep-sea diver might move in clogging water. But that was all the resistance the concrete seemed to offer to it, that sluggish impediment to its forward movement.

Behind it there was a faint swirl of luminosity, like phosphorescent water moving in the trail of a tiny boat. And the luminosity surrounded the thing like an aura.

And now we could see its face and I heard Belmont's whispered exclamation. For the face was as human as ours, with a straight nose, a firm, well-shaped mouth, and eyes glinting with intelligence.

With intelligence—and something else!

There was something deadly about those eyes peering at us through the misty concrete. Something that would have sent our hands leaping for our guns had not the thing been so little. You can't physically fear a doll only a foot and a half high.

"What on earth is it—and how can it move through solid concrete?" breathed Belmont.

I couldn't even guess the answer. But I had a theory that

sprang full grown into my mind at the first sight of the little figure. It was all I had to offer in the way of explanation later, and I gave it to Belmont for what it was worth at the time.

"We must be looking at a hitherto unsuspected freak of evolution," I said, instinctively talking in a whisper. "It must be that millions of years ago the human race split. Some of it stayed on top of the ground; some of it went into deep caves for shelter. As thousands of years passed, the under-earth beings went ever deeper as new rifts leading downward were discovered. But far down in the earth is terrific pressure, and heat. Through the ages their bodies adapted themselves. They compacted—perhaps in their very atomic structure.

"Now the density of their substance, and its altered atomic character, allows them to move through stuff that is solid to us. Like the concrete and the mush rock behind it, which is softer than the terrifically compressed stone around it."

"But the thing has eyes," murmured Belmont. "Anything living for generations underground would be blind."

"Animals, yes. But this is human; at least it has human intelligence. It has undoubtedly carried light with it."

The little mannikin was within a few inches of the surface of the wall now. It stood there, staring out at us as intently as we stared in at it. And I could see that Steve Boland had added no imaginative detail in his description of what he had seen.

The tiny thing was dressed in some sort of shiny stuff, like metal, that crisscrossed it in strips. It reminded me of something, and finally I got it. Our early airmen, trying for altitude records high in the stratosphere, had laced their bodies with heavy canvas strips to keep them from disrupting outward in the lessened pressure of the heights. The metallic-looking strips lacing this little body looked like those.

"It must be that the thing comes from depths that make this forty-thousand-foot level seem high and rarefied," I whispered to Belmont. "Hundreds of thousands of feet, perhaps. They've

heard us working at the ore, and have come far up here to
see what was happening.

"But to go through solid concrete—" muttered Belmont,
dazed.

"That would be due to the way the atoms of their substance have been compressed and altered. They might be like
the stuff on Sirius' companion, where substance weighs a ton
to the cubic inch. That would allow the atoms of their bodies
to slide through far-spaced atoms of ordinary stuff, as lead
shot could pour through a wide-meshed screen. . . ."

Belmont was so silent that I stared at him. He was paying
no attention to me, probably hadn't even heard me. His eyes
were wild and wide.

"There's another of them. And another! Frank—we're mad.
We must be."

Two more luminous swirls had appeared in the depths of
the concrete. Two more tiny little human figures slowly appeared as, breasting forward like deep-sea divers against
solid water, they plodded toward the face of the wall.

And now three mannikins, laced in with silvery-looking
metal strips, stared at us through several inches of the milky
appearing concrete. Belmont clutched my arm again.

"Their eyes!" he whispered. "They certainly don't like us,
Frank! I'm glad they're like things you see under a low
powered microscope instead of man-sized or bigger!"

Their eyes were most impressive—and threatening. They
were like human eyes, and yet unlike them. There was a lack
of something in them. Perhaps of the thing we call, for want
of a more definite term, Soul. But they were as expressive as
the eyes of intelligent children.

I read curiosity in them as intense as that which filled Belmont and me. But over and above the curiosity there was—
menace.

Cold anger shone from the soulless eyes. Chill outrage,
such as might shine from the eyes of a man whose home has
been invaded. The little men palpably considered us tres-
passers in these depths, and were glacially infuriated by our
presence.

And then both Belmont and I gasped aloud. For one of the little men had thrust his hands forward, and hands and arms had protruded from the wall, like the hands of a person groping a way out of a thick mist. Then the tiny body followed it. And as if at a signal, the other two little men moved forward out of the wall too.

The three metal-laced mannikins stood in the open air of the tunnel, with their backs to the wall that had offered no more resistance to their bodies than cheese offers to sharp steel. And behind them there were no holes where they had stepped from. The face of the concrete was unbroken.

The atomic theory must be correct, I thought. The compacted atoms of which they were composed slid through the stellar spaces between ordinary atoms, leaving them undisturbed.

But only a small part of my mind concerned itself with this. Nine-tenths of it was absorbed by a growing, indefinable fear. For now the three little men were walking slowly toward us. And in every line of their tiny bodies was a threat.

Belmont looked at me. Our hands went uncertainly toward our revolvers. But we did not draw them. You don't shoot at children, and the diminutive size of the three figures still made us consider them much as harmless children, though in the back of my mind, at least, if not in Belmont's, the indefinable fear was spreading.

The three stopped about a yard from us. Belmont was standing, and I was still seated, almost in a paralysis of wonder, on my rock fragment. They looked far up at Belmont and almost as far up at me. Three little things that didn't even come up to our knees!

And then Belmont uttered a hoarse cry and dragged out his gun at last. For one of the three slid his tiny hand into the metal lacing of his body and brought it out with a sort of rod in it about the size of a thick pin, half an inch long. And there was something about the look in the mannikin's eyes that brought a rush of frank fear to our hearts at last, though we couldn't even guess at the nature of the infinitesimal weapon he held.

The mannikin pointed the tiny rod at Belmont, and Belmont shot. I didn't blame him. I had my own gun out and trained on the other two. After all, we knew nothing of the nature of these fantastic creatures who had come up from unguessable depths below. We couldn't even approximate the amount of harm they might do, but their eyes told us they'd do whatever they could to hurt us.

An exclamation ripped from my lips as the roar of the shot thundered down the tunnel.

The bullet had hit the little figure. It couldn't have helped but hit it; Belmont's gun was within a yard of it, and he'd aimed point-blank.

But not a mark appeared on the mannikin, and he stood there apparently unhurt!

Belmont fired again, and to his shot I added my own. The bullets did the little men no damage at all.

"The slugs are going right through the things!" yelled Belmont, pointing.

Behind the mannikins, long scars in the rock floor told where the lead had ricocheted. But I shook my head in a more profound wonder than that of Belmont's.

"The bullets aren't going through them! They're going through the bullets! The stuff they're made of is denser than lead!"

The little man with the tiny rod took one more step forward. And then I saw something that had been lost for the time being in the face of things even more startling. I saw how the tiny tracks had been made.

As the mannikin stepped forward, I saw his advancing foot sink into the rock of the floor till the soles of his metallic-looking shoes were buried!

That small figure weighed so much that it sank into stone as a man would sink into ooze!

And now the microscopic rod flamed a little at the tip. And I heard Belmont scream—just once.

He fell, and I looked at him with a shock too great for comprehension, so that I simply stood there stupidly and saw without really feeling any emotion.

The entire right half of Belmont's chest was gone. It was only a crater—a crater that gaped out, as holes gape over spots where shells bury themselves deep and explode up and out.

There had been no sound, and no flash other than the minute speck of flame tipping the mannikin's rod. At one moment Belmont had been whole. At the next he was dead, with half his chest gone. That was all.

I heard myself screaming, and felt my gun buck in my hand as I emptied it. Then the infinitesimal rod turned my way, and I felt a slight shock and stared at my right wrist where a hand and a gun had once been.

I heard my own yells as from a great distance. I felt no pain; there are nerve shocks too great for pain-sensation. I felt only crazed, stupefied rage.

I leaped at the three little figures. With all my strength I swung my heavily booted foot at the one with the rod. There was death in that swing. I wanted to kill these three. I was berserk, with no thought in mind other than to rend and tear and smash. That kick would have killed an ox, I think.

It caught the little man in the middle of the back. And I screamed again and sank to the floor with the white-hot pain of broken small bones spiking my brain. That agony, less than the shock of losing a hand, I could feel all right. And in a blind haze of it I saw the little man smile bleakly and reach out his tiny hand toward Belmont, disregarding me as utterly as though I no longer existed.

And then through the fog of my agony I saw yet another wonder. The little man lifted Belmont's dead body.

With the one hand, and apparently with no more effort than I would have made to pick up a pebble, he swung the body two inches off the floor, and started toward the concrete wall with it.

I tried to follow, crawling on my knees, but one of the other little men dashed his fist against my thigh. It sank in my flesh till his arm was buried to the shoulder, and the mannikin staggered off-balance with the lack of resistance. He withdrew his arm. There was no mark in the fabric of my clothing and I could feel no puncture in my thigh.

The little man stared perplexedly at me, and then at his fist. Then he joined the other two. They were at the face of the concrete wall again.

I saw that they were beginning to look as though in distress. They were panting, and the one with the rod was pressing his hand against his chest. They looked at each other and I thought a message was passed among them.

A message of haste? I think so. For the one picked up Belmont again, and all three stepped into the concrete. I saw them forge slowly ahead through it. And I saw Belmont, at arm's length of the little man who dragged him, flattened against the smooth side of the stuff.

I think I went a little mad, then, as I understood at last just what had happened.

The little men had killed Belmont as a specimen, just as a man might kill a rare insect. They wanted to take him back to their own deep realms and study him. And they were trying to drag him through the solid concrete. It offered only normal resistance to their own compacted tons of weight, and it didn't occur to them that it would to Belmont's body.

I flung myself at the wall and clawed at it with my left hand. The body of my friend was suspended there, flattened against it as the little man within tried to make solid matter go through solid matter, ignorant of the limitations of the laws of physics as we on earth's surface know them.

They were in extreme distress now. Even in my pain and madness I could see that. Their mouths were open like the mouths of fish gasping in air. I saw one clutch the leader's arm and point urgently downward.

The leader raised his tiny rod. Once more I saw the infinitesimal flash at its tip. Then I saw a six-foot hole yawn in the concrete around Belmont's body. What was their ammunition? Tiny pellets of gas, so compressed at the depths they inhabited that it was a solid, and which expanded enormously when released at these pressures? No one will ever know—I hope!

In one last effort, the leader dragged the body of my friend into the hole in the concrete. Then, when it stubbornly refused to follow into the substance through which they could force their own bodies, they gave up. One of the three staggered and fell, sinking in the concrete as an overcome diver might sink through water to the ocean's bed. The other two picked him up and carried him. Down and away.

Down and away—down from the floor of the forty-thousand-foot level, and away from the surface of the concrete wall.

I saw the luminous trails they left in the concrete fade into indistinct swirls, and finally die. I saw my friend's form sag back from the hole in the concrete, to sink to the floor.

And then I saw nothing but the still form, and the ragged six-foot crater that had been blown soundlessly into the solid concrete by some mysterious explosive that had come from a thing no larger than a thick pin, and less than half an inch long. . . .

They found me an hour later—men who had come down to see why neither Belmont nor I answered the ring of the radio phone connecting the low level with the surface.

They found me raving beside Belmont's body, and they held my arms with straps as they led me to the shaft.

They tried me for murder and sabotage. For, next day, I got away from the men long enough to sink explosive into the forty-thousand-foot level and blow it up so that none could work there again. But the verdict was not guilty in both cases.

Belmont had died and I had lost my right hand in an explosion the cause of which was unknown, the military court decided. And I had been insane from shock when I destroyed the low level, which, even with the world famished for copper, was almost too far down to be commercially profitable anyway.

They freed me, and I wrote in my report, and some filing

clerk had, no doubt, shrugged at its impossibility and put it in a steel cabinet where it will be forever ignored.

But there is one thing that cannot be ignored. That is, those mannikins, those microscopic giants, if ever they decide to return by slow stages of pressure-acclimation to the earth's surface!

Myriads of them, tiny things weighing incredible tons, forging through labyrinths composed of soft veins of rock like little deep-sea divers plodding laboriously but normally through impeding water! Beings as civilized as ourselves, if not more so, with infinitely deadly weapons, and practically invulnerable to any weapons we might try to turn against them!

Will they tunnel upward some day and decide calmly and leisurely to take possession of a world that is green and fair, instead of black and buried?

If they do, I hope it will not be in my lifetime!

Anthony Boucher

# THE OTHER INAUGURATION

*Mr. Boucher is not often a pessimist in his writing, but in this uncomfortable tale of politics in two parallel worlds he comes out with a bitter conclusion. You might say that this is basically an intellectual terror tale; but terrible it is, if only because of its underlying implications for our times.*

*From the journal of Peter Lanroyd, Ph.D.:*

*Mon Nov 5 84:* To any man even remotely interested in politics, let alone one as involved as I am, every 1st Tue of every 4th Nov must seem like one of the crucial *if*-points of history. From every American presidential election stem 2 vitally different worlds, not only for U S but for world as a whole.

It's easy enough, esp for a Prof of Polit Hist, to find examples—1860, 1912, 1932 . . . & equally easy, if you're honest with yourself & forget you're a party politician, to think of times when it didn't matter much of a special damn who won an election. Hayes-Tilden . . . biggest controversy, biggest outrage on voters in U S history . . . yet how much of an *if*-effect?

But this is different. 1984 (damn Mr Orwell's long-dead soul! he jinxed the year!) is *the* key *if*-crux as ever was in U S hist. And on Wed Nov 7 my classes are going to expect a few illuminating remarks—wh are going to have to come from me, scholar, & forget about the County Central Comm.

So I've recanvassed my precinct (looks pretty good for a Berkeley Hill precinct, too; might come damn close to carrying it), I've done everything I can before the election itself, & I can put in a few minutes trying to be non-party-objective on why this year of race 1984 is so *if*-vital.

Historical b g:

A) U S always goes for 2-party system, whatever the names.

B) The Great Years 1952/76 when we had, almost for 1st time, honest 2-partyism. Gradual development (started 52 by Morse, Byrnes, Shivers, etc) of cleancut parties of "right" & "left" (both, of course, to the right of a European "center" party). Maybe get a class laugh out of how both new parties kept both old names, neither wanting to lose New England Repub votes or Southern Demo, so we got Democratic American Republican Party & Free Democratic Republican Party.

C) 1976/84 God help us growth of 3d party, American. (The bastards! The simple, the perfect name . . . !) Result: Gradual withering away of DAR, bad defeat in 1980 presidential, total collapse in 82 congressional election. Back to 2-party system: Am vs FDR.

So far so good. Nice & historical. But how tell a class, without accusations of partisanship, what an Am victory means? What a destruction, what a (hell! let's use their own word) subversion of everything American. . . .

Or am I being partisan? Can anyone be as evil, as anti-American, as to me the Senator is?

Don't kid yrself Lanroyd. If it's an Am victory, you aren't going to lecture on Wed. You're going to be in mourning for the finest working democracy ever conceived by man. And now you're going to sleep & work like hell tomorrow getting out the vote.

It was Tuesday night. The vote had been gotten out, and very thoroughly indeed, in Lanroyd's precinct, in the whole state of California, and in all 49 other states. The result was in, and the TV commentator, announcing the final electronic recheck of results from 50 state-wide electronic calculators, was being smug and happy about the whole thing. ("Conviction?" thought Lanroyd bitterly. "Or shrewd care in holding a job?")

". . . Yessir," the commentator was repeating gleefully, "it's such a landslide as we've never seen in all American history—and *American* history is what it's going to be from now on. For the Senator, five . . . hundred . . . and . . . eighty . . . nine electoral votes from forty . . . nine states. For the Judge, four electoral votes from one state.

"Way back in 1936, when Franklin Delano Roosevelt" (he pronounced the name as a devout Christian might say Judas Iscariot) "carried all but two states, somebody said, 'As Maine goes, so goes Vermont.' Well, folks, I guess from now on we'll have to say—ha! ha!—'As Maine goes . . . so goes Maine.' And it looks like the FDR party is going the way of the unlamented DAR. From now on, folks, it's Americanism for Americans!

"Now let me just recap those electoral figures for you again. For the Senator on the American ticket, it's five eighty-nine—that's five hundred and eighty-nine—electoral—"

Lanroyd snapped off the set. The automatic brought up the room lighting from viewing to reading level.

He issued a two-syllable instruction which the commentator would have found difficult to carry out. He poured a shot of bourbon and drank it. Then he went to hunt for a razor blade.

As he took it out of the cabinet, he laughed. Ancient Romans could find a good use for this, he thought. Much more comfortable nowadays, too, with thermostats in the bathtub. Drift off under constantly regulated temperature. Play hell with the M.E.'s report, too. Jesus! Is it hitting me so bad I'm thinking stream of consciousness? Get to work, Lanroyd.

One by one he scraped the political stickers off the window.

There goes the FDR candidate for State Assembly. There goes the Congressman—twelve-year incumbent. There goes the United States Senator. State Senator not up for reëlection this year, or he'd be gone too. There goes NO ON 13. Of course in a year like this State Proposition # 13 passed too; from now on, as a Professor at a State University, he was forbidden to criticize publicly any incumbent government official, and compelled to submit the reading requirements for his courses to a legislative committee.

There goes the Judge himself . . . not just a sticker but a full lumino-portrait. The youngest man ever appointed to the Supreme Court; the author of the great dissenting opinions of the '50s; later a Chief Justice to rank beside Marshall in the vitality of his interpretation of the Constitution; the noblest candidate the Free Democratic Republican Party had ever offered . . .

There goes the last of the stickers. . . .

Hey, Lanroyd, you're right. It's a symbol yet. There goes the last of the political stickers. You'll never stick 'em on your window again. Not if the Senator's boys have anything to say about it.

Lanroyd picked up the remains of the literature he'd distributed in the precincts, dumped it down the incinerator without looking at it, and walked out into the foggy night.

If . . .

All right you're a monomaniac. You're 40 and you've never married (and what a sweet damn fool you were to quarrel with Clarice over the candidates in 72) and you think your profession's taught you that politics means everything and so your party loses and it's the end of the world. But God damn it *this* time it *is*. This *is* the key-point.

If . . .

Long had part of the idea; McCarthy had the other part. It took the Senator to combine them. McCarthy got nowhere, dropped out of the DAR reorganization, failed with his third party, because he attacked and destroyed but didn't *give*. He appealed to hate, but not to greed, no what's-in-it-for-me, no porkchops. But add the Long technique, every-man-a-king,

fuse 'em together: "wipe out the socialists; I'll give you something better than socialism." That does it, Senator. Coming
Next Year: "wipe out the democrats; I'll give you something
better than democracy."

IF . . .

What was it Long said? "If totalitarianism comes to America, it'll be labeled *Americanism*." Dead Huey, now I find thy
saw of might. . . .

## IF

There was a lighted window shining through the fog. That
meant Cleve was still up. Probably still working on temporomagnetic field-rotation, which sounded like nonsense but
what did you expect from a professor of psionics? Beyond any
doubt the most unpredictable department in the University
. . . and yet Lanroyd was glad he'd helped round up the majority vote when the Academic Senate established it. No telling what might come of it . . . *if* independent research had
any chance of continuing to exist.

The window still carried a sticker for the Judge and a NO
ON 13. This was a good house to drop in on. And Lanroyd
needed a drink.

Cleve answered the door with a full drink in his hand.
"Have this, old boy," he said; "I'll mix myself another. Night
for drinking, isn't it?" The opinion had obviously been in-
fluencing him for some time; his British accent, usually all but
rubbed off by now, had returned full force as it always did
after a few drinks.

Lanroyd took the glass gratefully as he went in. "I'll sign
that petition," he said. "I need a drink to stay sober; I think
I've hit a lowpoint where I can't get drunk."

"It'll be interesting," his host observed, "to see if you're
right. Glad you dropped in. I needed drinking company."

"Look, Stu," Lanroyd objected. "If it wasn't for the stickers
on your window, I'd swear you were on your way to a happy
drunk. What's to celebrate for God's sake?"

"Well as to God, old boy, I mean anything that's to celebrate is to celebrate for God's sake, isn't it? After all . . . Pardon. I *must* be a bit tiddly already."

"I know," Lanroyd grinned. "You don't usually shove your Church of England theology at me. Sober, you know I'm hopeless."

"Point not conceded. But God does come into this, of course. My rector's been arguing with me—doesn't approve at all. Tampering with Divine providence. But A: how can mere me tamper with anything Divine? And B: if it's possible, it's part of the Divine plan itself. And C: I've defied the dear old boy to establish that it involves in any way the Seven Deadly Sins, the Ten Commandments, or the Thirty-Nine Articles."

"Professor Cleve," said Lanroyd, "would you mind telling me what the hell you are talking about?"

"Time travel, of course. What else have I been working on for the past eight months?"

Lanroyd smiled. "OK. Every man to his obsession. My world's shattered and yours is rosy. Carry on, Stu. Tell me about it and brighten my life."

"I say, Peter, don't misunderstand me. I am . . . well, really dreadfully distressed about . . ." He looked from the TV set to the window stickers. "But it's hard to think about anything else when . . ."

"Go on." Lanroyd drank with tolerant amusement. "I'll believe anything of the Department of Psionics, ever since I learned not to shoot craps with you. I suppose you've invented a time machine?"

"Well, old boy, I think I have. It's a question of . . ."

Lanroyd understood perhaps a tenth of the happy monolog that followed. As an historical scholar, he seized on a few names and dates. Principle of temporomagnetic fields known since discovery by Arthur McCann circa 1941. Neglected for lack of adequate power source. Mei-Figner's experiment with nuclear pile 1959. Nobody knows what became of M-F. Embarrassing discovery that power source remained chronostationary; poor M-F stranded somewhen with no return power. Hasselfarb Equations 1972 established that any adequate external power source must possess too much temporal inertia to move with traveler.

"Don't you see, Peter?" Cleve gleamed. "That's where everyone's misunderstood Hasselfarb. 'Any *external* power source . . .' Of course it baffled the physicists."

"I can well believe it," Lanroyd quoted. "Perpetual motion, or squaring the circle, would baffle the physicists. They're infants, the physicists."

Cleve hesitated, then beamed. "Robert Barr," he identified. "His Sherlock Holmes parody. Happy idea for a time traveler: Visit the Reichenbach Falls in 1891 and see if Holmes really was killed. I've always thought an impostor 'returned.'"

"Back to your subject, psionicist . . . which is a hell of a word for a drinking man. Here, I'll fill both glasses and you tell me why what baffles the physicists fails to baffle the ps . . ."

"'Sounds of strong men struggling with a word,'" Cleve murmured. They were both fond of quotation; but it took Lanroyd a moment to place this muzzily as Belloc. "Because the power source doesn't have to be *external*. We've been developing the *internal* sources. How can I regularly beat you at craps?"

"Psychokinesis," Lanroyd said, and just made it.

"Exactly. But nobody ever thought of trying the effect of PK power on temporomagnetic fields before. And it works and the Hasselfarb Equations don't apply!"

"You've done it?"

"Little trips. Nothing spectacular. Tiny experiments. *But*—and this, old boy, is the damnedest part—there's every indication that PK can *rotate* the temporomagnetic stasis!"

"That's nice," said Lanroyd vaguely.

"No, of course. You don't understand. My fault. Sorry, Peter. What I mean is this: We can not only travel in time; we can rotate into another, an alternate time. A world of If."

Lanroyd started to drink, then abruptly choked. Gulping and gasping, he eyed in turn the TV set, the window stickers and Cleve. "*If* . . ." he said.

Cleve's eyes made the same route, then focused on Lan-

royd. "What we are looking at each other with," he said softly, "is a wild surmise."

*From the journal of Peter Lanroyd, Ph.D.:*

*Mon Nov 12 84:* So I have the worst hangover in Alameda
County, & we lost to UCLA Sat by 3 field goals, & the American Party takes over next Jan; but it's still a wonderful world.

Or rather it's a wonderful universe, continuum, whatsit,
that includes both this world & the possibility of shifting to a
brighter alternate.

I got through the week somehow after Black Tue. I even
made reasonable-sounding non-subversive noises in front of
my classes. Then all week-end, except for watching the game
(in the quaint expectation that Cal's sure victory wd lift our
spirits), Stu Cleve & I worked.

I never thought I'd be a willing lab assistant to a psionicist.
But we want to keep this idea secret. God knows what a good
Am Party boy on the faculty (Daniels, for inst) wd think of
people who prefer an alternate victory. So I'm Cleve's fac-
totum & busbar-boy & I don't understand a damned thing I'm
doing but—

*It works.*

The movement in time anyway. Chronokinesis, Cleve calls
it, or CK for short. CK . . . PK . . . sound like a bunch of ex-
ecutives initialing each other. Cleve's achieved short CK.
Hasn't dared try rotation yet. Or taking me with him. But he's
sweating on my "psionic potential." Maybe with some results:
I lost only 2 bucks in a 2 hour crap game last night. And got
so gleeful about my ps pot that I got me this hangover.

Anyway, I know what I'm doing. I'm resigning fr the County Committee at tomorrow's meeting. No point futzing around
w politics any more. Opposition Party has as much chance
under the Senator as it did in pre-war Russia. And I've got
something else to focus on.

I spent all my non-working time in politics because (no
matter what my analyst might say if I had one) I wanted, in
the phrase that's true the way only corn can be, I wanted to

make a better world. All right; now I can really do it, in a
way I never dreamed of.

CK . . . PK . . . *OK!*

*Tue Dec 11:* Almost a month since I wrote a word
here. Too damned magnificently full a month tó try to syn-
opsize here. Anyway it's all down in Cleve's records. Main
point is development of my psionic potential. (Cleve says
anybody can do it, with enough belief & drive—wh is why
Psionics Dept & Psych Dept aren't speaking. Psych claims PK,
if it exists wh they aren't too eager to grant even now, is a
mutant trait. OK so maybe I'm a mutant. Still . . .

Today I made my first CK. Chronokinesis to you, old boy.
Time travel to you, you dope. All right, so it was only 10
min. So nothing happened, not even an eentsy-weentsy paradox. But I did it; & when we go, Cleve & I can go together.

So damned excited I forgot to close parenth above. Fine
state of affairs. So:)

*Sun Dec 30:* Used to really keep me a journal. Full of fascinating facts & political gossip. Now nothing but highpoints,
apptly. OK: latest highpoint:

Sufficient PK power *can* rotate the field.

Cleve never succeeded by himself. Now I'm good enough
to work with him. And together . . .

He picked a simple one. Purely at random, when he
thought we were ready. We'd knocked off work & had some
scrambled eggs. 1 egg was a little bad, & the whole mess was
awful. Obviously some alternate in wh egg was *not* bad. So
we went back (CK) to 1 p m just before Cleve bought eggs,
& we (how the hell to put it?) we . . . *worked.* Damnedest
sensation. Turns you inside out & then outside in again. If
that makes sense.

We bought the eggs, spent the same aft working as before,
knocked off work, had some scrambled eggs . . . delicious!

Most significant damned egg-breaking since Columbus!

*Sun Jan 20 85:* This is the day.

Inauguration Day. Funny to have it on a Sun. Hasn't been
since 57. Cleve asked me what's the inaugural augury. Told
him the odds were even. Monroe's 2d Inaug was a Sun . . . &

so was Zachary Taylor's 1st & only, wh landed us w Fillmore.

We've been ready for a week. Waited till today just to hear the Senator get himself inaugurated. 1st beginning of the world we'll never know.

TV's on. There the smug bastard is. Pride & ruin of 200,-000,000 people.

"Americans!"

Get that. Not "fellow Americans . . ."

"Americans! You have called me in clarion tones & I shall answer!"

Here it comes, all of it. ". . . my discredited adversaries . . ." ". . . strength, not in union, but in unity . . ." ". . . as you have empowered me to root out these . . ."

The one-party system, the one-system state, the one-man party-system-state . . .

Had enough, Stu? (Hist slogan current ca 46) OK: let's *work!*

Damn! Look what this pencil did while I was turning inside out & outside in again. (Note: Articles in contact w body move in CK. For reasons cf. Cleve's notebooks.) Date is now *Tue Nov 6 84:* TV's on. Same cheerful commentator:

". . . Yessir, it's 1 of the greatest landslides in American history. 524 electoral votes from 45 states, to 69 electoral votes from 5 states, all Southern, as the experts predicted. I'll repeat: That's 524 electoral votes for the Judge . . ."

We've done it! We're *there*. . . . then . . . whatever the hell the word is. I'm the first politician in history who ever made the people vote right against their own judgment!

Now, in this brighter better world where the basic tenets of American democracy were safe, there was no nonsense about Lanroyd's resigning from politics. There was too much to do. First of all a thorough job of party reorganization before the Inauguration. There were a few, even on the County and State Central Committees of the Free Democratic Republican Party, who had been playing footsie with the Senator's boys. A few well-planned parliamentary maneuvers weeded them out; a new set of by-laws took care of such contingencies in the future; and the Party was solidly unified and ready to back the Judge's administration.

Stuart Cleve went happily back to work. He no longer needed a busbar-boy from the History Department. There was no pressing need for secrecy in his work; and he possessed, thanks to physical contact during chronokinesis, his full notebooks on experiments for two and a half months which, in this world, hadn't happened yet—a paradox which was merely amusing and nowise difficult.

By some peculiar whim of alternate universes, Cal even managed to win the UCLA game 33–10.

In accordance with the popular temper displayed in the Presidential election, Proposition 13, with its thorough repression of all free academic thought and action, had been roundly defeated. A short while later, Professor Daniels, who had so actively joined the Regents and the Legislature in backing the measure, resigned from the Psychology Department. Lanroyd had played no small part in the faculty meetings which convinced Daniels that the move was advisable.

At last Sunday, January 20, 1985, arrived (or, for two men in the world, returned) and the TV sets of the nation brought the people the Inaugural Address. Even the radio stations abandoned their usual local broadcasts of music and formed one of their very rare networks to carry this historical highpoint.

The Judge's voice was firm, and his prose as noble as that of his dissenting or his possibly even greater majority opinions. Lanroyd and Cleve listened together, and together thrilled to the quietly forceful determination to wipe out every last vestige of the prejudices, hatreds, fears and suspicions fostered by the so-called American Party.

"A great man once said," the Judge quoted in conclusion, " 'We have nothing to fear but fear itself.' Now that a petty and wilful group of men have failed in their effort to undermine our very Constitution, I say to you: 'We have one thing to destroy. And that is destruction itself!' "

And Lanroyd and Cleve beamed at each other and broached the bourbon.

*From the journal of Peter Lanroyd, Ph. D.:*

*Sun Oct 20 85:* Exactly 9 mos. Obstetrical symbolism yet?

Maybe I shd've seen it then, at this other inauguration. Read betw the lines, seen the meaning, the true inevitable meaning. Realized that the Judge was simply saying, in better words (or did they sound better because I thought he was on My Side?), what the Senator said in the inaugural we escaped: "I have a commission to wipe out the opposition."

Maybe I shd've seen it when the Senator was arrested for inciting to riot. Instead I cheered. Served the sonofabitch right. (And it did, too. That's the hell of it. It's all confused. . . .)

He still hasn't been tried. They're holding him until they can nail him for treason. Mere matter of 2 constitutional amendments: Revise Art III Sec 3 Par 1 so "treason" no longer needs direct-witness proof of an overt act of war against the U S or adhering to their enemies, but can be anything yr Star Chamber wants to call it; revise Art I Sec 9 Par 3 so you can pass an ex post facto law. All very simple; the Judge's arguments sound as good as his dissent in U S v Feinbaum. (I shd've seen, even in the inaug, that he's not the same man in this world—the same mind turned to other ends. My ends? My end . . .) The const ams'll pass all right . . . except maybe in Maine.

I shd've seen it last year when the press began to veer, when the dullest & most honest columnist in the country began to blether about the "measure of toleration"—when the liberal Chronicle & the Hearst Examiner, for the 1st time in S F history, took the same stand on the Supervisors' refusal of the Civic Aud to a pro-Senator rally—when the NYer satirized the ACLU as something damned close to traitors. . . .

I began to see it when the County Central Committee started to raise hell about a review I wrote in the QPH. (God knows how a Committeeman happened to read that learned journal.) Speaking of the great old 2-party era, I praised both the DAR & the FDR as bulwarks of democracy. Very unwise. Seems as a good Party man I shd've restricted my praise to the FDR. Cd've fought it through, of course, stood on my

rights—hell, a County Committeeman's an elected representative of the people. But I resigned because . . . well, because
that was when I began to see it.

Today was what did it, though. 1st a gentle phone call fr
the Provost—in person, no secty—wd I drop by his office tomorrow? Certain questions have arisen as to some of the
political opinions I have been expressing in my lectures. . . .

That blonde in the front row with the teeth & the busy
notebook & the D's & F's . . .

So Cleve comes by & I think I've got troubles . . . !

He's finally published his 1st paper on the theory of CK &
PK-induced alternates. It's been formally denounced as "dangerous" because it implies the existence of better worlds. And
guess who denounced it? Prof Daniels of Psych.

Sure, the solid backer of # 13, the strong American Party
boy. He's a strong FDR man now. *He* knows. And he's back
on the faculty.

Cleve makes it all come out theological somehow. He says
that by forcibly setting mankind on the alternate *if*-fork that
*we* wanted, we denied man's free will. Impose "democracy"
against or without man's choice, & you have totalitarianism.
Our only hope is what he calls "abnegation of our own desire"
—surrender to, going along with, the will of man. We must
CK & PK ourselves back to where we started.

The hell with the theology; it makes sense politically too. I
was wrong. Jesus! I was wrong. Look back at every major
election, every major boner the electorate's pulled. So a boner
to me is a triumph of reason to you, sir. But let's not argue
which dates were the major boners. 1932 or 1952, take your
pick.

It's always worked out, hasn't it? Even 1920. It all straight-
ens out, in time. Democracy's the craziest, most erratic system ever devised . . . & the closest to perfection. At least it
keeps coming closer. Democratic man makes his mistakes—&
he corrects them in time.

Cleve's going back to make his peace with his ideas of God
& free will. I'm going back to show I've learned that a poli-

tician doesn't clear the hell & gone out of politics because he's
lost. Nor does he jump over on the winning side.

He works & sweats as a Loyal Opposition—hell, as an Underground if necessary, if things get as bad as that—but he
holds on & works to make men make their own betterment.

Now we're going up to Cleve's, where the field's set up . . .
& we're going back to the true world.


Stuart Cleve was weeping, for the first time in his adult
life. All the beautifully intricate machinery which created the
temporomagnetic field was smashed as thoroughly as a hydrogen atom over Novosibirsk.

"That was Winograd leading them, wasn't it?" Lanroyd's
voice came out oddly through split lips and missing teeth.

Cleve nodded.

"Best damn coffin-corner punter I ever saw . . . Wondered
why our friend Daniels was taking such an interest in athletes
recently."

"Don't oversimplify, old boy. Not all athletes. Recognized
a couple of my best honor students. . . ."

"Fine representative group of youth on the march . . . and
all wearing great big FDR buttons!"

Cleve picked up a shard of what had once been a chrono-
static field generator and fondled it tenderly. "When they
smash machines and research projects," he said tonelessly,
"the next step is smashing men."

". . . .d a fair job on us when we tried to stop them. Well . . .
these fragments we have shored against our madness. . . .
And now, to skip some three and a half centuries of theater
for our next quote, it's back to work we go! Hi-Ho! Hi-Ho!
Need a busbar-boy, previous experience guaranteed?"

"It took us ten weeks of uninterrupted work," Cleve said
hesitantly. "You think those vandals will let us alone that
long? But we have to try, I know." He bent over a snarled
mess of wiring which Lanroyd knew was called a magnetostat
and performed some incomprehensibly vital function. "Now
this looks almost servicea—" He jerked upright again, shaking
his head worriedly.

"Matter?" Lanroyd asked.

"My head. Feels funny. . . . One of our young sportsmen landed a solid kick when I was down."

"Winograd, no doubt. Hasn't missed a boot all season."

Perturbedly Cleve pulled out of his pocket the small dice-case which seemed to be standard equipment for all psionicists. He shook a pair in his fist and rolled them out in a clear space on the rubbage-littered floor.

"*Seven!*" he called.

A six turned up, and then another six.

"Sometimes," Cleve was muttering ten unsuccessful rolls later, "even slight head injuries have wiped out all psionic potential. There's a remote possibility of redevelopment; it *has* happened. . . ."

"And," said Lanroyd, "it takes both of us to generate enough PK to rotate." He picked up the dice. "Might as well check mine." He hesitated then let them fall. "I don't think I want to know. . . ."

They stared at each other over the ruins of the machinery that would never be rebuilt.

" 'I, a stranger and afraid . . .' " Cleve began to quote.

"In a world," Lanroyd finished, "I damned well made."

Alan E. Nourse

# NIGHTMARE BROTHER

*What is a man's breaking point? How much can he take? There are sure to be some situations in the complex world of tomorrow where a man will have to know that he cannot be defeated by illusion, or by loneliness, or by the horrors of the unknown. And there is only one way to make sure that such a man will have the necessary fortitude: that is, to test him for it first.*

*But consider the nature of the tests! Can they be much less than the expected situations themselves? This is the question explored, to a point of almost unbearable tension, in the following tale.*

HE WAS WALKING DOWN A TUNNEL.

At first it didn't even occur to him to wonder *why* he was walking down the tunnel, or how he had got there, or just what tunnel it was. He was walking quickly, with short, even steps, and it seemed, suddenly, as if he had been walking for hours.

It wasn't the darkness that bothered him at first. The tunnel wasn't bright, but it was quite light enough, for the walls glowed faintly with a bluish luminescence. Ahead of him the

Alan E. Nourse, NIGHTMARE BROTHER. Copyright 1953 in the United States and Great Britain by Street and Smith Publications, Inc. Reprinted by permission of Harry Altshuler from *Astounding Science Fiction*, February 1953.

glowing walls stretched as far as he could see. The tunnel was about ten feet wide, and ten feet high, with smooth walls arching into a perfectly smooth curve over his head. Under his feet the floor seemed cushiony, yielding slightly to the pressure as he walked, and giving off a soft, muffled sound in perfect measure to his tread. It was a pleasant, soothing sound, and he hardly thought to wonder at all just what he was doing. It was quite obvious, after all. As simple as simple could be. He was walking down a tunnel.

But then little tendrils of caution and question crept into his mind, and a puzzled frown crossed his quiet face. He stopped abruptly, standing stock-still in the tunnel as he squinted at the glowing walls in growing confusion. What a very odd place to be, he thought. A tunnel! He glanced about him, and cocked his head, listening for a long moment, until the stark silence of the place chilled him, forced him to sniff audibly, and scratch his head, and turn around.

My name is Robert Cox, he thought, and I am walking down a tunnel. He pondered for a moment, trying to remember. How long had he been walking? An hour? He shook his head. It must have been longer than that. Oddly, he couldn't remember *when* he had started walking. How had he got here? What had he been doing before he came into the tunnel? A chill of alarm crept up his spine as his mind groped. What had happened to his memory? Little doors in his mind seemed to snap quickly shut even as his memory approached them. Ridiculous, he thought, to be walking down a tunnel without even knowing where it was leading—

He peered forward in the silence. Quite suddenly he realized that he was absolutely alone. There was not a sound around him, not a stir, no sign of another human being, not even a flicker of life of any kind. The chill deepened, and he walked cautiously over to one wall, tapped it with his knuckles. Only a dull knock. For the merest fraction of a second an alarm rang in his mind, a cold, sharp intimation of deadly danger. He chuckled, uneasily. There was really no reason to be alarmed. A tunnel had to have an end, somewhere.

And then he heard the sound, and stared wide-eyed down the tunnel. It came to his ears very faintly, at first, the most curious sort of airy whistling, like a shrill pipe in the distance. It cut through the stillness cleanly, like a razor, leaving a strange tingle of dread in his mind. He listened, hardly breathing. Was the light growing fainter? Or were his eyes not behaving? He blinked, and sensed the light dimming even as the whistling sound grew louder and nearer, mingling with another, deeper sound. A throbbing roar came to his ears, overpowering the shrillness of the whistle, and then he saw the light, far down the tunnel, a single, round, yellow light, directly in the center of the passage, growing larger and larger as the roar intensified. A sharp wind suddenly stirred his dark hair as he stared fascinated by the yellow light bearing down on him. In a horrible flash, an image crossed his mind—the image of a man trapped on a railroad track as a dark engine approached with whistle screaming, bearing down like some hideous monster out of the night.

A cry broke from the man's lips. *It was a train!* Roaring down the tunnel toward him, it was moving like a demon, with no tracks, screeching its warning as it came, with the light growing brighter and brighter, blinding him. Relentlessly it came, filling the entire tunnel from side to side, hissing smoke and fire and steam from its valves, its whistle shrieking—

With a scream of sheer terror, Cox threw himself face down on the floor, trying frantically to burrow deeper into the soft mat of the tunnel floor, closing his mind down, blanking out everything but horrible, blinding fear. The light blazed to floodlight brilliance, and with a fearful rush of wind the roar rose to a sudden thundering bellow over his head. Then it gave way to the loud, metallic *clak-clak-clak* of steel wheels on steel rails beside his ears, and faded slowly into the distance behind him.

Trembling uncontrollably in every muscle, Cox stirred, trying to rise to his knees, groping for control of his mind. His eyes were closed tightly, and suddenly the floor was no longer soft matting, but a gritty stuff that seemed to run through his fingers.

He opened his eyes with a start, and a little cry came to his lips. The tunnel was gone. He was standing ankle-deep in the steaming sand of a vast, yellow desert, with a brassy sun beating down from a purple sky. He blinked, unbelieving, at the yellow dunes, and a twisted Joshua tree blinked back at him not ten feet away.

Two men and a girl stood in the room, watching the motionless body of the dark-haired man sprawled on the bed. The late afternoon sun came in the window, throwing bright yellow panels across the white bedspread, but the man lay quite still, his pale eyes wide open and glassy, oblivious to anything in the room. His face was deathly pale.

The girl gasped. "I think he's stopped breathing," she whispered.

The taller of the men, dressed in white, took her by the shoulder, gently turning her face away. "He's still breathing," he reassured her. "You shouldn't be here, Mary. You should go home, try to get some rest. He'll be all right."

The other man snorted, his pink face flushed with anger. "He shouldn't be here either," he hissed, jerking a thumb at the man on the bed. "I tell you, Paul, Robert Cox is not the man. I don't care what you say. He'll never get through."

Dr. Paul Schiml drew a deep breath, turning to face the other. "If Cox can't get through, there isn't a man in the Hoffman Medical Center who can—or ever will. You know that."

"I know that there were fifty others in the same training program who were better fitted for this than Bob Cox!"

"That's not true." Dr. Schiml's voice was sharp in the still room. "Reaction time, ingenuity, opportunism—not one in the group could hold a candle to Bob." He stared down at the red-faced man, his eyes glittering angrily. "Admit it, Connover. You're not worried for Bob Cox's sake. You're worried for your own neck. You've been afraid since the start, since the first ships came back to Earth, because you've been in charge of a program you don't believe in, and you're afraid of what will happen if Bob Cox doesn't come through. It wouldn't matter who was on that bed—you'd still be afraid." He sniffed in disgust. "Well, you needn't worry. Bob Cox will do it, if anyone can. He *has* to."

"And if he *doesn't* get through?"

The tall doctor stared angrily for a moment, then turned abruptly and walked over to the bedside. There was hardly a flicker of life in the man who lay there, only the shallowest respiration to indicate that he *was* alive. With gentle fingers Dr. Schiml inspected the small incision in the man's skull, checked again the multitude of tiny, glittering wires leading to the light panel by the bedside. He stopped, staring at the panel, and motioned sharply to Connover. "Here's the first, already," he whispered.

For a moment, only the faintest buzz sound could be heard from the panel; then Connover let out a soft whistle. "A tunnel. That makes sense. But what a device—" He turned wide-eyed to Schiml. "He could kill himself!"

"Of course he could. We've known that from the start."

"But *he* doesn't know—"

"He doesn't know anything." Schiml pointed to the panel. "A train ingenious? It's amazing. Could you think of anything worse?" He watched for a moment. "No room on either side for escape—he'll go under it."

All three watched, hardly breathing. Suddenly the girl was sobbing uncontrollably, burying her face on the doctor's shoulder. "It's horrible," she choked. "It's horrible . . . he'll never make it, never, he'll be killed—"

"No, Mary, not Robert. Not after the training he's had." The doctor's voice was grim. "You've got to believe that, Mary. This is the test, the final test. He can't let us down, not now—"

　　　　　　．　　　　　　　°　　　　　　　°

He could feel danger all about him. It was nothing at all tangible, just a deep, hollow voice in his mind, screaming out the danger. Cox shuddered, and glanced up at the brassy yellow sun, his forehead wet with perspiration. It was hot! Steaming hot, with an unrelenting heat that seemed to melt him down inside like soft wax. Every muscle in his body was tense; he stood poised, tingling, his pale eyes searching the barren yellow dunes of sand for the danger he knew was there—

Then the Joshua tree moved.

With a gasp, he threw himself on the sand, ten feet from it, watching it wide-eyed. Just a slight movement of the twisted arms of the thing—he could have been mistaken, his mind could have played tricks. He trembled as he squinted through the shimmering heat at the gaunt, twisted tree.

And then, quite suddenly, realization struck him. Desert! He had been in a *tunnel*—yes, that was right, a tunnel, and that light, that roaring thing—*what was he doing here?* He sat up slowly in the sand, ran his fingers through the hot grains, studying them with infinite curiosity. No doubt about it—it *was* desert! But how? How had he reached the tunnel in the first place? And what in the rational universe could have transported him to *this* place?

Eagerly his mind searched, striking against the curious, shadowy shield that blocked his memory. There was an answer, he knew; something was wrong, he shouldn't be there. Deep in his mind he knew he was in terrible danger, but such *idiotic* danger—if he could only think, somehow remember—

His shoulders tensed, and he froze, reactively, his eyes on the yellow mound of sand across the ridge from him. Hardly breathing, he watched, his mind screaming *danger, danger,* his eyes focusing on the yellow hillock. Then it moved again, swiftly, in the blinking of an eye, and froze again, ten feet closer—

It had looked in that fraction of a second, remarkably like a *cat*—a huge, savage, yellow cat. And then it had frozen into a hillock of sand.

Swiftly Cox moved, on hands and knees, at angles across the slope of sand from the thing. The sand burned his hands, and he almost cried out as the grit swirled up into his eyes, but he watched, every muscle tense. It moved again, at a tangent, swiftly sliding down the slope parallel to his movement, a huge, yellow, fanged thing, moving with the grace and flowing speed of molten gold, little red eyes fixed on him. Then it froze again, melting into the yellow, shimmering sand.

Stalking him!

In blind panic he pulled himself to his feet and ran down the sandy slope away from it, his eyes burning, running with the devil at his heels until a dune lay between him and the creature. Then he threw himself flat on the sand, peering over the rim of the dune. There was a swift blur of yellow movement, and the sand-cat was on the slope behind him, twenty yards closer, crouching against the sand, panting hungrily. Frantically, Cox glanced around him. Nothing! Nothing but yellow, undulating sand hills, the scorching sun, and the tall, twisted Joshua trees that moved! He looked back suddenly, and saw the sand-cat creeping toward him, slowly, slowly, not thirty yards away.

His breath came in panting gasps as he watched the creature. It was eight feet long, with lean, muscular haunches that quivered in the sun, the red eyes gleaming in savage hate. It moved with a sure confidence, a relentless certainty of its kill. Cox tried to think, tried to clear his mind of the fear and panic that gnawed at him, tried to clear away the screaming, incredulous puzzlement that tormented him. He had to get away, but he couldn't run. The creature was too fast. He knew his presence there was incredible; something in his mind tried to tell him not to believe it, that it wasn't true— but he felt the gritty sand under his sweating palms, and it was very, very real. And the sand-cat moved closer—

In a burst of speed he ran zigzagging down the slope and up the next, watching over his shoulder for the flash of yellow movement. With each change in direction, the sand-cat also shifted, stalking faithfully. If only he could get out of its sight for a moment! If it wasn't too bright, if that savage brain were starved enough, he might force it into a pattern response— He ran ten feet to the right, paused, and rushed on ten feet to the left, heading toward the huge boulder which stood up like a naked sentinel on the dune ahead. The sand-cat followed, moving to the right, then to the left. Again Cox sped, sure now that the pattern would be followed, moving right, then left. A long run away from the rock, then a long run toward it. The cat was closer, just twenty yards away, closing the distance between them with each run. Panting, Cox tried to catch his breath, taking a steel grip on his nerves. He knew that panic could kill him. Swiftly, he scuttled up over the edge of the dune, far to the right of the boulder, then abruptly switched back, keeping the boulder between him and the cat, reaching it, peering cautiously around—

Warm excitement flooded his mind. Slowly, ever so slowly the sand-cat was edging up over the dune, peering down in the direction he had run, slipping up over the dune on its belly, freezing, peering, a savage, baffled snarl coming from its dripping mouth. Eagerly Cox searched the sand around the boulder, picked up a chunk of sandstone as big as a brick. Then he took a huge breath, and plunged from behind the boulder, toward the cat, moving silently in the soft, hot sand. With a mixture of fury and fear he fell on the beast, raising the stone, bringing it down with all his might on the flat yellow head. The sand-cat snarled and whirled, claws slashing the air; his hot, rank breath caught Cox full, gagging him as he raised the stone again and again, bringing it down on the creature's skull. Razor claws ripped at his side, until the cat screamed and convulsed, and lay twitching—

And suddenly there was darkness, and a cold winter breeze in his face, and the stars were twinkling in the frigid night air above him. The sand-cat was gone, the desert, the Joshua trees. He lay in a ditch, half-soaked in icy mud, and his side was bleeding angrily.

•          •          •

He stared around him, and shivered. He was at the bottom of a ditch, his body lying in an icy rivulet of water. Above him, he could see the embankment, topped by a small iron fence. A road! Painfully he dragged himself up toward the top, peered over. The strip of polished metal gleamed in the starlight, as icy gusts of wind and snow swept down to bite his ears and bring tears to his eyes. The tears froze on his eyelids, and the sharp coldness of the dark air bit into his lungs, bringing pain with every breath.

In the distance he heard a rumbling sound, felt the road tremble as the gargantuan vehicles approached. Instinctively Cox ducked below the road surface, froze immobile as the long line of grotesque metallic monsters roared by, glimmering within their dull fluorescent force-shields. They showed no sign of life, but rumbled past him, moving steadily down the glittering highway. He could see the curious turrets, the gunlike projections, stark against the bleak night sky. Weapons, he thought, huge, tanklike engines which lumbered and roared along the road on some errand of death. Suddenly the last of the convoy lumbered past, and he eased himself cautiously up onto the road. A burst of thunder roared in his ears, and abruptly it began to pour, huge icy drops that splattered with the force of machine-gun bullets, stinging his skin and soaking his hair and clothes. He shuddered miserably, his mind groping in confusion. If he could only find a place to *think,* somewhere to rest and collect himself, somewhere to try to dress the wound in his side. In the gloom across the road he thought he could make out the gaunt ruins of a building standing against the starlight, and with infinite pain and slowness he dragged himself across the frigid steel strip, and down into the ditch on the other side. His feet were growing numb, and the pain in his side had turned to a dull, angry throbbing, but he somehow stumbled and staggered across the field, every ounce of his strength focused on reaching some sort of shelter.

It was a building—or it had been, once. Two walls had been completely shattered, bombed out, and the roof had fallen in, but one intact wall stood like a gaunt sentinel in the darkness. Inside, the building had been gutted by fire, and Cox was forced to rip rubble and debris away from the door. He forced it open on squeaking, long-neglected hinges. Finally he found a corner that was dry, and located a bit of blanket from the rubble inside. He sank into the corner, shaking his head, trying desperately to orient himself.

His side had stopped bleeding. A quick examination revealed four shallow, ugly-looking lacerations running down to his thigh. Four claws—the cat! Of course, the sand-cat had clawed him in its last, desperate snarl of rage. Cox leaned back, scratching his black hair with a grimy finger. The sand-cat was in the *desert*, not *here*. But before that, it was a tunnel, with a roaring train bearing down on him, a train that moved without tracks. And now, a frigid, war-beaten world—

It didn't add up. Desperately he tried to remember what had happened in between. Nothing, it seemed. He had slipped from one to the other in the blinking of an eye. But that was impossible! You just couldn't shift like that, from one place to another. At least—he didn't *think* it was possible.

He heard his breath, short and shallow, echoing in the silence of the ruined building. He was here. This building wa. real, the icy coldness and the darkness were very real. But the wound in his side was real, too. That hadn't happened here, that had happened somewhere else. How had he come here? Had he *wanted* to come? He shook his head angrily. It was ridiculous. But three different places— there *had* to be something in common, some common denominator. What had he found in all three places that was the same, what possible connection was there?

*Danger!* He sat bolt upright, staring into the blackness. That was it! A tunnel, and danger. A desert, and danger. Now this cold, hostile place, *and danger!* Not danger to anyone else, just danger to himself. *Pure, raw, naked danger.*

He pondered for a while, his mind whirling. Somehow, it seemed that danger had been his entire life, that all he could think of, the only thing he had ever known was danger. Could that be true? Instinctively, he knew it wasn't. There *had* been peace, before, somewhere, and love, and happy hours. But superimposed in his mind was the acute, barren awareness of imminent death, a sure knowledge that he could die

here, abruptly, at any moment, and only his own resourcefulness could save him.

It was like repeating the well-rehearsed words of a play.
Somebody had told him that. It wasn't original in his own
mind. It was propaganda, conditioned information, something
he had been *taught!*

*Could Mary have told him?*

He gasped. Mary! He repeated the name over and over,
excitedly. There was the link. Mary, his wife—certainly there
had been peace, and warmth, and comfort, and love. Mary
was his wife, he had known those things with her, in some
remote corner of his memory. He felt himself glow as he
suddenly remembered Mary's lovely face, the depth of love
in those dark eyes, the warmth of her arms around him, the
consuming peace and contentment in her sweet kisses and
soft, happy murmurings—somewhere there had been Mary,
who loved him beyond anything in the world.

The wind stirred through the ruined building, bringing a
sifting of damp snow into his face. There was no Mary here.
Somehow, he was here, and he was in danger, and there was
no warmth or love here. His mind swept back to reality with
a jolt. He hadn't wanted to come here. It *couldn't* have been
his will. There was only one other possible answer. *He had
been put here.*

His mind struck the idea, and trembled. Like the fit of a
hand in a glove, the thought settled down in his mind, filling a
tremendous gap. Yes, that was it, he had been placed here,
for some reason. He wasn't wilfully changing from place to
place, he was *being changed* from place to place, against his
will and volition. From danger into danger, he was being
shifted, like a chessman in some horrible game of death. But
no one was touching him, no one was near him—how could
these changes be happening? The answer sent a chill through
him, and his hand trembled. It was obvious. The changes
were happening in his own mind.

He rubbed his stubbled chin. If this were true, then these
things weren't really happening. He hadn't actually been in
the tunnel. There hadn't actually been a sand-cat. He wasn't

really lying here in a cold, damp corner, with deadly frost creeping up his legs. Angrily he rejected the thought. There was no room for doubt, these things were real, all right. The slashes on his side were real. He knew, beyond shadow of a doubt, that there *had* been a sand-cat. He knew it would have killed him if it could have, and if it had, he would have been quite dead.

*You can die, and only your own resourcefulness will save you*—who had said that? There had been a program, training him, somewhere, for something—something vastly important. His mind groped through the darkness, trying to penetrate the fuzzy uncertainty of his memory. Those words— from a small, red-faced man, and a tall, gaunt man in white—*Schiml!* Schiml had said those words, Schiml had put him here!

Suddenly he thought he saw the whole thing clearly. He was in danger, he must overcome the danger, he wasn't supposed to know that it wasn't really happening! There had been ι long training program, with Connover, and Schiml, and all the rest, and now he was on his own. But nothing, *nothing* could really hurt him, because these things were only figments of his imagination.

He shivered in the coldness. Somehow, he didn't quite dare to believe that.

.        .        .

Dr. Schiml sat down on the chair and wiped drops of perspiration from his brow. His eyes were bright with excitement as he glanced at the pallid form on the bed, and then back at the red-faced Connover. "He's taken the first step," he said hoarsely. "I was sure he would."

Connover scowled and nodded, his eyes fixed on the panel beside the bed. "Yes, he took the first step all right. He's figured out the source of his environment. That's not very much."

Schiml's eyes gleamed. "When we first computed the test, you wouldn't even concede the possibility of that. Now you see that he's made it. He'll make the other steps, too."

Connover whirled angrily on the doctor. "How can he? He

just *doesn't have the data!* Any fool could deduct that these
are subjective mental phenomena he's facing, under the circumstances. But you're asking for the impossible if you expect him to go any further along that line of reasoning. He
just doesn't have enough memory of reality to work with."

"He has Mary, and you, and me," the doctor snapped.
"He knows there's been a training program, and he knows
that he's being tested. And now he knows that he's living in
the nightmares of his own mind. He's got to solve the rest."

Connover snorted. "And that knowledge itself increases his
danger a thousand times. He'll be reckless, overconfident—"

The girl stirred. She had been staring blankly at the man
on the bed; her face was drawn and pallid, and her eyes were
red. She looked dully at Dr. Schiml. "Connover's right," she
said. "He has no way of knowing. He may just stand there
and let himself—" she broke off with a choked sob.

"Mary, can't you see? That's exactly what we've got to know.
We've got to know if the training was valid. He may get reckless, true, but never *too* reckless. The cat, remember? It hurt
him. It *really* hurt him. He'll take the next step, all right. He
may be hurt first, but he'll take it."

The girl's face flushed angrily. "It may kill him! You're
asking too much, he's not a superman, he's just an ordinary,
helpless human being like anybody else. He doesn't have any
magical powers."

The doctor's face was pale. "That's right. But he does have
some very unmagical powers, powers we've been drumming
into his mind for the past year. He'll just have to use them,
that's all. He'll *have* to."

Mary's eyes shifted once again to the motionless form on
the bed. "How much proof do you need?" she asked softly.
"How much more will he have to take before you stop it and
bring him back?"

The doctor's eyes drifted warily to Connover, then back to
Mary. A little smile crept onto his lips. "Don't worry," he said
gently, "I'll stop it soon enough. Just as soon as he's taken the
necessary steps. But not until then."

"And if he can't make them?"

She didn't see his hand tremble as he adjusted the panel light gently. "Don't worry," he said again. "He can make them."

     •         •         •

Gradually the numbness crept up Robert Cox's legs. He lay on the cold, grimy floor of the ruined building, staring into the blackness about him. His realization had brought him great relief; he was breathing more easily now, and he felt his mind relaxing from the strain he had been suffering. He knew, without question, that he was not in the midst of reality—that this cold, hostile place was *not* real, that it was merely some horrid nightmare dredged from the hidden depths of his own mind, thrust at him for some reason that he could not ponder, but thrust at him as an idiotic, horrible substitute for reality. Deep in his mind something whispered that no harm could really come. The sense of danger which pervaded his mind was false, a figment of the not-real world around him. They were testing him, it was quite obvious, though he couldn't pierce the murky shield of memory to understand why they were testing him, for what purpose. Still, having realized the unreality, the test must be ended. He couldn't be fooled any longer. He smiled to himself. Armed with that knowledge, there was no longer any danger. No real danger. Even the wound in his side was imagined, not really there—

And still the cold crept up his legs, insidiously, numbing them, moving higher and higher in his body. He didn't move. He simply waited. Because with the test all over, they would surely bring him back to reality.

Like an icy microtome blade, something slashed at his brain, swiftly, without warning. He screamed out, and his mind jerked and writhed in agony at the savage blow. He tried to sit upright, and found his muscles numb, paralyzed. Again the blow came, sharper, more in focus, striking with a horrid power that almost split his brain. He screamed again, closing his eyes tight, writhing on the floor. He tensed, steeling himself for another blow, and when it came his whole body jerked as he felt his own mental strength trying to rally like a protective barrier.

Frantically, he twisted and wriggled the upper part of his body, desperately and unthinkingly trying to stand and run, and toppled over onto his face in the rubble. Again the blow came, grating and screaming into his mind with an unrelenting savagery that baffled and appalled him. Twisting along the floor, he gained the door, peered sickly out into the blackness.

He could barely make out the gray shape of one of the steel monoliths he had seen rumbling down the road a little before. It was resting on the rocky frozen tundra of the field, standing motionless, the glow of power surrounding it like a ghostly aurora. He knew that the attack came from there, frightening, paralyzing bolts that shook him and sent his mind reeling helplessly, an attack of undreamed-of ferocity. He struggled, trying to erect some sort of mental patchwork against the onslaught. He had been wrong, he *could* be harmed, the test wasn't over—but why this horrible, jolting torture? Again and again the jolts came, until he screamed, and writhed, and waited in agonized anticipation of the next, and the next.

Then suddenly he felt his mind sucked down into a pool of velvet-soft warmth, of gentle sweetness, a welter of delightful tenderness. His mind wavered in sweet relief, relaxed to the throbbing, peaceful music that whirled through his mind, sinking easily into the trap, and then, abruptly, another savage blow, out of nowhere, threw him into a curled agonized heap on the floor. *No, no, no,* his mind screamed, *don't give up, fight it,* and he fought to reinforce a barrier of protection, tried feebly to strike back at the hideous, searing blows. This isn't real, he thought to himself, this isn't really happening, this is a ridiculous, impossible nightmare, and it *couldn't possibly hurt him*—but it *was* hurting him, terribly, until he couldn't stand it, he couldn't— Another blow came, more caustic, digging sharp, taloned fingers into his brain, wrenching and twisting it beyond endurance.

*He was going to die!* He knew it, in a horrible flash of realization. Whatever was out there in the field was going to kill him, going to wrench him into a blubbering mass of quivering protoplasm without mind, without life—*like the men who had come back on the starship.*

He took a gasping breath. Miraculously, he felt another link in the chain fall into place. *The starship*—he had seen it, sometime so long ago. Somewhere back in a remote corner of his mind he could remember the starship which had returned, after so many years, to its home on Earth, a gaunt, beaten hulk of a ship, with the lifeless, trampled men who had started it on its voyage. Men who were alive, but barely alive, men with records of unimaginable horror on their instruments, and nothing but babbling drivel coming from their lips. Men who had gone to the stars, and met alien savagery with which they could not cope; men who had been jolted from their lethargy into naked, screaming madness at the thought of ever, ever going back—

Was *this* why he was being tested? Was this why he had been trained, subjected to this mind-wrenching, gruelling ordeal? Another searing blow struck him, scraping at the feeble strength he had left, benumbing him, driving the picture from his mind. Was *this* what those men had faced? Was it this that had destroyed them, so infinitely far from their home, so very much alone on some alien world? Or was it something else, something a hundred-fold more horrible? He reeled and screamed, as anger beat through to his consciousness, a certain awareness that, imagination or not, the danger was *real*, so horribly real that he was falling apart under the onslaught, reaching that limit of his endurance beyond which was certain death.

Coldly, he searched for a weapon, coldly struggled to erect a shield to block the horrible blows—to fight horror with horror, to die fighting if need be. Grimly, he closed off his mind to hate and fear, dipped into the welter of horror and hatred in his mind, for something to match and conquer the monstrosity he was facing. With a howl of rage he sent out searing pictures of everything he knew of savagery, and hell-

ish violence, and diabolical hatred and destruction, matching
the alien onslaught blow for blow.

They could try to kill him, he knew they *could* kill him,
and he fought them with all the strength of mental power he
could drag from his brain, feeling the balance between his
mind and the shrieking horror from the field rise, and sway,
like a teeter-totter, back and forth, up and down, until somewhere he heard a scream, fading into silence, a scream of
alien fear and hatred and defeat.

And then he sank to the floor in exhaustion, his lips moving
feebly as he groaned, "I've got to fight them, or they'll kill me.
They'll kill me. They'll kill me."

    •           •           •

The girl's sobs echoed in the silent room. "Oh, stop it,"
she groaned, "stop it, Paul, please—he can't go on. Oh, it's
horrible—"

"I've had about as much as I want to watch," Connover
rasped hoarsely. His face had gone very pale, and he looked
ill. "How can you go on with this?"

"It's not me that's going on with it." Dr. Schiml's voice was
quiet. "I'm not concocting these things. All I'm doing is
applying tiny stimuli to tiny blocks of neural tissue. Nothing
more. The rest comes from his own mind—"

Mary turned to him, fiercely. "How could that be true?
How could there be such . . . such horror in his mind? *That*
isn't Robert, you know that. Robert's kind, and fine, and gentle
—how could he find such nightmares in his mind?"

"Everyone has nightmares in his mind, Mary. Even you.
And everyone has the power of death in his mind."

"But he's taken all the steps we planned," Connover cried.
"What more do you expect?"

"Some of the steps," Schiml corrected angrily. "Connover,
do you want to throw all these months of work out the
window? Of course he's come a long way. He's realized that
he's in danger that *can* kill him—that was desperately important—and he realizes the reason that he's being tested, too,
though he hasn't actually rationalized it out in that way. He's

beginning to realize why the starships failed. And he's realizing that he really *must* fight for survival. From the evidence he started with, he's gone a long way—a remarkably long way. Without the training, he wouldn't have survived the tunnel. But we can't stop now. He hasn't even approached the most vital realization of all. He's too strong, too confident, not desperate enough. I can't help him, Connover. He's got to do it himself."

"But he can't survive another attack like the last," Connover snapped. "Training or no training, no man could. You're deliberately letting him kill himself, Paul. Nobody could survive more of that—"

"He'll *have* to. The crews of the starships couldn't face what they found out there. That's why they came back—the way they did."

Connover's face was working. "Well, I wash my hands of it. I'm telling you to stop now. If that boy dies"—he glared at the tall doctor—"I won't be responsible."

"But you agreed—"

"Well, I've stopped agreeing. It's going too far."

Schiml stared at him for a long moment in disgust. Then he sighed. "If that's the way it's going to be"— he glanced at the girl—"I'll take full responsibility. But I've got to finish."

"And if he dies?"

Schiml's eyes were dull. "It's very simple," he said. "If he dies, we'll never have another chance. There'll never be another starship."

He couldn't tell how long he had been unconscious. Groggily, he raised his head, wincing as the pain stabbed through his brain, and blinked at the reflection of himself in the cold, mirror-steel wall. He stared at the reflection, startled to recognize himself. Robert Cox, his black hair muddy and caked, his face scratched in livid, grimy welts, his eyes red with strain and fatigue. With a groan, he rolled over on the polished floor, staring. Hesitantly he rubbed his side; the pain was still there, sharp under his probing fingers, and his head ached violently. But the room—

Then he knew that there had been another change. The room was perfectly enclosed, without a break, or window, or seam. It was a small, low-ceilinged room, with six sides—each side a polished mirror. The ceiling and floor also reflected his image as he struggled to his feet and sniffed the faint, sharp ozone-smell of the room. In the mirrors, a hundred Robert Coxes struggled unsteadily to their feet, blinking stupidly at him and at each other. A hundred haggard, grimy Robert Coxes, from every angle, from behind and above, reflecting and re-reflecting in the brilliant glow of the room.

And then he heard the scream. A long, piercing, agonized scream that reverberated from the walls of the room, nearly splitting his eardrums. It came again, louder, more piercing. Cox involuntarily clapped his fingers to his ears, but the sound came through them, pounding his skull. And then he heard the grinding sound along with the scream, a heavy, pervading grate of heavy-moving machinery, grinding, clanking, squealing in his ears. The scream came again, louder, more urgent, and a maddening whir joined the grating machinery. Cox stood poised in the center of the room, waiting, wary, ready for any sort of attack, his whole body geared to meet anything that came to threaten him. Deep in his mind a weariness was growing, a smoldering anger, at himself for being a party to this constantly-altering torture, at Dr. Schiml, and Connover, and anyone else who had a hand in this. What did they want? What conceivable point could there be to these attacks, this horrible instability? Why should he be subjected to such dangers that could kill him so easily? He felt a weakness, a terrible feeling that he couldn't go on, that he would have to lie down on the floor and be killed, that his limit was approaching, as he stood poised, fists clenched, waiting. How much could a man stand? What were they getting at, what did they want of him? And beyond all else, *when were they going to stop it?*

The thought broke off abruptly as a creeping chill slid up his spine, and he stared at the mirror opposite his face, almost gagging. He blinked at the image, then pawed at himself, unbelieving. Something was happening to him. Somehow, he wasn't the same any more—

Another scream cut through the air, a harsh, horrible whine of pain and torture, sending chills up his back as he winced. The image of him was different, somehow, melting and twisting before his eyes as he watched. Fascinated, he saw his hand melting away, twisting and turning into a tentacled slimy mess of writhing worms. He tore his eyes from the image, and glanced down at the hand—and a scream tore from his own throat. His cry echoed and re-echoed, as if every mirror image was screaming too, mocking him. No, he thought, *no*—it can't be happening, it *can't!* The room rumbled about him, with the cracking, grating sound of machinery with sand in its gears and the screams pierced out again and again. Now the arm was changing, too, twisting like something independently alive—

*He had to get out of that room!* With a scream of helpless rage he threw himself against the mirror, heard it give a strained twang as he bounced back in a heap on the floor. His mind raced, seeking a way out; his eyes peered about, searching for a door, but there was nothing but mirrors, mirrors doing hideous things to his arm, creeping toward his shoulder. Every time he looked for a door in one wall, he could see nothing but the reflection of another wall, and another. Down on his hands and knees, he crept about the room—four, five, six walls—was it seven and eight? Or was he repeating? He couldn't tell. Every glance drew his eyes back to the horrible, changing arm, until with superhuman control he reached down, seized the writhing thing with his good hand, and wrenched it away, a twisting, quivering, jellylike mass. And the stump continued to melt and change, and he couldn't see anything but the mirror.

A thought slid through his mind, and he caught it, frantically, a straw in the wind. Reflection. He couldn't see anything but the reflection. How many walls? He couldn't count. He couldn't be sure. But he had to get out of that room, he *had* to get out! He closed his eyes, closing out some of the brilliant light, bringing the piercing screams still closer to his mind. Slowly, painfully, he backed up to the wall of the room, keeping his eyes tightly closed, refusing to follow his actions in the mirrors, groping behind him with his good arm, seeking over the smooth surface—

A crack. Follow it. Smoothness—then metal. A knob! With a cry that was half a sob of relief he twisted the knob, felt the wall give, slipped outside onto rough, uneven ground with his eyes still closed, and slammed the door behind him. He stood panting as the grinding and the screams peeled away like a cloak, leaving him in absolute, almost palpable silence.

There was light. He opened his eyes, then closed them again with a swift gasp, his mind rocking with shock and fear. Cautiously he opened them a slit, peering down, fighting back the terrible, age-old fear, and then slammed them shut again in a rush of vertigo.

He was standing on the top of a thousand-foot pinnacle!

Instantly he fell down flat, gripping the smooth edges of rock with a desperate grip. The section of flat rock on which he stood was the size of a coffin, six feet long and three wide. Above him was a cool, blue sky with fleecy white clouds. But on all sides, inches from where he stood, was a sheer, cruel, breathtaking drop to the pounding sea below.

A shadow passed over him, and he glanced up, tense, fearful. High above he saw huge black wings, a long, naked red neck, cruel talons, black and shiny, and a hooked beak that glinted in the sunlight. A bird like he had never seen before, sweeping down toward him, then away, making huge circles in the bright blue sky. A bird far larger than he, with evil little button-eyes that stared down at him, unblinking—he sobbed, clinging for dear life to the rock, watching the bird circling lower and lower. Why? Why didn't they stop this torture? Why didn't they stop it, bring him back?

He sensed that the end was near—his strength was failing, his will was failing. Little streamers of hopelessness and despair were nibbling at his brain, despair of holding out much longer, despair that was almost overpowering the fear of death which had sustained him so long. The bird was so low he could hear the hungry flap of its wings as the steel-tipped talons scraped nearer and nearer to his shoulders. He peered over the edge of the precipice, seeking some kind of descent, some toe hold, finding none. He *had* to get down, he could never fight the creature. He blinked down at the blue water so far below. To climb down would be imbecility. He could feel the shredded end of his arm, loose in the cloth of his sleeve. With only one arm to hold on with, he couldn't hope to fight off the bird, even if there were a way to climb down.

A steely talon ripped his shirt as the bird skimmed by, sending a stab of pain through him, crystallizing his mad idea into action. Such a sheer drop above the water *could* mean a sheer drop below its level. An impossible choice, but there was nothing else to do. Taking a gasp of air he edged to the rim of the drop, gathered his strength, and threw himself off into space—and pure hope.

The water struck with a horrible impact, driving the wind from him, but he fought desperately toward the surface with his good arm, waiting for release, his mind begging that they would now be satisfied, that now they would stop, bring him back, not make him take any more. Finally he broke surface, and then, quite abruptly, felt solid ground under his feet. Glancing back, he saw that the pinnacle was gone, and the sky had turned a horrid orange-yellow color. Panting, his strength spent, he staggered up on the shore.

But the shore wasn't right. With a burst of anger he saw the fearful, distorted shore line upon which he stood, the sand under his feet writhing and alive as little wisps of it rose about his ankles, twisting them, as if to throw him down to his knees. Stars were blinking up at him from the ground, and great boulders of black granite scudded through the sky, whizzing past his ears like huge, unearthly cannon balls. The world was changing, turning and twisting into impossible shapes and contortions, and he smelled the dank, sharp odor of chlorine in the pungent air.

With a scream of rage he threw himself onto the writhing

sand, pounding his fist against it in helpless fury, screaming out again and again. He couldn't stand it any longer, this was the end, he couldn't fight any more— They'd *have* to bring him back now, they'd *have* to stop—

A horrible thought split into his mind, bringing him to his knees abruptly. His eyes were wide, hollow-rimmed as he stared unseeing at the impossibly distorted landscape. Fear struck into him, deep, hollow fear that screamed out in his mind, a desolate, empty fear. Carefully he reviewed his ordeal, everything he had thought, and seen, and felt. For so long, he had been running, fighting—enough to satisfy any test, as much as he was humanly capable of fighting. To test his re-actions, conscious and unconscious, his resourcefulness in the face of danger, his ingenuity, his resiliency, his fight, his drive, his spirit—they couldn't ask for more. Yet they still hadn't brought him back. Surely, if any human being had ever proved himself capable of surviving the fearful alienness of the stars and the worlds around the stars, he had proved himself.

*But they hadn't brought him back—*

The thought came again, strongly, growing into horrible certainty. He shuddered, a huge sob breaking from his lips. He knew, he was sure. He had been waiting, hoping, fighting until he had satisfied them and they would stop. But now he saw the picture, from a different angle, with terrible clarity.

*They weren't going to stop.* They were *never* going to stop subjecting him to these horrors. No matter how much he took, no matter how long he kept going, they would never stop.

He had been fighting for a lost cause, fighting to satisfy the insatiable. And he could keep fighting, and running, and fighting, *until he toppled over dead.*

Anger broke through the despair, blinding anger, anger that tore at his heart and twisted his mouth into a snarl of rage. He had been bilked, fooled, sold down the river. He was just another experiment, a test case, to see how much a live danger-trained spaceman could stand, to be run to death on a treadmill like a helpless, mindless guinea pig—

For the greater good of humanity, they had said. He spat on the sand. He didn't care about humanity any more. To enable men to go to the stars! *Bother the stars!* He was a man, he'd fought a grueling battle, he'd faced death in the most horrible forms his own mind could conceive. He wasn't going to die, not in the face of the worst that Connover and Schiml and their psych-training crews could throw at him!

He leaned back on the sand, red anger tearing through his veins. It was his own mind he was fighting, these things had come from his own mind, directed by Schiml's probing needles, stimulated by tiny electrical charges, horribly real, but coming from his own mind nevertheless. They could kill him, oh yes, he never lost sight of that fact.

But he could kill *them*, too.

He saw the huge rock coming at quite a distance. It was black, and jagged, like a monstrous chunk of coal, speeding straight for his head, careening through the air like some idiotic missile from hell. With bitter anger Robert Cox stood up, facing the approaching boulder, fixing his mind in a single, tight channel, and screamed *"Stop!"* with all the strength he had left.

And the boulder faltered in mid-flight, and slowed, and vanished in a puff of blue light.

Cox turned to face the shifting, junglelike shore line, his muscles frozen, great veins standing out in his neck. It's not true, his mind screamed to him, you can wake yourself up, they won't help you, but you can do it yourself, you can make it all go away, *you yourself can control this mind of yours—*

And then, like the mists of a dream, the world began fading away around him, twisting like wraiths in the thin, pungent air, changing, turning, changing again, as the last of his strength crept out of his beaten body, and his mind sank with the swirling world into a haze of unconsciousness. And the last thing he saw before blackout was a girl's sweet face, tearful and loving, hovering close to his, calling his name—

．　　　　　．　　　　　．

He was awake quite suddenly. Slowly he stared around the

bright, cheerful hospital room. His bed was by a window, and he looked out at the cool morning sun beaming down on the busy city below. Far below he could see the spreading buildings and grounds of the Hoffman Medical Center, like a green oasis in the teeming city. And far in the distance he saw the gleaming silver needlepoints of the starships that he knew were waiting for him.

He turned his face toward the tall, gaunt man in white by his bedside. "Paul," he said softly, "I came through."

"You came through." The doctor smiled happily, and sat down on the edge of the bed.

"But I had to terminate the test all by myself. You couldn't have stopped it for me."

Schiml nodded gravely. "That was the last step you had to take, the really critical step of the whole test. I couldn't have told the others about it, of course. They'd never have let me start the test if they had known. Connover wouldn't even stick with the part that he'd agreed upon. But without that last step, the test would have been worthless. Can you see that?"

Cox nodded slowly. "I had to rise above the physical reaction level, somehow, I had to force myself—"

"There's no way for us to know what you'll find, out there, when you go," Schiml said slowly. "All we knew was what the others found, and what it did to them. They couldn't survive what they found. But we knew that training in reactive, fight-or-flight level of response to danger wouldn't be good enough, either. You would have to have razor-sharp reactions *plus* full rational powers, even at the very end of your physical rope. We *had* to know that you had that—" He reached over to inspect Cox's bandaged head for a moment, his fingers infinitely gentle. "If the horrors you faced had been fakes, to be turned off when the going got tough, you wouldn't have been driven to that last ebb of resourcefulness that will save you—when you go to the stars. That was the final jump, the one the others didn't realize—that you had to discover, finally: That *we* weren't going to help you; that if you were to be saved, ultimately, it *had* to depend on you and you alone. You see, when you go where the other star-men went, no one will be with you to help. It'll be you and you alone. But whatever alien worlds you find, you'll have a strange sort of guardian angel to help you."

"The training—"

"That's right. Training on an unconscious level, of course, but there in your mind nevertheless, a sharpening of your senses, of your analytical powers—an overwhelmingly acute fight-or-flight sense to protect you, no matter what nightmares you run into."

Cox nodded. "I know. Like you called it, at the beginning of training—a sort of a brother, hidden, but always there. And this testing was the final step, to see if I *could* survive such nightmares."

"And you'll take it with you to the stars, the nightmare knowledge and experience. It's hidden deep in your mind, but it'll be there when you need it. You'll be the next man to go—you and your nightmare brother."

Cox stared out the window for a long moment. "Mary's all right?" he asked softly.

"She's waiting to see you."

Robert Cox sat up slowly, his mind clear in the remembrance of the ordeal he had been through—a hideous ordeal. Terrible, but necessary so that when he came back, he would not be like the others had been. So that men could go to the stars with safety, and come back with safety.

Slowly he remembered his anger. He gripped the doctor's hand, squeezed it tightly. "Thanks, Paul," he said. "If I come back—"

"You mean, when you come back," said Dr. Schiml, grinning. "When you come back, we'll all have a beer together. That's what we'll do."

Murray Leinster

# PIPELINE TO PLUTO

> *Two kinds of criminals are discussed in this narrative
> of interplanetary flight in a possible tomorrow: the
> criminal who* thinks *he knows how to get something
> for very nearly nothing, and the criminal who* knows
> *he can. And when one type preys on the other, the
> results can be remarkably sinister—particularly when
> one of them has found that he has been deluded.*

F AR, FAR OUT ON PLUTO, WHERE THE SUN IS ONLY A VERY
bright star and a frozen, airless globe circles in emptiness; far
out on Pluto, there was motion. The perpetual faint starlight
was abruptly broken. Yellow lights shone suddenly in a circle,
and men in spacesuits waddled to a space tug—absurdly
marked *Betsy-Anne* in huge white letters. They climbed up
its side and went in the airlock. Presently a faint, jetting glow
appeared below its drivetubes. It flared suddenly and the tug
lifted, to hover expertly a brief distance above what seemed
an unmarred field of frozen atmosphere. But that field heaved
and broke. The nose of a Pipeline carrier appeared in the
center of a cruciform opening. It thrust through. It stood half
its length above the surface of the dead and lifeless planet.

Murray Leinster, PIPELINE TO PLUTO. Copyright 1945 in the
United States and Great Britain by Street and Smith Publications,
Inc. Reprinted by permission of Oscar J. Friend from *Astounding
Science Fiction*, August 1945.

The tug drifted above it. Its grapnel dropped down, jetted minute flames, and engaged in the monster tow ring at the carrier's bow.

The tug's drivetubes flared luridly. The carrier heaved abruptly up out of its hiding place and plunged for the heavens behind the tug. It had a huge classmark and number painted on its side, which was barely visible as it whisked out of sight. It went on up at four gravities acceleration, while the spacetug lined out on the most precise of courses and drove fiercely for emptiness.

A long, long time later, when Pluto was barely a pallid disk behind, the tug cast off. The carrier went on, sunward. Its ringed nose pointed unwaveringly to the sun toward which it would drift for years. It was one of a long, long line of carriers drifting through space, a day apart in time but millions of miles apart in distance. They would go on until a tug from Earth came out and grappled them, and towed them in to their actual home planet.

But the *Betsy-Anne,* of Pluto, did not pause for contemplation of the two-billion-mile-long line of orecarriers taking the metal of Pluto back to Earth. It darted off from the line its late tow now followed. Its radio-locator beam flickered invisibly in emptiness. Presently its course changed. It turned about. It braked violently, going up to six gravities deceleration for as long as half a minute at a time. Presently it came to rest and there floated toward it an object from Earth, a carrier with great white numerals on its sides. It had been hauled off Earth and flung into an orbit which would fetch it out to Pluto. The *Betsy-Anne's* grapnel floated toward it and jetted tiny sparks until the tow ring was engaged. Then the tug and its new tow from Earth started back to Pluto.

There were two long lines of white-numbered carriers floating sedately through space. One line drifted tranquilly in to Earth. One drifted no less tranquilly out past the orbits of six planets to reach the closed-in, underground colony of the mines on Pluto.

Together they made up the Pipeline.

The evening Moon-rocket took off over to the north and went straight up to the zenith. Its blue-white rocket-flare changed color as it fell behind, until the tail-end was a deep, rich crimson. The Pipeline docks were silent, now, but opposite the yard the row of flimsy eating- and drinking-places rattled and muttered to themselves from the lower-than-sound vibrations of the Moon-ship.

There was a youngish, battered man named Hill in the Pluto Bar, opposite the docks. He paid no attention to the Moon-rocket, but he looked up sharply as a man came out of the Pipeline gate and came across the street toward the bar. But Hill was staring at his drink when the door opened and the man from the dock looked the small dive over. Besides Hill—who looked definitely tough, and as if he had but recently recovered from a ravaging illness—there was only the bartender, a catawheel-truck driver and his girl having a drink together, and another man at a table by himself and fidgeting nervously as if he were waiting for someone. Hill's eyes flickered again to the man in the door. He looked suspicious. But then he looked back at his glass.

The other man came in and went to the bar.

"Evenin', Mr. Crowder," said the bartender.

Hill's eyes darted up, and down again. The bartender reached below the bar, filled a glass, and slid it across the mahogany.

"Evenin'," said Crowder curtly. He looked deliberately at the fidgety man. He seemed to note that the fidgety man was alone. He gave no sign of recognition, but his features pinched a little, as some men's do when they feel a little, crawling unease. But there was nothing wrong except that the fidgety man seemed to be upset because he was waiting for someone who hadn't come.

Crowder sat down in a booth, alone. Hill waited a moment, looked sharply about him, and then stood up. He crossed purposefully to the booth in which Crowder sat.

"I'm lookin' for a fella named Crowder," he said huskily. "That's you, ain't it?"

Crowder looked at him, his face instantly masklike. Hill's

looks matched his voice. There was a scar under one eye. He had a cauliflower ear. He looked battered, and hard-boiled—and as if he had just recovered from some serious injury or illness. His skin was reddened in odd patches.

"My name is Crowder," said Crowder suspiciously. "What is it?"

Hill sat down opposite him.

"My name's Hill," he said in the same husky voice. "There was a guy who was gonna come here tonight. He'd fixed it up to be stowed away on a Pipeline carrier to Pluto. I bought 'im off. I bought his chance. I came here to take his place."

"I don't know what you're talking about," said Crowder coldly.

But he did. Hill could see that he did. His stomach-muscles knotted. He was uneasy. Hill's gaze grew scornful.

"You're the night super of th' Pipeline yards, ain't you?" he demanded truculently.

Crowder's face stayed masklike. Hill looked tough. He looked like the sort of yegg who'd get into trouble with the police because he'd never think things out ahead. He knew it, and he didn't care. Because he had gotten in trouble—often —because he didn't think things out ahead. But he wasn't that way tonight. He'd planned tonight in detail.

"Sure I'm the night-superintendent of the Pipeline yards," said Crowder shortly. "I came over for a drink. I'm going back. But I don't know what you're talking about."

Hill's eyes grew hard.

"Listen, fella," he said truculently—but he had been really ill, and the signs of it were plain—"they're payin' five hundred credits a day in the mines out on Pluto, ain't they? A guy works a year out there, he comes back rich, don't he?"

"Sure!" said Crowder. "The wages got set by law when it cost a lot to ship supplies out. Before the Pipeline got going."

"An' they ain't got enough guys to work, have they?"

"There's a shortage," agreed Crowder coldly. "Everybody knows it. The liners get fifty thousand credits for a one-way passage, and it takes six months for the trip."

Hill nodded, truculently.

"I wanna get out to Pluto," he said huskily. "See? They don't ask too many questions about a guy when he turns up out there. But the spaceliners, they do, an' they want too many credits. So I wanna go out in a carrier by Pipeline. See?"

Crowder downed his drink and stood up.

"There's a law," he said uncompromisingly, "that says the Pipeline can't carry passengers or mail."

"Maybe," said Hill pugnaciously, "but you promised to let a guy stow away on the carrier tonight. He told me about it. I paid him off. He sold me his place. I'm takin' it, see?"

"I'm night superintendent at the yards," Crowder told him. "If there are arrangements for stowaways, I don't know about them. You're talking to the wrong man."

He abruptly left the table. He walked across the room to the fidgety man, who seemed more and more uneasy because somebody hadn't turned up. Crowder's eyes were viciously angry when he bent over the fidgety man.

"Look here, Moore!" he said savagely, in a low tone. "That guy is on! He says he paid your passenger to let him take his place. That's why your man hasn't showed up. You picked him out and he sold his place to this guy. So I'm leaving it right in your lap! I can lie myself clear. They couldn't get any evidence back, anyhow. Not for years yet. But what he told me is straight, he's got to go or he'll shoot off his mouth! So it's in your lap!"

The eyes of Moore—the fidgety man—had a hunted look in them. He swallowed as if his mouth were dry. But he nodded.

Crowder went out. Hill scowled after him. After a moment he came over to Moore.

"Lookahere," he said huskily. "I wanna know somethin'. That guy's night super for Pipeline, ain't he?"

Moore nodded. He licked his lips.

"Lissen!" said Hill angrily, "there's a Pipeline carrier leaves here every day for Pluto, an' one comes in from Pluto every day. It's just like gettin' on a 'copter an' goin' from one town to another on the Pipeline, ain't it?"

Moore nodded again—this time almost unnoticeably.

"That's what a guy told me," said Hill pugnaciously. "He said he'd got it all fixed up to stow away on a carrier-load of grub. He said he'd paid fifteen hundred credits to have it fixed up. He was gonna leave tonight. I paid him off to let me take his place. Now this guy Crowder tells me I'm crazy!"

"I . . . wouldn't know anything about it," said Moore, hesitantly. "I know Crowder, but that's all."

Hill growled to himself. He doubled up his fist and looked at it. It was a capable fist. There were scars on it as proof that things had been hit with it.

"O.K.!" said Hill. "I guess that guy kidded me. He done me outta plenty credits. I know where to find him. He's goin' to a hospital!"

He stirred, scowling.

"W-wait a minute," said Moore. "It seems to me I heard something, once—"

Carriers drifted on through space. They were motorless, save for the tiny drives for the gyros in their noses. They were a hundred feet long, and twenty feet thick, and some of them contained foodstuffs in air-sealed containers—because everything will freeze, in space, but even ice will evaporate in a vacuum. Some carried drums of rocket fuel for the tugs and heaters and the generators for the mines on Pluto. Some contained tools and books and visiphone records and caviar and explosives and glue and cosmetics for the women on Pluto. But all of them drifted slowly, leisurely, unhurriedly, upon their two-billion-mile journey.

There were over twelve hundred of them in each line going each way, a day apart in time and millions of miles apart in space. They were very lonely, those long cylinders with their white-painted numbers on their sides. The stars were the only eyes to look upon the while they traveled, and it took three years to drift from one end of the pipeline to the other.

But nevertheless there were daily arrivals and departures on the Pipeline, and there was continuous traffic between the two planets.

Moore turned away from the pay-visiphone, into which he had talked in a confidential murmur while the screen remained blank. The pugnacious, battered Hill scowled impatiently behind him.

"I'm not sure," said Moore uneasily. "I talked to somebody I thought might know something, but they're cagey. They'd lose their jobs and maybe get in worse trouble if anybody finds out they're smuggling stowaways to Pluto. Y'see, the space lines have a big pull in politics. They've got it fixed so the Pipeline can't haul anything but freight. If people could travel by Pipeline, the space liners 'ud go broke. So they watch close."

He looked uneasy as he spoke. But Hill said sourly:

"O.K.! I'm gonna find the guy that sold me his place, an' I'm gonna write a message on him with a blowtorch. The docs'll have fun readin' him, an' why he's in the hospital!"

Moore swallowed.

"Who was it? I've heard something—"

Hill bit off the name. Moore swallowed again—as if the name meant something. As if it were right.

"I . . . I'll tell you, guy," said Moore. "It's none of my business, but I . . . well . . . I might be able to fix things up for you. It's risky, though, butting in on something that ain't my business—"

"How much?" said Hill shortly.

"Oh . . . f-five hundred," said Moore uneasily.

Hill stared at him. Hard. Then he pulled a roll out of his pocket. He displayed it.

"I got credits," he said huskily. "But I'm givin' you just one hundred of 'em. I'll give you nine hundred more when I'm all set. That's twice what you asked for. But that's all, see? I got a reason to get off Earth, an' tonight I'll pay to manage it. But if I'm double-crossed, somebody gets hurt!"

Moore grinned nervously.

"No double-crossing in this," he said quickly. "Just . . . well . . . it is ticklish."

"Yeah," said Hill. He waved a battered-knuckle hand. "Get goin'. Tell those guys I'm willin' to pay. But I get stowed away, or I'll fix that guy who sold me his place so he'll tell all he knows! I'm goin' to Pluto, or else!"

Moore said cautiously:

"M-maybe you'll have to pay out a little more . . . but not much! But you'll get there! I've heard . . . just heard, you understand . . . that the gang here smuggles a fella into the Pipeline yard and up into the nose of a carrier. They pick out a carrier loaded with grub. Champagne and all that. He can live high on the way, and not worry because out on Pluto they're so anxious to get a man to work that they'll square things. They need men bad, out on Pluto! They pay five hundred credits a day!"

"Yeah," said Hill grimly. "They need 'em so bad there ain't no extradition either. I'm int'rested in that, too. Now get goin' an' fix me up!"

The Pipeline was actually a two-billion-mile arrangement of specks in infinity. Each of the specks was a carrier. Each of the carriers was motorless and inert. Each was unlighted. Each was lifeless. But—some of them had contained life when they started.

The last carrier out from Earth, to be sure, contained nothing but its proper cargo of novelties, rocket fuel, canned goods and plastic base. But in the one beyond that, there was what had been a hopeful stowaway. A man, with his possessions neatly piled about him. He'd been placed up in the nose of the carrier, and he'd waited, mousy-still, until the space tug connected with the tow ring and heaved the carrier out to the beginning of the Pipeline. As a stowaway, he hadn't wanted to be discovered. The carrier ahead of that—many millions of miles farther out—contained two girls, who had heard that stenographers were highly paid on Pluto, and that there were so few women that a girl might take her pick of husbands. The one just before that had a man and woman in it. There were four men in the carrier beyond them.

The hundred-foot cylinders drifting out and out and out toward Pluto contained many stowaways. The newest of them still looked quite human. They looked quite tranquil. After all, when a carrier is hauled aloft at four gravities acceleration the air flows out of the bilge-valves very quickly, but the cold comes in more quickly still. None of the stowaways had actually suffocated. They'd frozen so suddenly they probably did not realize what was happening. At sixty thousand feet the temperature is around seventy degrees below zero. At a hundred and twenty thousand feet it's so cold that figures simply haven't any meaning. And at four gravities acceleration you reach a hundred and twenty thousand feet before you've really grasped the fact that you paid all your money to be flung unprotected into space. So you never quite realize that you're going on out into a vacuum which will gradually draw every atom of moisture from every tissue of your body.

But, though there were many stowaways, not one had yet reached Pluto. They would do so in time, of course. But the practice of smuggling stowaways to Pluto had only been in operation for a year and a half. The first of the deluded ones had not quite passed the halfway mark. So the stowaway business should be safe and profitable for at least a year and a half more. Then it would be true that a passenger entered the Pipeline from Earth and a passenger reached Pluto on the same day. But it would not be the same passenger, and there would be other differences. Even then, though, the racket would simply stop being profitable, because there was no extradition either to or from Pluto.

The battered youngish man said coldly:

"Well? You fixed it?"

Moore grinned nervously.

"Yeah. It's all fixed. At first they thought you might be an undercover man for the passenger lines, trying to catch the Pipeline smuggling passengers so they could get its charter canceled. But they called up the man whose place you took, and it's straight. He said he gave you his place and told you to see Crowder."

Hill said angrily:

"But Crowder stalled me!"

Moore licked his lips.

"You'll get the picture in a minute. We cross the street and go in the Pipeline yard. You have to slip the guard something. A hundred credits for looking the other way."

Hill growled:

"No more stalling!"

"No more stalling," promised Moore. "You go out to Pluto in the next carrier."

They went out of the Pluto Bar. They crossed the street, which was thin, black, churned-up mud from the catawheel trucks which hauled away each day's arrival of freight from Pluto. They moved directly and openly for the gateway. The guard strolled toward them.

"Slim," said Moore, grinning nervously, "meet my friend Hill."

"Sure!" said the guard.

He extended his hand, palm up. Hill put a hundred-credit note in it.

"O.K.," said the guard. "Luck on Pluto, fella."

He turned his back. Moore snickered almost hysterically and led the way into the dark recesses of the yard. There was the landing field for the space tugs. There were six empty carriers off to one side. There was one in a loading pit, sunk down on a hydraulic platform until only its nose now showed above-ground. It could be loaded in its accelerating position, that way, and would not need to be upended after reaching maximum weight.

"Take-off is half an hour before sunrise today," said Moore jerkily. "You'll know when it's coming because the hydraulic platform shoves the carrier up out of the pit. Then you'll hear the grapnel catching in the tow ring. Then you start. The tug puts you in the Pipeline and hangs around and picks up the other carrier coming back."

"That's speed!" said Hill. "Them scientists are great stuff, huh? I start off in that, an' before I know it I'm on Pluto!"

"Yeah," said Moore. He smirked with a twitching, ghastly effect. "Before you know it. Here's the door where you go in."

Crowder came around the other side of the carrier's cone-shaped nose. He scowled at Hill, and Hill scowled back.

"You sounded phony to me," said Crowder ungraciously. "I wasn't going to take any chances by admitting anything. Moore told you it's going to cost you extra?"

"For what?" demanded Hill, bristling.

"Because you've got to get away fast," said Crowder evenly. "Because there's no extradition from Pluto. We're not in this for our health. Two thousand credits more."

Hill snarled:

"Thief—" Then he said sullenly. "O.K."

"And my nine hundred," said Moore eagerly.

"Sure," said Hill, sardonically. He paid. "O.K. now? Whadda I do now?"

"Go in the door here," said Crowder. "The cargo's grub. Get comfortable and lay flat on your back when you feel the carrier coming up to be hitched on for towing. After the acceleration's over and you're in the Pipeline, do as you please."

"Yeah!" said Moore, giggling nervously. "Do just as you please."

Hill said tonelessly:

"Right. I'll start now."

He moved with a savage, infuriated swiftness. There was a queer, muffled cracking sound. Then a startled gasp from Moore, a moment's struggle, and another sharp crack.

Hill went into the nose of the carrier. He dragged them in. He stayed inside for minutes. He came out and listened, swinging a leather blackjack meditatively. Then he went over to the gate. He called cautiously to the guard.

"You! Slim! Crowder says come quick—an' quiet! Somethin's happened an' him an' Moore got their hands full."

The guard blinked, and then came quickly. Hill hurried behind him to the loading pit. The guard called tensely:

"Hey, Crowder, what's the matter—"

Hill swung the blackjack again, with deft precision. The guard collapsed.

A little later Hill had finished his work. The three men were bound with infinite science. They not only could not escape, they could not even kick. That's quite a trick—but it can be done if you study the art. And they were not only gagged, but there was tape over their mouths beyond the gag, so that they could not even make a respectable groaning noise. And Hill surveyed the three of them by the light of a candle he had taken from his pocket—as he had taken the rope from about his waist—and said in husky satisfaction:

"O.K. O.K.! I'm givin' you fellas some bad news. You're headin' out to Pluto."

Terror close to madness shone in the three pairs of eyes which fixed frantically upon him. The eyes seemed to threaten to start from their sockets.

"It ain't so bad," said Hill grimly. "Not like you think it is. You'll get there before you know it. No kidding! You'll go snakin' up at four gravities, an' the air'll go out. But you won't die of that. Before you strangle, you'll freeze—an' fast! You'll freeze so fast y'won't have time to die, fellas. That's the funny part. *You freeze so quick you ain't got time to die!* The Space Patrol found out a year or so back that that can happen, when things are just right—an' they will be, for you. So the Space Patrol will be all set to bring you back, when y' get to Pluto. But it does hurt, fellas. It hurts like hell! I oughta know!"

He grinned at them, his mouth twisted and his eyes grim.

"I paid you fellas to send me out to Pluto last year. But it happened I didn't get to Pluto. The Patrol dragged my carrier out o' the Pipeline an' over to Callisto because they hadda shortage o' rocket fuel there. Callisto—moon of Jupiter, you know. Less than an eighth of the distance to Pluto. See? So I been through it, an' it hurts! I wouldn't tell on you fellas, because I wanted you to have it, so I took my bawlin' out for stowin' away an' come back to send you along. So you' goin', fellas! An' you' goin' all the way to Pluto! And remember this, fellas! It's gonna be good! After they bring you back, out there on Pluto, every fella an' every soul you sent off as stowaways, they'll be there on Pluto waitin' for you! It's gonna be good, guys! It's gonna be good!"

He looked at them in the candlelight, and seemed to take a vast satisfaction in their expressions. Then he blew out the candle, and closed the nose door of the carrier, and went away.

Half an hour before sunrise next morning the hydraulic platform pushed the carrier up. A space tug hung expertly overhead; its grapnel came down and hooked in the tow ring. Then the carrier jerked skyward at four gravities acceleration.

Far out from Earth the carrier went on, the latest of a long line of specks in infinity which constituted the Pipeline to Pluto. Many of those specks contained things which had been human—and would be human again. But now each one drifted sedately away from the sun, and in the later carriers the stowaways still looked completely human and utterly tranquil. What had happened to them had come so quickly that they did not realize what it was. But in the last carrier of all, with three bound, gagged figures in its nose, the expressions were not tranquil at all. Because those men did know what had happened to them. More—they knew what was yet to come.

# Philip K. Dick

# IMPOSTOR

*In all the variations on the theme of aliens from space visiting us, the kind that is most terrifying is that in which galactic entities are able to imitate the shape of man perfectly. We would not know they were among us. They could gradually infiltrate our planet and eventually take it over!*

*But here is a tale which goes one frightening final step further, the step in which the aliens imitate me, and you, and you. How, as Horace Gold put it in his introductory note to this story when it ran in* Galaxy Science Fiction, *could we prove we were ourselves?*

*We couldn't!*

"ONE OF THESE DAYS I'M GOING TO TAKE TIME OFF," Spence Olham said at first-meal. He looked around at his wife. "I think I've earned a rest. Ten years is a long time."

"And the Project?"

"The war will be won without me. This ball of clay of ours isn't really in much danger." Olham sat down at the table and lit a cigarette. "The news-machines alter dispatches to make it appear the Outspacers are right on top of us. You know what I'd like to do on my vacation? I'd like to take a camping trip

Philip K. Dick, IMPOSTOR. Copyright 1953 by Galaxy Publishing Corp. Reprinted by permission of Scott Meredith from *Galaxy*, June 1953.

in those mountains outside of town, where we went that time. Remember? I got poison oak and you almost stepped on a gopher snake."

"Sutton Wood?" Mary began to clear away the food dishes. "The Wood was burned a few weeks ago. I thought you knew. Some kind of a flash fire."

Olham sagged. "Didn't they even try to find the cause?" His lips twisted. "No one cares any more. All they can think of is the war." He clamped his jaws together, the whole picture coming up in his mind, the Outspacers, the war, the needle-ships.

"How can we think about anything else?"

Olham nodded. She was right, of course. The dark little ships out of Alpha Centauri had by-passed the Earth cruisers easily, leaving them like helpless turtles. It had been one-way fights, all the way back to Terra.

All the way, until the protec-bubble was demonstrated by Westinghouse Labs. Thrown around the major Earth cities and finally the planet itself, the bubble was the first real defense, the first legitimate answer to the Outspacers—as the news-machines labeled them.

But to win the war, that was another thing. Every lab, every project was working night and day, endlessly, to find something more: a weapon for positive combat. His own project, for example. All day long, year after year.

Olham stood up, putting out his cigarette. "Like the Sword of Damocles. Always hanging over us. I'm getting tired. All I want to do is take a long rest. But I guess everybody feels that way."

He got his jacket from the closet and went out on the front porch. The shoot would be along any moment, the fast little bug that would carry him to the Project.

"I hope Nelson isn't late." He looked at his watch. "It's almost seven."

"Here the bug comes," Mary said, gazing between the rows of houses. The sun glittered behind the roofs, reflecting against the heavy lead plates. The settlement was quiet; only a few people were stirring. "I'll see you later. Try not to work beyond your shift, Spence."

Olham opened the car door and slid inside, leaning back against the seat with a sigh. There was an older man with Nelson.

"Well?" Olham said, as the bug shot ahead. "Heard any interesting news?"

"The usual," Nelson said. "A few Outspace ships hit, another asteroid abandoned for strategic reasons."

"It'll be good when we get the Project into final stage. Maybe it's just the propaganda from the news-machines, but in the last month I've gotten weary of all this. Everything seems so grim and serious, no color to life."

"Do you think the war is in vain?" the older man said suddenly. "You are an integral part of it, yourself."

"This is Major Peters," Nelson said. Olham and Peters shook hands. Olham studied the older man.

"What brings you along so early?" he said. "I don't remember seeing you at the Project before."

"No, I'm not with the Project," Peters said, "but I know something about what you're doing. My own work is altogether different."

A look passed between him and Nelson. Olham noticed it and he frowned. The bug was gaining speed, flashing across the barren, lifeless ground toward the distant rim of the Project buildings.

"What is your business?" Olham said. "Or aren't you permitted to talk about it?"

"I'm with the government," Peters said. "With FSA, the Security Organ."

"Oh?" Olham raised an eyebrow. "Is there any enemy infiltration in this region?"

"As a matter of fact I'm here to see you, Mr. Olham."

Olham was puzzled. He considered Peters' words, but he could make nothing of them. "To see me? Why?"

"I'm here to arrest you as an Outspace spy. That's why I'm up so early this morning. *Grab him, Nelson—*"

The gun drove into Olham's ribs. Nelson's hands were shaking, trembling with released emotion, his face pale. He took a deep breath and let it out again.

"Shall we kill him now?" he whispered to Peters. "I think we should kill him now. We can't wait."

Olham stared into his friend's face. He opened his mouth to speak, but no words came. Both men were staring at him steadily, rigid and grim with fright. Olham felt dizzy. His head ached and spun.

"I don't understand," he murmured.

At that moment the shoot car left the ground and rushed up, heading into space. Below them the Project fell away, smaller and smaller, disappearing. Olham shut his mouth.

"We can wait a little," Peters said. "I want to ask him some questions, first."

Olham gazed dully ahead as the bug rushed through space.

"The arrest was made all right," Peters said into the vidscreen. On the screen the features of the Security chief showed. "It should be a load off everyone's mind."

"Any complications?"

"None. He entered the bug without suspicion. He didn't seem to think my presence was too unusual."

"Where are you now?"

"On our way out, just inside the protec-bubble. We're moving at maximum speed. You can assume that the critical period is past. I'm glad the take-off jets in this craft were in good working order. If there had been any failure at that point—"

"Let me see him," the Security chief said. He gazed directly at Olham where he sat, his hands in his lap, staring ahead. "So that's the man." He looked at Olham for a time. Olham said nothing. At last the chief nodded to Peters. "All right. That's enough." A faint trace of disgust wrinkled his features. "I've seen all I want. You've done something that will be remembered for a long time. They're preparing some sort of citation for both of you."

"That's not necessary," Peters said.

"How much danger is there now? Is there still much chance that—"

"There is some chance, but not too much. According to my understanding, it requires a verbal key phrase. In any case we'll have to take the risk."

"I'll have the Moon base notified you're coming."

"No." Peters shook his head. "I'll land the ship outside, beyond the base. I don't want it in jeopardy."

"Just as you like." The chief's eyes flickered as he glanced again at Olham. Then his image faded. The screen blanked.

Olham shifted his gaze to the window. The ship was already through the protec-bubble, rushing with greater and greater speed all the time. Peters was in a hurry; below him, rumbling under the floor, the jets were wide open. They were afraid, hurrying frantically, because of him.

Next to him on the seat, Nelson shifted uneasily. "I think we should do it now," he said. "I'd give anything if we could get it over with."

"Take it easy," Peters said. "I want you to guide the ship for a while so I can talk to him."

He slid over beside Olham, looking into his face. Presently he reached out and touched him gingerly, on the arm and then on the cheek.

Olham said nothing. *If I could let Mary know,* he thought again. *If I could find some way of letting her know.* He looked around the ship. How? The vidscreen? Nelson was sitting by the board, holding the gun. There was nothing he could do. He was caught, trapped.

*But why?*

"Listen," Peters said, "I want to ask you some questions. You know where we're going. We're moving Moonward. In an hour we'll land on the far side, on the desolate side. After we land you'll be turned over immediately to a team of men waiting there. Your body will be destroyed at once. Do you understand that?" He looked at his watch. "Within two hours your parts will be strewn over the landscape. There won't be anything left of you."

Olham struggled out of his lethargy. "Can't you tell me—"

"Certainly, I'll tell you." Peters nodded. "Two days ago we received a report that an Outspace ship had penetrated the protec-bubble. The ship let off a spy in the form of a humanoid robot. The robot was to destroy a particular human being and take his place."

Peters looked calmly at Olham.

"Inside the robot was a U-Bomb. Our agent did not know how the bomb was to be detonated, but he conjectured that it might be by a particular spoken phrase, a certain group of words. The robot would live the life of the person he killed, entering into his usual activities, his job, his social life. He had been constructed to resemble that person. No one would know the difference."

Olham's face went sickly chalk.

"The person whom the robot was to impersonate was Spence Olham, a high-ranking official at one of the Research projects. Because this particular project was approaching crucial stage, the presence of an animate bomb, moving toward the center of the Project—"

Olham stared down at his hands. *"But I'm Olham!"*

"Once the robot had located and killed Olham, it was a simple matter to take over his life. The robot was probably released from the ship eight days ago. The substitution was probably accomplished over the last week end, when Olham went for a short walk in the hills."

"But I'm Olham." He turned to Nelson, sitting at the controls. "Don't you recognize me? You've known me for twenty years. Don't you remember how we went to college together?" He stood up. "You and I were at the University. We had the same room." He went toward Nelson.

"Stay away from me!" Nelson snarled.

"Listen. Remember our second year? Remember that girl? What was her name—" He rubbed his forehead. "The one with the dark hair. The one we met over at Ted's place."

"Stop!" Nelson waved the gun frantically. "I don't want to hear any more. You killed him! You . . . machine."

Olham looked at Nelson. "You're wrong. I don't know what

happened, but the robot never reached me. Something must have gone wrong. Maybe the ship crashed." He turned to Peters. "I'm Olham. I know it. No transfer was made. I'm the same as I've always been."

He touched himself, running his hands over his body. "There must be some way to prove it. Take me back to Earth. An X-ray examination, a neurological study, anything like that will show you. Or maybe we can find the crashed ship."

Neither Peters nor Nelson spoke.

"I am Olham," he said again. "I know I am. But I can't prove it."

"The robot," Peters said, "would be unaware that he was not the real Spence Olham. He would become Olham in mind as well as body. He was given an artificial memory system, false recall. He would look like him, have his memories, his thoughts and interests, perform his job.

"But there would be one difference. Inside the robot is a U-Bomb, ready to explode at the trigger phrase." Peters moved a little away. "That's the one difference. That's why we're taking you to the Moon. They'll disassemble you and remove the bomb. Maybe it will explode, but it won't matter, not there."

Olham sat down slowly.

"We'll be there soon," Nelson said.

He lay back, thinking frantically, as the ship dropped slowly down. Under them was the pitted surface of the Moon, the endless expanse of ruin. What could he do? What would save him?

"Get ready," Peters said.

In a few minutes he would be dead. Down below he could see a tiny dot, a building of some kind. There were men in the building, the demolition team, waiting to tear him to bits. They would rip him open, pull off his arms and legs, break him apart. When they found no bomb they would be surprised; they would know, but it would be too late.

Olham looked around the small cabin. Nelson was still holding the gun. There was no chance there. If he could get to a doctor, have an examination made—that was the only way. Mary could help him. He thought frantically, his mind racing. Only a few minutes, just a little time left. If he could contact her, get word to her some way.

"Easy," Peters said. The ship came down slowly, bumping on the rough ground. There was silence.

"Listen," Olham said thickly. "I can prove I'm Spence Olham. Get a doctor. Bring him here—"

"There's the squad." Nelson pointed. "They're coming." He glanced nervously at Olham. "I hope nothing happens."

"We'll be gone before they start work," Peters said. "We'll be out of here in a moment." He put on his pressure suit. When he had finished he took the gun from Nelson. "I'll watch him for a moment."

Nelson put on his pressure suit, hurrying awkwardly. "How about him?" He indicated Olham. "Will he need one?"

"No." Peters shook his head. "Robots probably don't require oxygen."

The group of men were almost to the ship. They halted, waiting. Peters signaled to them.

"Come on!" He waved his hand and the men approached warily; stiff, grotesque figures in their inflated suits.

"If you open the door," Olham said, "it means my death. It will be murder."

"Open the door," Nelson said. He reached for the handle.

Olham watched him. He saw the man's hand tighten around the metal rod. In a moment the door would swing back, the air in the ship would rush out. He would die, and presently they would realize their mistake. Perhaps at some other time, when there was no war, men might not act this way, hurrying an individual to his death because they were afraid. Everyone was frightened, everyone was willing to sacrifice the individual because of the group fear.

He was being killed because they could not wait to be sure of his guilt. There was not enough time.

He looked at Nelson. Nelson had been his friend for years. They had gone to school together. He had been best man at his wedding. Now Nelson was going to kill him. But Nelson was not wicked; it was not his fault. It was the times. Perhaps it had been the same way during the plagues. When men had shown a spot they probably had been killed, too, without a moment's hesitation, without proof, on suspicion alone. In times of danger there was no other way.

He did not blame them. But he had to live. His life was too precious to be sacrificed. Olham thought quickly. What could he do? Was there anything? He looked around.

"Here goes," Nelson said.

"You're right," Olham said. The sound of his own voice surprised him. It was the strength of desperation. "I have no need of air. Open the door."

They paused, looking at him in curious alarm.

"Go ahead. Open it. It makes no difference." Olham's hand disappeared inside his jacket. "I wonder how far you two can run."

"Run?"

"You have fifteen seconds to live." Inside his jacket his fingers twisted, his arm suddenly rigid. He relaxed, smiling a little. "You were wrong about the trigger phrase. In that respect you were mistaken. Fourteen seconds, now."

Two shocked faces stared at him from the pressure suits. Then they were struggling, running, tearing the door open. The air shrieked out, spilling into the void. Peters and Nelson bolted out of the ship. Olham came after them. He grasped the door and dragged it shut. The automatic pressure system chugged furiously, restoring the air. Olham let his breath out with a shudder.

One more second—

Beyond the window the two men had joined the group. The group scattered, running in all directions. One by one they threw themselves down, prone on the ground. Olham seated himself at the control board. He moved the dials into place. As the ship rose up into the air the men below scrambled to their feet and stared up, their mouths open.

"Sorry," Olham murmured, "but I've got to get back to Earth."

He headed the ship back the way it had come.

It was night. All around the ship crickets chirped, disturbing the chill darkness. Olham bent over the vidscreen. Gradually the image formed; the call had gone through without trouble. He breathed a sigh of relief.

"Mary," he said. The woman stared at him. She gasped.

"Spence! Where are you? What's happened?"

"I can't tell you. Listen, I have to talk fast. They may break this call off any minute. Go to the Project grounds and get Dr. Chamberlain. If he isn't there, get any doctor. Bring him to the house and have him stay there. Have him bring equipment, X-ray, fluoroscope, everything."

"But—"

"Do as I say. Hurry. Have him get it ready in an hour." Olham leaned toward the screen. "Is everything all right? Are you alone?"

"Alone?"

"Is anyone with you? Has . . . has Nelson or anyone contacted you?"

"No. Spence, I don't understand."

"All right. I'll see you at the house in an hour. And don't tell anyone anything. Get Chamberlain there on any pretext. Say you're very ill."

He broke the connection and looked at his watch. A moment later he left the ship, stepping down into the darkness. He had a half mile to go.

He began to walk.

One light showed in the window, the study light. He watched it, kneeling against the fence. There was no sound, no movement of any kind. He held his watch up and read it by starlight. Almost an hour had passed.

Along the street a shoot bug came. It went on.

Olham looked toward the house. The doctor should have already come. He should be inside, waiting with Mary. A thought struck him. Had she been able to leave the house? Perhaps they had intercepted her. Maybe he was moving into a trap.

But what else could he do?

With a doctor's records, photographs and reports, there was a chance, a chance of proof. If he could be examined, if he could remain alive long enough for them to study him—

He could prove it that way. It was probably the only way. His one hope lay inside the house. Dr. Chamberlain was a respected man. He was the staff doctor for the Project. He would know, his word on the matter would have meaning. He could overcome their hysteria, their madness, with facts.

Madness— That was what it was. If only they would wait, act slowly, take their time. But they could not wait. He had to die, die at once, without proof, without any kind of trial or examination. The simplest test would tell, but they had not time for the simplest test. They could think only of the danger. Danger, and nothing more.

He stood up and moved toward the house. He came up on the porch. At the door he paused, listening. Still no sound. The house was absolutely still.

Too still.

Olham stood on the porch, unmoving. They were trying to be silent inside. Why? It was a small house; only a few feet away, beyond the door, Mary and Dr. Chamberlain should be standing. Yet he could hear nothing, no sound of voices, nothing at all. He looked at the door. It was a door he had opened and closed a thousand times, every morning and every night.

He put his hand on the knob. Then, all at once, he reached out and touched the bell instead. The bell pealed, off some place in the back of the house. Olham smiled. He could hear movement.

Mary opened the door. As soon as he saw her face he knew.

He ran, throwing himself into the bushes. A Security officer shoved Mary out of the way, firing past her. The bushes burst apart. Olham wriggled around the side of the house. He leaped up and ran, racing frantically into the darkness. A searchlight snapped on, a beam of light circling past him.

He crossed the road and squeezed over a fence. He jumped down and made his way across a backyard. Behind him men were coming, Security officers, shouting to each other as they came. Olham gasped for breath, his chest rising and falling.

Her face— He had known at once. The set lips, the terrified, wretched eyes. Suppose he had gone ahead, pushed open the door and entered! They had tapped the call and come at once, as soon as he had broken off. Probably she believed their account. No doubt she thought he was the robot, too.

Olham ran on and on. He was losing the officers, dropping them behind. Apparently they were not much good at running. He climbed a hill and made his way down the other side. In a moment he would be back at the ship. But where to, this time? He slowed down, stopping. He could see the ship already, outlined against the sky, where he had parked it. The settlement was behind him; he was on the outskirts of the wilderness between the inhabited places, where the forests and desolation began. He crossed a barren field and entered the trees.

As he came toward it, the door of the ship opened.

Peters stepped out, framed against the light. In his arms was a heavy boris-gun. Olham stopped, rigid. Peters stared around him, into the darkness. "I know you're there, some place," he said. "Come on up here, Olham. There are Security men all around you."

Olham did not move.

"Listen to me. We will catch you very shortly. Apparently you still do not believe you're the robot. Your call to the woman indicates that you are still under the illusion created by your artificial memories.

"But you *are* the robot. You are the robot, and inside you is the bomb. Any moment the trigger phrase may be spoken, by you, by someone else, by anyone. When that happens the bomb will destroy everything for miles around. The Project, the woman, all of us will be killed. Do you understand?"

Olham said nothing. He was listening. Men were moving toward him, slipping through the woods.

"If you don't come out, we'll catch you. It will be only a matter of time. We no longer plan to remove you to the

Moon-base. You will be destroyed on sight, and we will have to take the chance that the bomb will detonate. I have ordered every available Security officer into the area. The whole county is being searched, inch by inch. There is no place you can go. Around this wood is a cordon of armed men. You have about six hours left before the last inch is covered."

Olham moved away. Peters went on speaking; he had not seen him at all. It was too dark to see anyone. But Peters was right. There was no place he could go. He was beyond the settlement, on the outskirts where the woods began. He could hide for a time, but eventually they would catch him.

Only a matter of time.

Olham walked quietly through the wood. Mile by mile, each part of the county was being measured off, laid bare, searched, studied, examined. The cordon was coming all the time, squeezing him into a smaller and smaller space.

What was there left? He had lost the ship, the one hope of escape. They were at his home; his wife was with them, believing, no doubt, that the real Olham had been killed. He clenched his fists. Some place there was a wrecked Outspace needle-ship, and in it the remains of the robot. Somewhere nearby the ship had crashed, crashed and broken up.

And the robot lay inside, destroyed.

A faint hope stirred him. What if he could find the remains? If he could show them the wreckage, the remains of the ship, the robot—

But where? Where would he find it?

He walked on, lost in thought. Some place, not too far off, probably. The ship would have landed close to the Project; the robot would have expected to go the rest of the way on foot. He went up the side of a hill and looked around. Crashed and burned. Was there some clue, some hint? Had he read anything, heard anything. Some place close by, within walking distance. Some wild place, a remote spot where there would be no people.

Suddenly Olham smiled. Crashed and burned—

Sutton Wood.

He increased his pace.

It was morning. Sunlight filtered down through the broker trees, onto the man crouching at the edge of the clearing. Ol ham glanced up from time to time, listening. They were no far off, only a few minutes away. He smiled.

Down below him, strewn across the clearing and into the charred stumps that had been Sutton Wood, lay a tangled mass of wreckage. In the sunlight it glittered a little, gleaming darkly. He had not had too much trouble finding it. Sutton Wood was a place he knew well; he had climbed around it many times in his life, when he was younger. He had known where he would find the remains. There was one peak that jutted up suddenly, without warning.

A descending ship, unfamiliar with the Wood, had little chance of missing it. And now he squatted, looking down at the ship, or what remained of it.

Olham stood up. He could hear them, only a little distance away, coming together, talking in low tones. He tensed himself. Everything depended on who first saw him. If it were Nelson, he had no chance. Nelson would fire at once. He would be dead before they saw the ship. But if he had time to call out, hold them off for a moment— That was all he needed. Once they saw the ship he would be safe.

But if they fired first—

A charred branch cracked. A figure appeared, coming forward uncertainly. Olham took a deep breath. Only a few seconds remained, perhaps the last seconds of his life. He raised his arms, peering intently.

It was Peters.

"Peters!" Olham waved his arms. Peters lifted his gun, aiming. "Don't fire!" His voice shook. "Wait a minute. Look past me, across the clearing."

"I've found him," Peters shouted. Security men came pouring out of the burned woods around him.

"Don't shoot. Look past me. The ship, the needle-ship. The Outspace ship. Look!"

Peters hesitated. The gun wavered.

"It's down there," Olham said rapidly. "I knew I'd find it

here. The burned wood. Now you believe me. You'll find the remains of the robot in the ship. Look, will you?"

"There is something down there," one of the men said nervously.

"Shoot him!" a voice said. It was Nelson.

"Wait." Peters turned sharply. "I'm in charge. Don't anyone fire. Maybe he's telling the truth."

"Shoot him," Nelson said. "He killed Olham. Any minute he may kill us all. If the bomb goes off—"

"Shut up." Peters advanced toward the slope. He stared down. "Look at that." He waved two men up to him. "Go down there and see what that is."

The men raced down the slope, across the clearing. They bent down, poking in the ruins of the ship.

"Well?" Peters called.

Olham held his breath. He smiled a little. It must be there; he had not had time to look, himself, but it had to be there. Suddenly doubt assailed him. Suppose the robot had lived long enough to wander away? Suppose his body had been completely destroyed, burned to ashes by the fire?

He licked his lips. Perspiration came out on his forehead. Nelson was staring at him, his face still livid. His chest rose and fell.

"Kill him," Nelson said. "Before he kills us."

The two men stood up.

"What have you found?" Peters said. He held the gun steady. "Is there anything there?"

"Looks like something. It's a needle-ship, all right. There's something beside it."

"I'll look." Peters strode past Olham. Olham watched him go down the hill and up to the men. The others were following after him, peering to see.

"It's a body of some sort," Peters said. "Look at it!"

Olham came along with them. They stood around in a circle, staring down.

On the ground, bent and twisted into a strange shape, was a grotesque form. It looked human, perhaps; except that it was bent so strangely, the arms and legs flung off in all directions. The mouth was open, the eyes stared glassily.

"Like a machine that's run down," Peters murmured.

Olham smiled feebly. "Well?" he said.

Peters looked at him. "I can't believe it. You were telling the truth all the time."

"The robot never reached me," Olham said. He took out a cigarette and lit it. "It was destroyed when the ship crashed. You were all too busy with the war to wonder why an out-of-the-way woods would suddenly catch fire and burn. Now you know."

He stood smoking, watching the men. They were dragging the grotesque remains from the ship. The body was stiff, the arms and legs rigid.

"You'll find the bomb, now," Olham said. The men laid the body on the ground. Peters bent down.

"I think I see the corner of it." He reached out, touching the body.

The chest of the corpse had been laid open. Within the gaping tear something glinted, something metal. The men stared at the metal without speaking.

"That would have destroyed us all, if it had lived," Peters said. "That metal box, there."

There was silence.

"I think we owe you something," Peters said to Olham. "This must have been a nightmare to you. If you hadn't escaped, we would have—" He broke off.

Olham put out his cigarette. "I knew, of course, that the robot had never reached me. But I had no way of proving it. Sometimes it isn't possible to prove a thing right away. That was the whole trouble. There wasn't any way I could demonstrate that I was myself."

"How about a vacation?" Peters said. "I think we might work out a month's vacation for you. You could take it easy, relax."

"I think right now I want to go home," Olham said.

"All right, then," Peters said. "Whatever you say."

Nelson had squatted down on the ground, beside the

corpse. He reached out toward the glint of metal visible within the chest.

"Don't touch it," Olham said. "It might still go off. We better let the demolition squad take care of it later on."

Nelson said nothing. Suddenly he grabbed hold of the metal, reaching his hand inside the chest. He pulled.

"What are you doing?" Olham cried.

Nelson stood up. He was holding onto the metal object. His face was blank with terror. It was a metal knife, an Outspace needle-knife, covered with blood.

"This killed him," Nelson whispered. "My friend was killed with this." He looked at Olham. "You killed him with this and left him beside the ship."

Olham was trembling. His teeth chattered. He looked from the knife to the body. "This can't be Olham," he said. His mind spun, everything was whirling. "Was I wrong?"

He gaped.

"But if that's Olham, then I must be—"

He did not complete the sentence, only the first phrase. The blast was visible all the way to Alpha Centauri.

# Robert A. Heinlein

# THEY

---

*The persecution complex is one of the familiar symptoms of mental illness, and one of the most intractable. The victim is sure that he is being followed, watched, subtly misled, for reasons which he is never quite able to pin down logically. For its victim, the disease is so vividly frightening that it often drives him to violence. He knows his illusions are not illusions, that they are real, and unbearably menacing. But, perhaps, there is something even worse than being the victim of your illusions, something like what happened to the man in THEY.*

---

THEY WOULD NOT LET HIM ALONE.

They never would let him alone. He realized that that was part of the plot against him—never to leave him in peace, never to give him a chance to mull over the lies they had told him, time enough to pick out the flaws, and to figure out the truth for himself.

That damned attendant this morning! He had come busting in with his breakfast tray, waking him, and causing him to

---

Robert A. Heinlein, THEY. Copyright 1941 in the United States and Canada by Street and Smith Publications, Inc.; copyright 1951 by Twayne Publishers, Inc., for *World of Wonder*, edited by Fletcher Pratt. Reprinted by permission of Lurton Blassingame from *Unknown*, April 1941.

forget his dream. If only he could remember that dream—

Someone was unlocking the door. He ignored it.

"Howdy, old boy. They tell me you refused your breakfast?" Dr. Hayward's professionally kindly mask hung over his bed.

"I wasn't hungry."

"But we can't have that. You'll get weak, and then I won't be able to get you well completely. Now get up and get your clothes on and I'll order an eggnog for you. Come on, that's a good fellow!"

Unwilling, but still less willing at that moment to enter into any conflict of wills, he got out of bed and slipped on his bathrobe. "That's better," Hayward approved. "Have a cigarette?"

"No, thank you."

The doctor shook his head in a puzzled fashion. "Darned if I can figure you out. Loss of interest in physical pleasures does not fit your type of case."

"What is my type of case?" he inquired in flat tones.

"Tut! Tut!" Hayward tried to appear roguish. "If medicos told their professional secrets, they might have to work for a living."

"What is my type of case?"

"Well—the label doesn't matter, does it? Suppose *you* tell me. I really know nothing about your case as yet. Don't you think it is about time you talked?"

"I'll play chess with you."

"All right, all right." Hayward made a gesture of impatient concession. "We've played chess every day for a week. If you will talk, I'll play chess."

What could it matter? If he was right, they already understood perfectly that he had discovered their plot; there was nothing to be gained by concealing the obvious. Let them try to argue him out of it. Let the tail go with the hide! To hell with it!

He got out the chessmen and commenced setting them up. "What do you know of my case so far?"

"Very little. Physical examination, negative. Past history, negative. High intelligence, as shown by your record in school and your success in your profession. Occasional fits of moodiness, but nothing exceptional. The only positive information was the incident that caused you to come here for treatment."

"To be brought here, you mean. Why should it cause comment?"

"Well, good gracious, man—if you barricade yourself in your room and insist that your wife is plotting against you, don't you expect people to notice?"

"But she *was* plotting against me—and so are you. White, or black?"

"Black—it's your turn to attack. Why do you think we are 'plotting against you'?"

"It's an involved story, and goes way back into my early childhood. There was an immediate incident, however—" He opened by advancing the white king's knight to KB3. Hayward's eyebrows raised.

"You make a piano attack?"

"Why not? You know that it is not safe for me to risk a gambit with you."

The doctor shrugged his shoulders and answered the opening. "Suppose we star . with your early childhood. It may shed more light than more recent incidents. Did you feel that you were being persecuted as a child?"

"No!" He half rose from his chair. "When I was a child I was sure of myself. I knew then. I tell you; I knew! Life was worth while, and I knew it. I was at peace with myself and my surroundings. Life was good and I was good, and I assumed that the creatures around me were like myself."

"And weren't they?"

"Not at all! Particularly the children. I didn't know what viciousness was until I was turned loose with other 'children.' The little devils! And I was expected to be like them and play with them."

The doctor nodded. "I know. The herd compulsion. Children can be pretty savage at times."

"You've missed the point. This wasn't any healthy roughness; these creatures were *different*—not like myself at all.

They *looked* like me, but they were *not* like me. If I tried to say anything to one of them about anything that mattered to me, all I could get was a stare and a scornful laugh. Then they would find some way to punish me for having said it."

Hayward nodded. "I see what you mean. How about grown-ups?"

"That is somewhat different. Adults don't matter to children at first—or, rather, they did not matter to me. They were too big, and they did not bother me, and they were busy with things that did not enter into my considerations. It was only when I noticed that my presence affected them that I began to wonder about them."

"How do you mean?"

"Well, they never did the things when I was around that they did when I was not around."

Hayward looked at him carefully. "Won't that statement take quite a lot of justifying? How do you know what they did when you weren't around?"

He acknowledged the point. "But I used to catch them just stopping. If I came into a room, the conversation would ꭅ ꭘ suddenly, and then it would pick up about the weau... something equally inane. Then I took to hiding and listening and looking. Adults did not behave the same way in my presence as out of it."

"Your move, I believe. But see here, old man—that was when you were a child. Every child passes through that phase. Now that you are a man, you must see the adult point of view. Children *are* strange creatures and have to be protected—at least, we do protect them—from many adult interests. There is a whole code of conventions in the matter that—"

"Yes, yes," he interrupted impatiently, "I know all that. Nevertheless, I noticed enough and remembered enough that was never clear to me later. And it put me on my guard to notice the next thing."

"Which was?" He noticed that the doctor's eyes were averted as he adjusted a castle's position.

"The things I saw people doing and heard them talking

about were never of any importance. They *must* be doing something else."

"I don't follow you."

"You don't choose to follow me. I'm telling this to you in exchange for a game of chess."

"Why do you like to play chess so well?"

"Because it is the only thing in the world where I can see all the factors and understand all the rules. Never mind—I saw all around me this enormous plant, cities, farms, factories, churches, schools, homes, railroads, luggage, roller coasters, trees, saxophones, libraries, people and animals. People that looked like me and who should have felt very much like me, if what I was told was the truth. But what did they appear to be doing? 'They went to work to earn the money to buy the food to get the strength to go to work to earn the money to buy the food to get the strength to go to work to earn the money to buy the food to get the strength to go to—' until they fell over dead. Any slight variation in the basic pattern did not matter, for they always fell over dead. And everybody tried to tell me that I should be doing the same thing. I knew better!"

The doctor gave him a look apparently intended to denote helpless surrender and laughed. "I can't argue with you. Life does look like that, and maybe it is just that futile. But it is the only life we have. Why not make up your mind to enjoy it as much as possible?"

"Oh, no!" He looked both sulky and stubborn. "You can't peddle nonsense to me by claiming to be fresh out of sense. How do I know? Because all this complex stage setting, all these swarms of actors, could not have been put here just to make idiot noises at each other. Some other explanation, but not that one. An insanity as enormous, as complex as the one around me had to be planned. I've found the plan!"

"Which is?"

He noticed that the doctor's eyes were again averted.

"It is a play intended to divert me, to occupy my mind and confuse me, to keep me so busy with details that I will not have time to think about the meaning. You are all in it, every one of you." He shook his finger in the doctor's face. "Most of them may be helpless automatons, but you're not. You are one of the conspirators. You've been sent in as a trouble-shooter to try to force me to go back to playing the role assigned to me!"

He saw that the doctor was waiting for him to quiet down.

"Take it easy," Hayward finally managed to say. "Maybe it is all a conspiracy, but why do you think that you have been singled out for special attention? Maybe it is a joke on all of us. Why couldn't I be one of the victims as well as yourself?"

"Got you!" He pointed a long finger at Hayward. "That is the essence of the plot. All of these creatures have been set up to look like me in order to prevent me from realizing that I was the center of the arrangements. But I have noticed the key fact, the mathematically inescapable fact, that I am unique. Here am I, sitting on the inside. The world extends outward from me. I am the center—"

"Easy, man, easy! Don't you realize that the world looks that way to me, too. We are each the center of the universe—"

"Not so! That is what you have tried to make me believe, that I am just one of millions more just like me. Wrong! If they were like me, then I could get into communication with them. I can't. I have tried and tried and I can't. I've sent out my inner thoughts, seeking some one other being who has them, too. What have I gotten back? Wrong answers, jarring incongruities, meaningless obscenity. I've tried, I tell you. God!—how I've tried! But there is nothing out there to speak to me—nothing but emptiness and otherness!"

"Wait a minute. Do you mean to say that you think there is nobody home at my end of the line? Don't you believe that I am alive and conscious?"

He regarded the doctor soberly. "Yes, I think you are probably alive, but you are one of the others—my antagonists. But you have set thousands of others around me whose faces are blank, not *lived in*, and whose speech is a meaningless re-flex of noise."

"Well, then, if you concede that I am an ego, why do you insist that I am so very different from yourself?"

"Why? Wait!" He pushed back from the chess table and strode over to the wardrobe, from which he took out a violin case.

While he was playing, the lines of suffering smoothed out of his face and his expression took a relaxed beatitude. For a while he recaptured the emotions, but not the knowledge, which he had possessed in dreams. The melody proceeded easily from proposition to proposition with inescapable, unforced logic. He finished with a triumphant statement of the essential thesis and turned to the doctor. "Well?"

"Hm-m-m." He seemed to detect an even greater degree of caution in the doctor's manner. "It's an odd bit, but remarkable. 'Spity you didn't take up the violin seriously. You could 'ave made quite a reputation. You could even now. Why don't you do it? You could afford to, I believe."

He stood and stared at the doctor for a long moment, then shook his head as if trying to clear it. "It's no use," he said slowly, "no use at all. There is no possibility of communication. I am alone." He replaced the instrument in its case and returned to the chess table. "My move, I believe?"

"Yes. Guard your queen."

He studied the board. "Not necessary. I no longer need my queen. Check."

The doctor interposed a pawn to parry the attack.

He nodded. "You use your pawns well, but I have learned to anticipate your play. Check again—and mate, I think."

The doctor examined the new situation. "No," he decided, "no—not quite." He retreated from the square under attack. "Not checkmate—stalemate at the worst. Yes, another stalemate."

He was upset by the doctor's visit. He *couldn't* be wrong, basically, yet the doctor had certainly pointed out logical holes in his position. From a logical standpoint the whole world might be a fraud perpetrated on everybody. But logic meant nothing—logic itself was a fraud, starting with un-proved assumptions and capable of proving anything. The world is what it is!—and carries its own evidence of trickery.

But does it? What did he have to go on? Could he lay down a line between known facts and everything else and then make a reasonable interpretation of the world, based on facts alone—an interpretation free from complexities of logic and no hidden assumptions of points not certain. Very well—

First fact, himself. He knew himself directly. He existed.

Second facts, the evidence of his "five senses," everything that he himself saw and heard and smelled and tasted with his physical senses. Subject to their limitations, he must believe his senses. Without them he was entirely solitary, shut up in a locker of bone, blind, deaf, cut off, the only being in the world.

And that was not the case. He knew that he did not invent the information brought to him by his senses. There had to be something else out there, some *otherness* that produced the things his senses recorded. All philosophies that claim that the physical world around him did not exist except in his im-agination were sheer nonsense.

But beyond that, what? Were there any third facts on which he could rely? No, not at this point. He could not afford to believe anything that he was told, or that he read, or that was implicitly assumed to be true about the world around him. No, he could not believe any of it, for the sum total of what he had been told and read and been taught in school was so contradictory, so senseless, so widely insane that none of it could be believed unless he personally confirmed it.

Wait a minute— The very telling of these lies, these sense-less contradictions, was a fact in itself, known to him directly. To that extent they were data, probably very important data.

The world as it had been shown to him was a piece of un-reason, an idiot's dream. Yet it was on too mammoth a scale to be without some reason. He came wearily back to his original point: Since the world could not be as crazy as it appeared to be, it must necessarily have been arranged to appear crazy in order to deceive him as to the truth.

Why had they done it to him? And what was the truth behind the sham? There must be some clue in the deception itself. What thread ran though it all? Well, in the first place he had been given a superabundance of explanations of the world around him, philosophies, religions, "common sense" explanations. Most of them were so clumsy, so obviously inadequate, or meaningless, that they could hardly have expected him to take them seriously. They must have intended them simply as misdirection.

But there were certain basic assumptions running through all the hundreds of explanations of the craziness around him. It must be these basic assumptions that he was expected to believe. For example, there was the deep-seated assumption that he was a "human being," essentially like millions of others around him and billions more in the past and the future.

That was nonsense! He had never once managed to get into real communication with all those *things* that looked so much like him but were so different. In the agony of his loneliness, he had deceived himself that Alice understood him and was a being like him. He knew now that he had suppressed and refused to examine thousands of little discrepancies because he could not bear the thought of returning to complete loneliness. He had needed to believe that his wife was a living, breathing being of his own kind who understood his inner thoughts. He had refused to consider the possibility that she was simply a mirror, an echo—or something unthinkably worse.

He had found a mate, and the world was tolerable, even though dull, stupid, and full of petty annoyance. He was moderately happy and had put away his suspicions. He had accepted, quite docilely, the treadmill he was expected to use, until a slight mischance had momentarily cut through the fraud—then his suspicions had returned with impounded force; the bitter knowledge of his childhood had been confirmed.

He supposed that he had been a fool to make a fuss about it. If he had kept his mouth shut they would not have locked him up. He should have been as subtle and as shrewd as they, kept his eyes and ears open and learned the details of and the reasons for the plot against him. He might have learned how to circumvent it.

But what if they had locked him up—the whole world was an asylum and all of them his keepers.

A key scraped in the lock, and he looked up to see an attendant entering with a tray. "Here's your dinner, sir."

"Thanks, Joe," he said gently. "Just put it down."

"Movies tonight, sir," the attendant went on. "Wouldn't you like to go? Dr. Hayward said you could—"

"No, thank you. I prefer not to."

"I wish you would, sir." He noticed with amusement the persuasive intentness of the attendant's manner. "I think th doctor wants you to. It's a good movie. There's a Mickey Mouse cartoon—"

"You almost persuade me, Joe," he answered with passive agreeableness. "Mickey's trouble is the same as mine, essentially. However, I'm not going. They need not bother to hold movies tonight."

"Oh, there will be movies in any case, sir. Lots of our other guests will attend."

"Really? Is that an example of thoroughness, or are you simply keeping up the pretense in talking to me? It isn't necessary, Joe, if it's any strain on you. I *know* the game. If I don't attend, there is no point in holding movies."

He liked the grin with which the attendant answered this thrust. Was it possible that this being was created just as he appeared to be—big muscles, phlegmatic disposition, tolerant, dog-like? Or was there nothing going on behind those kind eyes, nothing but robot reflex? No, it was more likely that he was one of them, since he was so closely in attendance on him.

The attendant left and he busied himself at his supper tray, scooping up the already-cut bites of meat with a spoon, the only implement provided. He smiled again at their caution and thoroughness. No danger of that—he would not destroy this body as long as it served him in investigating the truth of the matter. There were still many different avenues of research available before taking that possibly irrevocable step.

After supper he decided to put his thoughts in better order by writing them; he obtained paper. He should start with a general statement of some underlying postulate of the credos that had been drummed into him all his "life." Life? Yes, that was a good one. He wrote:

I am told that I was born a certain number of years ago and that I will die in a similar number of years hence. Various clumsy stories have been offered me to explain to me where I was before birth and what becomes of me after death, but they are rough lies, not intended to deceive, except as misdirection. In every other possible way the world around me assures me that I am mortal, here but a few years, and a few years hence gone completely—nonexistent.

WRONG—I am immortal. I transcend this little time axis; a seventy-year span on it is but a casual phase in my experience. Second only to the prime datum of my own existence is the emotionally convincing certainty of my own continuity. I may be a closed curve, but, closed or open, I neither have a beginning nor an end. Self-awareness is not relational; it is absolute, and cannot be reached to be destroyed, or created. Memory, however, being a relational aspect of consciousness, may be tampered with and possibly destroyed.

It is true that most religions which have been offered me teach immortality, but note the fashion in which they teach it. The surest way to lie convincingly is to tell the truth unconvincingly. They did not wish me to believe.

Caution: Why have they tried so hard to convince me that I am going to "die" in a few years? There must be a very important reason. I infer that they are preparing me for some sort of a major change. It may be crucially important for me to figure out their intentions about this —probably I have several years in which to reach a decision. Note: Avoid using the types of reasoning they have taught me.

The attendant was back. "Your wife is here, sir."

"Tell her to go away."

"Please, sir—Dr. Hayward is most anxious that you should see her."

"Tell Dr. Hayward that I said that he is an excellent chess player."

"Yes, sir." The attendant waited for a moment. "Then you won't see her, sir?"

"No, I won't see her."

He wandered around the room for some minutes after the attendant had left, too distrait to return to his recapitulation. By and large they had played very decently with him since they had brought him here. He was glad that they had allowed him to have a room alone, and he certainly had more time free for contemplation than had ever been possible on the outside. To be sure, continuous effort to keep him busy and to distract him was made, but, by being stubborn, he was able to circumvent the rules and gain some hours each day for introspection.

But, damnation!—he did wish they would not persist in using Alice in their attempts to divert his thoughts. Although the intense terror and revulsion which she had inspired in him when he had first rediscovered the truth had now aged into a simple feeling of repugnance and distaste for her company, nevertheless it was emotionally upsetting to be reminded of her, to be forced into making decisions about her.

After all, she *had* been his wife for many years. *Wife?* What was a wife? Another soul like one's own, a complement, the other necessary part to the couple, a sanctuary of understanding and sympathy in the boundless depths of aloneness. *That* was what he had thought, what he had needed to believe and had believed fiercely for years. The yearning need for companionship of his own kind had caused him to see himself reflected in those beautiful eyes and had made him quite uncritical of occasional incongruities in her responses.

He sighed. He felt that he had sloughed off most of the typed emotional reactions which they had taught him by precept and example, but Alice had gotten under his skin, way under, and it still hurt. He had been happy—what if it had been a dope dream? They had given him an excellent, a beautiful mirror to play with—the more fool he to have looked behind it!

Wearily he turned back to his summing up.

The world is explained in either one of two ways: the common-sense way which says that the world is pretty much as it appears to be and that ordinary human conduct and motivations are reasonable, and the religio-mystic solution which states that the world is dream stuff, unreal, insubstantial, with reality somewhere beyond.

WRONG—both of them. The common-sense scheme has no sense to it of any sort. "Life is short and full of trouble. Man born of woman is born to trouble as the sparks fly upward. His days are few and they are numbered. All is vanity and vexation." Those quotations may be jumbled and incorrect, but that is a fair statement of the common-sense world-is-as-it-seems in its only possible evaluation. In such a world, human striving is about as rational as the blind dartings of a moth against a light bulb. The "common-sense world" is a blind insanity, out of nowhere, going nowhere, to no purpose.

As for the other solution, it appears more rational on the surface, in that it rejects the utterly irrational world of common sense. But it is not a rational solution, it is simply a flight from reality of any sort, for it refuses to believe the results of the only available direct communication between the ego and the Outside. Certainly the "five senses" are poor enough channels of communication, but they are the only channels.

He crumpled up the paper and flung himself from the chair. Order and logic were no good—his answer was right because it smelled right. But he still did not know all the answers. Why the grand scale to the deception, countless creatures, whole continents, an enormously involved and minutely detailed matrix of insane history, insane tradition, insane culture? Why bother with more than a cell and a strait jacket?

It must be, it had to be, because it was supremely important to deceive him completely, because a lesser deception would not do. Could it be that they dared not let him suspect his real identity no matter how difficult and involved the fraud?

He had to know. In some fashion he must get behind the deception and see what went on when he was not looking. He had had one glimpse; this time he must see the actual workings; catch the puppet masters in their manipulations.

Obviously the first step must be to escape from this asylum, but to do it so craftily that they would never see him, never catch up with him, not have a chance to set the stage before him. That would be hard to do. He must excel them in shrewdness and subtlety.

Once decided, he spent the rest of the evening in considering the means by which he might accomplish his purpose. It seemed almost impossible—he must get away without once being seen and remain in strict hiding. They must lose track of him completely in order that they would not know where to center their deceptions. That would mean going without food for several days. Very well—he could do it. He must not give them any warning by unusual action or manner.

The lights blinked twice. Docilely he got up and commenced preparations for bed. When the attendant looked through the peephole he was already in bed, with his face turned to the wall.

Gladness! Gladness everywhere! It was good to be with his own kind, to hear the music swelling out of every living thing, as it always had and always would—good to know that everything was living and aware of him, participating in him, as he participated in them. It was good to be, good to know the unity of many and the diversity of one. There had been

one bad thought—the details escaped him—but it was gone—
it had never *been;* there was no place for it.

The early morning sounds from the adjacent ward penetrated the sleep-laden body which served him here and gradually recalled him to awareness of the hospital room. The
transition was so gentle that he carried over full recollection
of what he had been doing and why. He lay still, a gentle
smile on his face, and savored the uncouth, but not unpleasant, languor of the body he wore. Strange that he had ever
forgotten despite their tricks and stratagems. Well, now that
he had recalled the key, he would quickly set things right in
this odd place. He would call them in at once and announce
the new order. It would be amusing to see old Glaroon's expression when he realized that the cycle had ended—

The click of the peephole and the rasp of the door being
unlocked guillotined his line of thought. The morning attendant pushed briskly in with the breakfast tray and placed it
on the tip table. "Morning, sir. Nice, bright day—want it in
bed, or will you get up?"

Don't answer! Don't listen! Suppress this distraction! This
is part of their plan— But it was too late, too late. He felt himself slipping, falling, wrenched from reality back into the
fraud world in which they had kept him. It was gone, gone
completely, with no single association around him to which
to anchor memory. There was nothing left but the sense of
heartbreaking loss and the acute ache of unsatisfied catharsis.

"Leave it where it is. I'll take care of it."

"Okey-doke." The attendant bustled out, slamming the
door, and noisily locked it.

He lay quite still for a long time, every nerve end in his
body screaming for relief.

At last he got out of bed, still miserably unhappy, and attempted to concentrate on his plans for escape. But the
psychic wrench he had received in being recalled so suddenly
from his plane of reality had left him bruised and emotionally
disturbed. His mind insisted on rechewing its doubts, rather
than engage in constructive thought. Was it possible that the

doctor was right, that he was not alone in his miserable dilemma? Was he really simply suffering from paranoia, delusions of self-importance?

Could it be that each unit in this yeasty swarm around him was the prison of another lonely ego—helpless, blind, and speechless, condemned to an eternity of miserable loneliness? Was the look of suffering which he had brought to Alice's face a true reflection of inner torment and not simply a piece of play-acting intended to maneuver him into compliance with their plans?

A knock sounded at the door. He said "Come in," without looking up. Their comings and goings did not matter to him.

"Dearest—" A well-known voice spoke slowly and hesitantly.

"Alice!" He was on his feet at once, and facing her. "Who let you in here?"

"Please, dear, please— I had to see you."

"It isn't fair. It isn't fair." He spoke more to himself than to her. Then: "Why did you come?"

She stood up to him with a dignity he had hardly expected. The beauty of her childlike face had been marred by line and shadow, but it shone with an unexpected courage. "I love you," she answered quietly. "You can tell me to go away, but you can't make me stop loving you and trying to help you."

He turned away from her in an agony of indecision. Could it be possible that he had misjudged her? Was there, behind that barrier of flesh and sound symbols, a spirit that truly yearned toward his? Lovers whispering in the dark— "You *do* understand, don't you?"

"Yes, dear heart, I understand."

"Then nothing that happens to us can matter, as long as we are together and understand—" Words, words, rebounding hollowly from an unbroken wall—

No, he *couldn't* be wrong! Test her again— "Why did you keep me on that job in Omaha?"

"But I didn't make you keep that job. I simply pointed out that we should think twice before—"

"Never mind. Never mind." Soft hands and a sweet face preventing him with mild stubbornness from ever doing the thing that his heart told him to do. Always with the best of intentions, the best of intentions, but always so that he had never quite managed to do the silly, unreasonable things that *he* knew were worth while. Hurry, hurry, hurry, and strive, with an angel-faced jockey to see that you don't stop long enough to think for yourself—

"Why did you try to stop me from going back upstairs that day?"

She managed to smile, although her eyes were already spilling over with tears. "I didn't know it really mattered to you. I didn't want us to miss the train."

It had been a small thing, an unimportant thing. For some reason not clear even to him he had insisted on going back upstairs to his study when they were about to leave the house for a short vacation. It was raining, and she had pointed out that there was barely enough time to get to the station. He had surprised himself and her, too, by insisting on his own way in circumstances in which he had never been known to be stubborn.

He had actually pushed her to one side and forced his way up the stairs. Even then nothing might have come of it had he not—quite unnecessarily—raised the shade of the window that faced toward the rear of the house.

It was a very small matter. It had been raining, hard, out in front. From this window the weather was clear and sunny, with no sign of rain.

He had stood there quite a long while, gazing out at the impossible sunshine and rearranging his cosmos in his mind. He re-examined long-suppressed doubts in the light of this one small but totally unexplainable discrepancy. Then he had turned and had found that she was standing behind him.

He had been trying ever since to forget the expression that he had surprised on her face.

"What about the rain?"

"The rain?" she repeated in a small, puzzled voice. "Why, it was raining, of course. What about it?"

"But it was *not* raining out my study window."

"What? But of course it was. I did notice the sun break through the clouds for a moment, but that was all."

"Nonsense!"

"But, darling, what has the weather to do with you and me? What difference does it make whether it rains or not—to us?" She approached him timidly and slid a small hand between his arm and side. "Am I responsible for the weather?"

"I think you are. Now please go."

She withdrew from him, brushed blindly at her eyes, gulped once, then said in a voice held steady: "All right. I'll go. But remember—you *can* come home if you want to. And I'll be there, if you want me." She waited a moment, then added hesitantly: "Would you . . . would you kiss me good-by?"

He made no answer of any sort, neither with voice nor eyes. She looked at him, then turned, fumbled blindly for the door, and rushed through it.

The creature he knew as Alice went to the place of assembly without stopping to change form. "It is necessary to adjourn this sequence. I am no longer able to influence his decisions."

They had expected it, nevertheless they stirred with dismay.

The Glaroon addressed the First for Manipulation. "Prepare to graft the selected memory track at once."

Then, turning to the First for Operations, the Glaroon said: "The extrapolation shows that he will tend to escape within two of his days. This sequence degenerated primarily through your failure to extend that rainfall all around him. Be advised."

"It would be simpler if we understood his motives."

"In my capacity as Dr. Hayward, I have often thought so," commented the Glaroon acidly, "but if we understood his motives, we would be part of *him*. Bear in mind the Treaty! He almost remembered."

The creature known as Alice spoke up. "Could he not have the Taj Mahal next sequence? For some reason he values it."

"You are becoming assimilated!"

"Perhaps. I am not in fear. Will he receive it?"

"It will be considered."

The Glaroon continued with orders: "Leave structures standing until adjournment. New York City and Harvard University are now dismantled. Divert him from those sectors.

"Move!"

Chad Oliver

# LET ME LIVE IN A HOUSE

*The effect of loneliness and of unknown horrors upon spacemen driving their timeless way through the dark of interstellar nothingness, or dragging out a dreary tour of duty in an isolated observation post on a far planet or satellite, has been a frequent theme among modern science fiction writers. Alan Nourse's story (page 158) tells how space pilots may be conditioned against these terrors. Here, on the other hand, Mr. Oliver describes how one man—among four people—defeats the real thing: loneliness, monotony, and the final terror of an unexpected visitor where no visitor should ever be able to come. Gordon Collier achieves a victory—but a costly one, as you will see . . .*

IT WAS ALL EXACTLY PERFECT, DOWN TO THE LAST SCRATCH on the white picket fence and the frigidaire that wheezed asthmatically at predictable intervals throughout the night.

The two white cottages rested lightly on their fresh green lawns, like contented dreams. They were smug in their completeness. They had green shutters and substantial brass door

knockers. They had clean, crisp curtains on the windows, and
knickknacks on the mantelpieces over the fireplaces. They
had a fragment of poetry, caught in dime-store frames in the
halls: *Let me live in a house by the side of the road and be a
friend to man.*

One of the cottages had a picture of crusty old Grandfather
Walters, and that was important.

Soft and subtle sounds hummed through the warm air. One
of the sounds was that of a copter, high overhead, but you
couldn't *see* it, of course. A breeze sighed across the grass, but
the grass was motionless. Somewhere, children laughed and
shouted as they clambered and splashed in the old swimming hole.

There were no children, naturally—nor any swimming hole
for that matter.

It was all exactly perfect, though. *Exactly.* If you didn't
know better, you'd swear it was real.

Gordon Collier breathed in the smell of flowers that didn't
exist and stared without enthusiasm at the white clouds that
drifted along through a robin's-egg-blue sky.

"Damn it all," he said.

He kicked at the green grass under his feet and failed to
dent it. Then he walked into his snug white cottage and
slammed the door behind him, hard.

Helen called from the kitchen: "Don't slam the door, dear."

"I'm sorry," Gordon said. "It slipped."

Helen came bustling in. She was an attractive, if hardly
spectacular, woman of thirty. She had brown hair and eyes,
and a domestic manner. She kissed her husband lightly. "Been
over at the Walters'?" she asked.

"How did you guess?" Gordon said. Where did she *think*
he had been—outside?

"Now, Gordey," Helen admonished him. "You needn't snap
my head off for asking a civil question."

"Please don't call me 'Gordey,' " Gordon said irritably. Then
he relented—it wasn't her fault, after all. He gave her the
news about the Walters. "Bart's playing football," he related
for the millionth time, "and Mary is watching tri-di."

"Will they be dropping over for cards tonight?" Helen asked.

*She's playing the game to the hilt,* Gordon thought. *She's learned her part like a machine. I wish I could do that.*

"They'll be over," he said.

Helen's eyes lighted up happily. She had always loved company, Gordon remembered. "My!" she exclaimed. "I'd better see about supper." She smiled eagerly, like a dog at a rabbit, and hustled away back to the kitchen.

Gordon Collier watched his wife go, not without admiration of a sort. They had certainly picked well when they picked Bart, who could ^c for hours with his electric football game, reliving the past, or who could with equal absorption paint charmingly naive pictures about the stars. Mary, too, was fine—as long as she had her tri-di set, her life was complete. But when they had picked his wife, they had hit the nail on the head. She was perfect in her part—she gave the impression of actually *believing* in it.

Gordon frowned sourly at himself. "The trouble with you, Gordon," he said softly, "is that you just haven't learned your lines very well."

There was a reason for that, too—but he preferred not to think about it.

After supper—steak and fried potatoes and salad and coffee —the doorbell rang. It was, of course, the Walters.

"Well!" exclaimed Helen. "If it isn't Bart and Mary!"

In they came—Mary, gray at forty, looking to see if the tri-di was on, and Barton, big and wholesome as a vitamin ad, bounding through the door as though it were the enemy goal line.

*Four people,* Gordon thought. *Four people, utterly alone. Four human beings, pretending to be a society.*

*Four people.*

They exchanged such small talk as there was. Since they had all been doing precisely the same things for seven months, there wasn't much in the way of startling information to be passed back and forth. The bulk of the conversation was taken up with Mary's opinion of the latest tri-di shows, and it developed that she liked them all.

She turned on Gordon's set, which didn't please him unduly, and for half an hour they watched a variety show—canned and built into the set, of course—that was mainly distinguished by its singular lack of variety of any sort. Finally, in desperation, Gordon got out the cards.

"We'll make it poker tonight," he decided as they all sat down at the collapsible green card table. He dealt out four hands of three-card draw, shoved a quarter into the center of the table, and settled back to enjoy the game as best he could.

It wasn't easy. Mary turned up the tri-di in order to hear better, and Barton engaged with furious energy in his favorite pastime—replaying the 1973 Stanford-Notre Dame game, with himself in the starring role.

At eleven o'clock sharp Helen served the cheese and crackers.

At midnight, they heard the new sound.

It was a faint whistle, and it hissed over their heads like an ice-coated snake. It sizzled in from far away, and then there was a long, still pause. Finally, there was a shadowy suggestion of a thump.

Gordon instantly cut off the tri-di set. They all listened. He opened a window and looked out. He couldn't see anything—the blue sky had switched to the deep purple of night and the only glimmer of light came from the porch lamp on the cottage next door. There was nothing to see, and all that he heard were the normal sounds that weren't really there—the chirp of crickets, the soft sigh of the breeze.

"Did you hear it?" he asked the others.

They nodded, uncertain and suddenly alone. *A new sound.* How could that be?

Gordon Collier walked nervously out of the room, followed by Barton. He clenched his fists, feeling the clammy sweat in the palms of his hands, and fought to keep the fear from surging up within him. They walked into a small hall and Gordon pressed a button. A section of the wall slid smoothly back on oiled runners, and the two men walked into the white, brightly-lighted equipment room.

Gordon kept his hand steady and flipped on the outside scanners. He couldn't see a thing. He tried the tracer screen, and it was blank. Barton tried the radio, on the off chance that someone was trying to contact them. There was silence.

They checked the radar charts for the past hour. They were all quite normal—except the last one. That one had a streak on it, a very sharp and clear and unmistakable streak. It was in the shape of an arc, and it curved down in a grimly familiar way. It started far out in space and it ended. Outside—Outside in the ice and the rocks and the cold.

"Probably a meteor," Barton suggested.

"Probably," Gordon agreed dubiously, and made a note to that effect in the permanent record.

"Well, what else *could* it have been?" Barton challenged.

"Nothing," Gordon admitted. "It was a meteor."

They swung the wall shut again, covering the tubes and screen and coils with flowered wallpaper and Gainsborough's *Blue Boy*. They returned to the living room, where their wives still sat around the card table waiting for them. The room was as comfortable as ever, and the tri-di set was on again.

It was all just as they had left it, Gordon thought—but it was different. The room seemed smaller, constricted, isolated. The temperature had not changed, but it was colder. Millions and millions of miles flowed into the room and crawled around the walls. . . .

"Just a meteor, I guess," Gordon said.

They went on with their game for another hour, and then Barton and Mary went home to bed. Before they left, they invited Gordon and Helen to visit them the next night.

The house was suddenly empty.

Gordon Collier held his wife in his arms and listened to the frigidaire wheezing in the kitchen and the water dripping from a half-closed faucet. Outside, there were only the crickets and the wind.

"It was only a meteor," he said.

"I know," said his wife.

They went to bed then, but sleep was slow in coming. They had a home, of course, a little white cottage in a green yard. They had two nice neighbors and blue skies and a tri-di set. It was all exactly perfect, and there was certainly nothing to be afraid of.

But it was a long way back, and they had no ship.

When Gordon Collier awoke in the morning, he knew instantly that something was wrong. He swung himself out of bed and stood in the middle of the room, half-crouched, not sure what he was looking for.

The room seemed normal enough. The twin beds were in their proper places, the rug was smooth, his watch was still on the dresser where he had left it. He looked at the alarm clock and saw that it hadn't gone off yet. His wife was still asleep. What had awakened him?

He stood quite still and listened. At once, he heard it. It came from outside, out by the green lawn and the blue skies. He walked to the window to make certain that his senses weren't playing tricks on him. The sound was still there—another *new* sound. Another new sound where there could *be* no new sounds, but only the old ones, repeating themselves over and over again. . . .

He closed the window, trying to shut it out. Perhaps, he told himself, it wasn't exactly a new sound after all; perhaps it was only the old sound distorted by a faulty speaker or a bad tube. There had been gentle breezes before, summery puffs and wisps of air, and even the gentle patter of light rain once every two weeks. He listened again, straining his ears, but he did not open the window. His heart beat spasmodically in his chest. No, there could be no doubt of it!

*The wind was rising.*

Helen moaned in her sleep and Gordon decided not to waken her. She might need her sleep and then some before this was over, he knew. He dressed and walked out into the hall, pressed the button that opened the equipment room, and went inside. He checked everything—dials, scanners, tracers, charts. Again, they were all quite normal except one. One of he tracers showed a faint line coming in from the ice and the ocks, in toward the two isolated cottages that huddled under he Bubble.

Presumably, it was still there—whatever it was.

The significant question was easily formulated: what did he line represent, the line that had curved down out of space and had now cut across the ice almost to his very door? What *could* it represent?

Gordon Collier forced himself to think logically, practically. It wasn't easy, not after seven months of conditioned living that had been specially designed so that he *wouldn't* think in rational terms. He closed the door, shutting off the little white house and all that it represented. He sat down on a hard metal chair with only the gleaming machines for company. He tried.

It was all too plain that he couldn't contact Earth. His radio wouldn't reach that far, and, anyhow, who was there to listen at the other end? The ship from Earth wasn't due for another five months, so he could expect no help from that source. In an emergency, the two women wouldn't be of much help. As for Bart, what he would do would depend on what *kind* of an emergency he had to face.

What kind of an emergency *was* it? He didn't know, had no way of knowing. The situation was unprecedented. It was nothing much on the face of it—a whistle and a thump and a few lines on a tracer. *And the wind,* his mind whispered, *don't forget the wind.* Nothing much, but he was afraid. He looked at his white, trembling hands and doubted himself. What could he do?

*What was out there?*

The wall slid open behind him and he bit his lip to keep from crying out.

"Breakfast is ready, dear," his wife said.

"Yes, yes," Gordon murmured shakily. "Yes, I'm coming."

He got to his feet and followed his wife out of the room, back into the comfortable cottage that he knew so well. He kept his eyes straight ahead of him as he walked and tried

not to listen to the swelling moan of the wind that couldn'
blow.

Gordon Collier drank his coffee black and dabbled at the
poached converter eggs, trying to fake an appetite that he did
not feel. His wife ate her breakfast in normal fashion, chat
tering familiar morning-talk in an inconsequential stream
Gordon didn't pay much attention until a stray sentence or
two struck home:

"Just listen to that wind, Gordey," she said, with only a
trace of strain in her voice. "I declare, I believe we're in for a
storm!"

Collier forced himself to go on drinking his coffee, but he
was badly shaken. *Her mind won't even accept the situation
for what it is,* he thought with a chill. *She's going to play the
game out to the bitter end. I'm ALONE.*

"That's right, dear," he said evenly, fighting to keep his
voice steady. "We're in for a storm."

Outside, the wind whined around the corners of the little
cottage and something that might have been thunder rumbled
in from far away.

The afternoon was a nightmare.

Gordon Collier stood at the window and watched. He
didn't want to do it, but something deep within him would
not let him turn away. His wife stayed huddled in front of the
tri-di, watching a meaningless succession of pointless programs, and doubtless she was better off than he was. But he
had to watch, even if it killed him. Dimly, he sensed that it
was his responsibility to watch.

There wasn't much to see, of course. The robin's-egg-blue
sky had turned an impossible, leaden gray, and the fleecy
white clouds were tinged with a dismal black. The neat green
grass seemed to have lost some of its vitality; it looked dead,
like the artificial thing that it was. From far above his head—
almost to the inner surface of the Bubble, he judged—little
flickerings of light played across the sky.

The visual frequencies were being tampered with, that was all. It wouldn't do to get all excited about it.

The sounds were worse. Thunder muttered and rolled down from above. The faint hum of a copter high in the sky changed to a high-pitched screech, the sound of an aircraft out of control and falling. He waited and waited for the crash, but of course it never came. There was only the screech that went on and on and on, forever.

The auditory frequencies were being tampered with, that was all. *It wouldn't do to get all excited about it.*

When the laughing children who were splashing in the old swimming hole began to scream, Gordon Collier shut the window.

He sank down in a chair and buried his face in his hands. He wanted to shout, throw things, cry, *anything*. But he couldn't. His mind was numb. He could only sit there in the chair by the window and wait for the unknown.

It was almost evening when the rain came. It came in sheets and torrents and splattered on the window panes. It ran down the windows in gurgling rivulets and made puddles in the yard. It was *real* rain.

Gordon Collier looked at the water falling from a place where water could not be and began to whimper with fright.

Precisely at nine o'clock, Gordon and Helen dug up two old raincoats out of the hall closet and walked next door through the storm. They rang the doorbell and stood shivering in the icy rain until Mary opened the door and spilled yellow light out into the blackness.

They entered the cottage, which was an exact replica of their own except for the austerely frowning portrait of Grandfather Walters in the front hall. They stood dripping on the rug until Bart came charging in from the living room, grinning with pleasure at seeing them again.

"What a storm!" he said loudly. "Reminds me of the time we played UCLA in a cloudburst—here, let me take your coats."

Gordon clenched his fists helplessly. Bart and Mary weren't

facing the situation either; they were simply adapting to it frantically and hoping it would go away. *Well,* his mind demanded, *what else can they do?*

They went through the ritual of playing cards. This time it was bridge instead of poker, but otherwise it was the same. It always was, except for holidays.

Outside, the incredible storm ripped furiously at the cottage. The roof began to leak, ever so slightly, and a tiny drip began to patter away ironically in the middle of the bridge table. No one said anything about it.

Gordon played well enough to keep up appearances, but his mind wasn't on the game. He loaded his pipe with his own ultra-fragrant bourbon-soaked tobacco, and retreated behind a cloud of smoke.

He had himself fairly well under control now. The worst was probably over, for him. He could at least think about it—that was a triumph, and he was proud of it.

Here they were, he thought—four human beings on a moon as big as a planet, three hundred and ninety million miles from the Earth that had sent them there. Four human beings, encased in two little white cottages under an air bubble on the rock and ice that was Ganymede. Here they were—waiting. Waiting in an empty universe, sustained by a faith in something that had almost been lost.

They were skeleton crews, waiting for the firm flesh to come and clothe their bones. It would not happen today, and it would not happen tomorrow. It might never happen—now.

It was unthinkable that any ship from Earth could be in the vicinity. It was unthinkable that their equipment could have broken down, changed, by itself.

So they were waiting, he thought—but not for the ship from Earth. No, they were waiting for—what?

At eleven o'clock, the storm stopped abruptly and there was total silence.

At midnight, there was a knock on the door.

It was one of those moments that stand alone, cut off and isolated from the conceptual flow of time. It stood quite still, holding its breath.

The knock was repeated—impatiently.

"Someone is at the door," Mary said dubiously.

"That's right," Bart said. "We must have visitors."

No one moved. The four human beings sat paralyzed around the table, their cards still in their hands, precisely as though they were waiting for some imaginary servant to open the door and see who was outside. Gordon Collier found himself relatively calm, but he knew that it was not a natural calmness. He was conditioned too, like the rest of them. He studied them with intense interest. Could they even swallow this insane knock on the door, digest it, fit it somehow into their habitual thought patterns?

Apparently, they could.

"See to the door, dear," Mary told her husband. "I wonder who it could be this time of night?"

The knock was repeated a third time. Whoever—or whatever—was outside, Gordon thought, sounded irritated.

Reluctantly, Bart started to get up. Gordon beat him to it, however, pushing back his chair and getting to his feet. "Let me go," he said. "I'm closer."

He walked across the room to the door. It seemed a longer way than he had ever noticed before. The stout wood door seemed very thin. He put his hand on the doorknob, and was dimly conscious of the fact that Bart had gotten up and followed him across the room. He looked at the door, a scant foot before his eyes. The knock came again—sharply, impatiently, a no-nonsense knock. Gordon visualized the heavy brass door knocker on the other side of the door. To whom, or what, did the hand that worked that knocker belong? Or *was* it a hand?

Almost wildly, Gordon remembered a string of jokes that had made the rounds when he was a boy. Jokes about the little man who turned off the light in the refrigerator when you closed the door. Jokes about a little man—what had they called him?

*The little man who wasn't there.*

Gordon shook his head. That kind of reaction wouldn't do,

he told himself. He had to be calm. He asked himself a question: *What are you waiting for?*

He gritted his teeth and opened the door, fast.

The little man *was* there, and he was tapping his foot. But he was not exactly a little man, either. He was somewhat vague, amorphous—he was, you might say, *almost* a little man.

"It's about time," the almost-man said in a blurred voice. "But first, a word from our sponsor. May I come in?"

Stunned, Gordon Collier felt himself moving aside and the little man hustled past him into the cottage.

The almost-man stood apart from the others, hesitating. He wasn't really a little man, Gordon saw with some relief; that is, he wasn't a gnome or an elf or anything like that. Gordon recognized with a start the state of his own mental processes that had even allowed him to imagine that it *could* be some supernatural creature out there on the green lawn, knocking at the door. He fought to clear his mind, and knew that he failed.

Gordon caught one thought and held on, desperately: *If this is an alien, all that I have worked for is finished. The dream is ended.*

The almost-man—changed. He soli-fied, became real. He *was* a man—elderly, a bit pompous, neatly dressed in an old-fashioned business suit with a conservative blue tie. He had white hair and a neat, precise moustache. His blue eyes twinkled.

"I am overwhelmed," he said clearly, waving a thin hand in the air. "My name is John. You are too kind to a poor old country boy."

Gordon stared. The man was a dead ringer for the portrait of Grandfather Walters on the wall.

Bart and Mary and Helen just looked blankly at the man, trying to adjust to the enormity of what had happened. Bart had resumed his seat at the bridge table, and had even picked up his hand. Helen was watching Gordon, who still stood by the door. Mary sat uncertainly, dimly realizing that she was the hostess here, and waiting for the proper stimulus that would prod her into a patterned routine of welcome. The house waited—a stage set for a play, with the actors all in place and the curtain half-way up.

Gordon Collier slammed the door, fighting to clear his mind from the gentle fog that lapped at it, that made everything all right. "What in the hell is the big idea?" he asked the man who looked like Grandfather Walters and whose name was John.

"Gordey!" exclaimed Helen.

"That's no way to talk to company," Mary said.

John faced Gordon, ignoring the others. His moustache bristled. He spread his hands helplessly. "I am a simple wayfaring stranger," he said. "I happened to pass by your door, and since you live in a house by the side of the road, I assumed that you would wish to be a friend to man."

Gordon Collier started to laugh hysterically, but smothered it before the laughter exploded nakedly into the room. "*Are* you a man?" he asked.

"Certainly not," John said indignantly.

Gordon Collier clenched his fists until his fingernails drew blood from the palms of his hands. He tried to use his mind, to free it, to fight. He could not, and he felt the tears of rage in his eyes. *I must,* he thought, *I must, I must, I MUST*.

He closed his eyes. The ritual had been broken, the lulling pattern was no more. He told himself: *Somewhere in this madness there is a pattern that will reduce it to sanity. It is up to me to find it; that is why I am here. I must fight this thing, whatever it is. I must clear my mind and I must fight. I must get behind the greasepaint and the special effects and deal with whatever is underneath. This is the one test I must not fail.*

"Would you care for a drink?" he asked the man who looked like Grandfather Walters.

"Not particularly," John told him. "In fact, the thought appalls me."

Gordon Collier turned and walked out into the kitchen, took a bottle of Bart's best Scotch out of the cupboard, and drank two shots straight. Then he methodically mixed a Scotch and soda, and stood quite still, trying to think.

He *had* to think.

This wasn't insane, he had to remember that. It *seemed* to be, and that was important. Things didn't just happen, he knew; there was always an explanation, if you could just find it. Certainly, these two little cottages out here on Ganymede were fantastic enough unless you knew the story behind them. You would never guess, looking at them, that they were the tail end of a dream, a dream that man was trying to stuff back into the box . . .

Again, the thought came: *If this is an alien, all that I have worked for is finished. The dream is ended.* And a further thought: *Unless they never find out, back on Earth.*

Those thoughts. They drummed so insistently through his mind. Were they his, really? Or were they, too, part of the conditioning? He shook his head. He could not think clearly, his mind was clogged. He would have to feel his way along.

He was desperately aware that he was not reacting rationally to the situation in which he found himself. None of it made sense; there was too much trickery. But how could he cut through to the truth?

He didn't know.

He *did* know that there was danger with him in the house, danger that was beyond comprehension.

He tried to be calm. He walked back into the living room, to face the three people who were less than human and the strange man who had walked in out of infinity.

Gordon Collier entered the room and stopped. He forced his mind to accept the scene in matter-of-fact terms. He reached out for reality and held on tight.

There was the bridge table, and there Helen and Mary and Bart, their cards in their hands, caught between action and non-action. There was the homey furniture, and the knick-knacks on the mantelpiece over the non-functional fireplace. Out in the kitchen, the frigidaire wheezed. There was the line of poetry: *Let me live in a house by the side of the road and be a friend to man.* There was the portrait of old Grandfather Walters.

There sat the man named *John,* who *was* Grandfather Walters, down to the last precise hair in his white moustache, the last wrinkle in his dreary gray business suit.

Outside, in a night alive with shadows, there was no sound at all.

"You have returned, as time will allow," John said. "No doubt you have your questions ready." He lit a cigarette, and the brand he smoked had not existed for twenty years. He dropped ashes on the rug.

"I can ask you questions, then," Gordon Collier said hesitantly.

"Certainly, my man. Please do. Valuable prizes."

Gordon frowned, not caring for the phrase "my man." And the oddly misplaced tri-di jargon was disconcerting, vaguely horrible. He fought to clear his mind.

"Are you our friend?"

"No."

"Our enemy?"

"No."

The three people at the bridge table watched, unmoving.

"Are you trying to—ummm—conquer the Earth?"

"My good man, what on Earth for?"

Gordon Collier tried to ignore the pun. It didn't fit. Nothing fitted. That was why he could not force his mind to see it all objectively, then. It was completely outside his experience, all of it.

*Somewhere there is a pattern—*

"What is this all about? What is going on?"

John's blue eyes twinkled. He lit another cigarette, dropping the other one on the rug and grinding it out with his neatly polished black shoe. He said: "I have already told you that I am not a man. It follows that I am, from your point of view, an alien. I have nothing to hide. My actions are irrational to you, just as yours are to me. You are, in a way, a preliminary to food. There, is that clear?"

Gordon Collier stared at the man who looked like Grandfather Walters. *If this is an alien—*

His mind rebelled at the thought. It was absurd, fantastic. He tried to find another explanation, ignoring the shrieking danger signals in his mind. Suppose, now, that this was all a trick, a monstrous trick. John was not an alien at all—of course he wasn't—but a clever agent from Earth, out to wreck the dream.

"You say that you are an alien," he told John. "Prove it."

John shrugged, dropping ashes into the little pile on the rug. "The best proof would be highly unpleasant for you," he said. "But I can—the words are difficult, we're a little late, folks —take a story out of your mind and—the words are very hard —project it back to you again. Will that be good enough?"

"Prove it," Gordon Collier repeated, trying to be sure of himself. "Prove it."

John nodded agreeably. He looked around him, smiling.

The clock in the hall struck two.

Gordon Collier sat down. He leaned forward. . . .

He saw a ship. It was very cold and dark. He saw—shadows —in the ship. He followed the ship. It had no home. It was nomadic. It fed on energy that it—absorbed—from other cultures. He saw one of the—shadows—more clearly. There were many shadows. They were watching him. He strained forward, could almost see them—

"I beg your pardon," John said loudly. "How clumsy of me."

The room was taut with fear.

"If at first you don't succeed," John said languidly, "try, try again. Let's see, my m⸺ —where shall we start?"

The question was rhetorical. Gordon Collier felt a jolt hit his mind. He felt himself slipping, tried to hold on. He failed. It began to come, out of the past.

Disjointed, at first. Jerky headlines, and then more . . .

MAN CONQUERS SPACE!

YANK SHIP LANDS ON MOON!

NEXT STOP MARS SCIENTIST SAYS!

There had been more, under the headlines. Articles about how the space stations were going to end war by a very logical alchemy. Articles about rockets and jets and atomics. Articles about how to build a nice steel base on the moon.

Gordon Collier laughed aloud and then stopped, suddenly.

The three people at the bridge table stared at him mindlessly. John stabbed in his brain . . .

They had chattered away quite glibly about weightlessness and gravity strains. They had built a perfect machine.

But there had been an imperfect machine inside it.

His name was man.

There were imperfect machines outside it, too. Villages and towns and cities filled to overflowing with them. Once the initial steps had been taken, once man was really in space at last, the reaction came. The true enormity of the task became all too obvious.

Space stations didn't cure wars, of course, any more than spears or rifles or atomic bombs had cured wars. Wars were culturally determined patterns of response to conflict situations; to get rid of wars, you had to change the pattern, not further implement it.

Space killed men. It sent them shrieking into the unknown in coffins of steel. It ripped them out of their familiar, protective cultures and hurled them a million miles into Nothing.

Space wasn't profitable. It gobbled up millions and billions into its gaping craw and it was never satiated. It didn't care about returning a profit. There was no profit to return.

Space was for the few. It was expensive. It took technical skills and training as its only passport. It was well to speak of dreams, but this dream had to be paid for. It took controls and taxes. Who paid the taxes? Who wanted the controls?

*I work eight hours a day in a factory,* the chorus chanted into the great emptiness. *I got a wife and kids and when I come home at night I'm too tired to dream. I work hard. I earn my money. Why should I foot the bill for a four-eyed Glory Joe?*

Space was disturbing. Sermons were spoken against it. Editorials were written against it. Laws were enacted against it—subtle laws, for controls were not wanted.

The rockets reached Luna and beyond—Mars and Venus and the far satellites of Jupiter and Saturn. Equipment was set up, the trail was blazed at last.

But who would follow the trail? Where did it go? What did it get you when you got there?

Starburn leaves scars on the soul. Some men could not give up. Some men knew that man could not turn back.

Starburned men knew that dreams never really die.

They dwelt in fantastic loneliness, many of them, waiting. They waited for a few of their fellows on Earth to win over a hostile planet with advertising and lectures and closed-door sessions with industrialists. They fought to lay the long-neglected foundations for a skyscraper that already teetered precariously up into the sky and beyond.

Far out in space, the fragile network of men and ships held on tight and hoped.

"Let us revert to verbal communication again," John said with startling suddenness. "Projection is quite tiring."

Gordon Collier jerked back to the present and tried to adjust. He was aware, dimly, that he was being played with consummate skill. He thought of a fish that knew it had a hook in its mouth. What could he do about it? He tried to think. . . .

"Of course," John went on—quite smoothly now—and lighting yet another cigarette, "your scientists, if I may apply the word to them, belatedly discovered that they could not simply isolate a man, or a man and a woman, in a steel hut on an alien world and go off and leave him for six months or a year, to employ your ethnocentric time scale. A man is so constituted that he is naked and defenseless without his culture, something he can live by and believe in."

Gordon Collier gripped his empty glass until he thought the glass would shatter. Could this man be reading his thoughts? A word came to him: *hypnosis*. It sounded nice. He tried to believe in it.

"In the long run, you see," John continued, "it is the totality of little things that goes to make up a culture. A man such as yourself does not simply sit in a room; he sits in a room of a familiar type, with pictures on the walls and dust in the corners and lamps on the tables. A man does not just eat; he eats special kinds of food that he has been conditioned to want, served as he has been trained to want them to be served, in containers he is accustomed to, in a social setting that he is familiar with, that he fits into, that he *belongs* in. All intelligent life is like that, you see."

Gordon waited, trying to think. He had almost had something there, but it was slipping away. . . .

"Someone had to stay in space, of course," John said, dropping more ashes on the rug. "Someone had to man the stations and look after the equipment, and there was a more subtle reason; it was a distinct psychological advantage to have men already *in* space, to prove that it could be done. The machines couldn't do everything, unfortunately for you, and so someone had to stay out here, and he had to stay sane —sane by your standards, of course."

Gordon Collier looked across at the three people who sat as though frozen around the forgotten bridge table, staring at him with blank dead-fish eyes. Helen, his wife. Bart and Mary. Sane? What did that mean? What was the price of sanity?

"And so," John continued in a bored voice, "man took his culture with him—the more provincial and reassuring and fixed the better. He took little white cottages and neighborly customs, rooted them up out of their native soil, sealed them in cylinders of steel, and rocketed them off to barren little worlds of ice and darkness. I must say, Collier, that your mind has a frightfully melodramatic way of looking at things. Perhaps that was why the little white cottages and the neighbors were not enough; in any event, conditioning was also necessary. No person operating at his full level of perception could possibly enact this farce you are living out here. And yet, without the farce you go mad. It is difficult to imagine a people less suited to space travel, don't you agree?"

Gordon Collier shrugged, feeling the cold sweat gathering in the palms of his hands.

"And there you are," John said, lighting another cigarette. "They are *much* milder. I have tried to demonstrate projection to you, on several different levels. I hope you will excuse the scattered editorial comments?"

Gordon Collier defensively reached out for a single line of

reasoning and clung to it. If this were an alien, and the news got back to Earth, then the dream of space travel was finished. An advanced race already in space, added to all the other perils, would be the last straw. He, Gordon Collier, had dedicated his life to the dream. Therefore, it could not end. Therefore, John was human. It was all a trick.

His mind screamed its warning, but he thrust it aside.

He leaned forward, breathing hard. "I'll excuse them," he said slowly, "but I'll also call you a liar."

Outside, the night was still.

The sound had been turned off.

There was no storm now—no rain, nor thunder, nor lightning. There was no wind, not even whispers of a summer breeze. There were no crickets, and no night rustlings in the stuff that looked like grass.

Bart and Mary and Helen sat uncertainly at their bridge table, trying to somehow adapt themselves to a situation that they were in no way prepared to face. It wasn't their fault, Gordon knew. They had not been conditioned to handle *new* elements. That was his job. That was what he had been chosen for. He was the change factor, the mind that had been left free enough to function.

But not wholly free. He felt that keenly, here in the room with the man called John. He was fuzzy and approximate. He needed to be clear and exact. He tried to believe he had figured it all out. *Hypnosis.* That was a good word.

He hoped that it was good enough.

"A liar?" The man who looked like Grandfather Walters laughed in protest and blew smoke in Collier's eyes. "The projection was incorrect?"

Collier shook his head, ignoring the smoke, trying not to be distracted. "The information was correct. That proves nothing."

John arched his bushy eyebrows. "Oh? Come now, my man."

"Look here," Gordon Collier said decisively, believing it now. "You look like a man to me. All I have to contradict my impression is your unsupported statement and some funny tricks that can be explained in terms of conditioning and hypnosis. If you came from Earth, as you obviously did, then you would know the story as well as I do. The rest is tricks. The real question is: who sent you here, and why?"

It was cold in the room. Why was it so cold?

John deftly added more ashes to the small mountain at his feet. "Your logic is excellent, if primitive," he said. "The trouble with logic is that its relationship with reality is usually obscure. It *is* logical that I am from Earth. It is not, however, true."

"I don't believe you," Gordon Collier said.

John smiled patiently. "The trouble is," he said, "that you have a word, 'alien,' and no concept to go with it. You persist in reducing me to non-alien terms, and I assure you that I will not reduce. I am, by definition, not human."

The doubt came again, gnawing at him. He fought himself. He felt an icy chill trip along his spine. He tried to convince himself and he said: "There is a reason for the storms and the build-up and the screams. I think it is a human reason. I think you have been sent here by the interests on Earth who are fighting space expansion, to try to scare us off. I think you're a good actor, but I don't think you're good enough."

The thought came again: *If this is an alien . . .*

Nonsense.

Helen, at the bridge table, suddenly stirred. She said, "My, but it's late." That was all.

John ignored her. "I assure you," he said, "that I have not the slightest interest in whether your little planet gets into space or not. Your ethnocentrism is fantastic. Can't you see, man? I don't care, not at all, not in any particular. It just isn't part of my value system."

"Go back and tell them it didn't work," Gordon Collier said.

"Oh, no," John said, shocked. "I'm spending the night."

The silence tautened.

Mary moved at the bridge table. The button had been

punched, and she tried to respond. "Bart," she said, "set up the spare bed for the nice man."

Bart didn't move.

"You're not staying," Gordon Collier said flatly. He shook his head. He was so confused. If only—

John smiled and lit another cigarette from his endless supply. "I really must, you know," he said cheerfully. "Look at it this way. The star cluster to which you refer as *the* galaxy —quaint of you—is inhabited by a multitude of diverse cultural groups. A moment's reflection should show you that uniformity of organization over so vast a territory is impossible. The problem of communications alone would defeat such a plan, even were it desirable, which it isn't.

"One of these cultures, of which I happen to be a member, has no territorial identification, except with space itself. Our ship is our home. We are, in a manner of speaking, nomads. Our economy, since we produce nothing, is based upon what we are able to extract from others."

Gordon Collier listened to his heart. It drummed liquidly in his ears.

"The closest similarity I can find in your mind is that of the ancient Plains Indians in the area you think of as North America," John continued, his blue eyes sparkling. "How charming that you should regard them as primitive! Sedentary economies are so dull, you know. We have become rather highly skilled, if I do say so myself, at imitating dominant life forms. Contacting aliens for preliminary 'typing' is a prestige mechanism with us, just as counting *coup* served an analogous purpose among your Plains Indians, when a brave would sneak into an enemy camp at night and touch a sleeping warrior or cut loose a picketed horse. This gave him prestige in his tribe, and without it he was nothing; he had no status. With us there is a further motive. Suppose, to extrapolate down to your level, you wish to pick apples. It will be to your advantage, then, to try to look and act like the farmer who owns them, will it not? Our culture has found it expedient to 'type' members of an alien culture in a controlled situation, before setting out to, so to speak, pick apples in earnest. The individual who does the 'typing' gains prestige in proportion to the danger involved. Am I getting through to you?"

Gordon Collier got to his feet, slowly. He could not think, not really. In a way, he realized this. He tried to go ahead regardless, to do what he could. His brain supplied a thought: *What would the ship from Earth pick up five months from tonight in this silent cottage? Would it be human beings— or something else?*

Of course, John *was* a human being.

A hypnotist, perhaps.

Why was it so cold in the house?

He started for the man called John, slowly, step by step. He did not know why he did it; he only knew that he had to act, act now, act before it was too late, act despite the cost. The impulse came from down deep, beyond the conditioning.

"You're a liar," he said again, biting the words out thickly, believing in them. "You're a liar. We don't believe in you. Get out, get out, get *out—*"

*If this is an alien, the dream is ended. Unless—*

The man called John slid out of his chair and back way. His blue eyes glittered coldly. The cigarette between his fingers shredded itself to the floor, squeezed in two.

"Stop," said John.

Gordon Collier kept on coming.

The man called John—changed.

Gordon Collier screamed.

It was an animal scream.

He staggered back, back against the wall. His eyes were shut, jammed shut as tightly as he could force them. His mouth was open, to let the endless scream rip and tear itself out from the matrix of his being. He cowered, crouched against the wall, a creature in agony.

He was afraid that he would not die.

His hands shook, and they were clammy with the cold sweat that oozed from his palms. A white flash of indescribable pain seared up from his toes, burned like molten lead through his body. It hissed along his naked nerves and howled into his cringing brain with the numbing, blinding impact of a razor-sharp chisel on a rotten tooth. Blood trickled wetly from his nostrils.

He clawed the floor, not feeling the splinters in his nails.

The scream screeched to a piercing climax that bulged his eyes from their sockets.

Something snapped.

His body relaxed, trembling quietly. His mind was clean and empty, like a flower washed with the summer rain. He breathed in great choking mouthfuls of air. He remembered—

It had *bubbled*.

He shut it out. He lay quite still for a long minute, letting the life wash warmly back through his veins. His breathing slowed. He felt a tiny thrill of triumph course through his body.

His mind was clean.

He could think again.

He took a deep breath and turned around.

The cottage was still there. The frigidaire wheezed in the kitchen. The living room was unchanged. There were the chairs, the tri-di, the picture of Grandfather Walters, the ashes on the rug, the three motionless figures at the bridge table. Bart and Mary and Helen.

They were very still.

Yes, of course. Their conditioned minds had been strained past the tolerance point and they had blanked out. Short-circuited. The fuse had blown. They were out of it, for now.

He was alone.

The man called John was seated again in his armchair, blue eyes twinkling, moustache neat and prim, the pile of ashes at his feet. He had lit another cigarette. He was smiling, quite himself again.

Or, rather, he was *not* himself again.

Gordon Collier got to his feet. It took him a long time, and he did it clumsily. He was shaken and weak in the knees. He had lost the fuzziness which had partially protected him.

But he had his mind back.

It was, he thought, a fair trade.

"I fear the shock has been too much for your dull friends," John said languidly, crossing his legs carefully so as not to disturb the neat crease in his trousers. "I tried to warn you, you know."

Gordon said: "You can't stay here." The words were thick and he licked his lips with his parched tongue.

John hesitated, but recovered quickly. "On the contrary," he said, "I can and I will. A charming place, really. I'd like to get to know you better."

"I can imagine," said Gordon Collier.

The silence beat at his ears. It was uncanny. He had never heard no-sound before.

Black despair settled within him like cold ink. The situation, he now saw, was frightening in its simplicity. He had to accept it for what it was. The thing was alien. It didn't *care* what the effects of its visit would be on the future of Earth. Human beings were to it what pigs were to a man.

Does the hungry man worry about whether or not pigs have dreams?

"You're going to get out," he told it.

The man called John raised an eyebrow in polite doubt.

Gordon Collier was not sure, now, that man *should* leave the Earth. It was odd, he thought, that his concern was still with the dream. Regardless of his actions here, all the human beings would not be "eaten." Many would escape, and the species would recover. But if this thing, or even any news of it, reached the Earth, then the dream was finished. The whole shaky, crazy structure that had put man into space would collapse like a card house in a hurricane. Man—or what was left of him—would retreat, build a wall around himself, try to hide.

And if he did get into space to stay?

Gordon Collier didn't know. There were no simple answers. If the aliens, or even the intelligence that there *were* such aliens, reached the Earth, then man was through, dead in his insignificance. If not, he had a chance to shape his own destiny. He had won time. It was as simple as that.

Gordon Collier again faced the man called John. He smiled.
Two cultures, locked in a room.

From the bridge table, three sluggish statues turned to
watch.

To Gordon Collier, the only sound in the room was that of
his own harsh breathing in his ears.

"As I was saying," said the man called John, "I'm afraid
I really must ignore your lamentable lack of hospitality and
stay on for awhile. I am, you might say, the man who came
to dinner. You are quite helpless, Gordon Collier, and I can
bring my people here at any time. Enough of them, you see,
to fill both your houses and the air bubble beyond. It will be
alive with my people. You are quite helpless, Gordon Collier
and I can bring my people here at any time. Enough of them,
you see, to fill . . ."

Gordon Collier refused to listen to the voice that tried to
lull him back to sleep. He shut it out of his mind. He had but
one weapon, and that was his mind. He had to keep it clear
and uncluttered.

John kept talking, melodically.

Gordon Collier tried to think, tried to organize his thoughts,
collect his data, relate it to a meaningful whole.

*Somewhere there is a pattern.*

Several pieces of information, filed away by his conditioned
brain until it could assemble them, clicked into place like
parts of a puzzle. Now that the fog was gone, a number of
facts were clear.

He used his mind, exultantly.

For one thing, of course, the man called John had given
him more information than was strictly necessary. Why? Well,
he had explained about the prestige mechanism involved—
and the more danger there was, the more prestige. An important fact followed: if he, Gordon Collier, were in fact utterly helpless, then there was no danger, and no prestige.

And *that* indicated . . .

". . . lamentable lack of hospitality and stay on for awhile,"
the voice droned on in his ears. "I am, you might say, the man

who came to dinner. You are quite helpless, Gordon Collier, and I can . . ."

So John had armed him with information. He had been playing a game of sorts, a game for keeps. He had given his opponent clues. What were they? *What were they?*

". . . bring my people here at any time. Enough of them, you see . . ."

"*The trouble is,*" John had said, "*that you have a word, 'alien,' and no concept to go with it.*"

Gordon Collier stood motionless, between John and the three immobile figures at the bridge table, looking for the string that would untie the knot. John's voice buzzed on, but he ignored it.

From the first, he remembered, John had kept himself apart from the human beings. He had walked in, hesitated, said his stilted tri-di derived introductory remarks, and seated himself as Grandfather Walters. He had remained isolated He had never come really close to any of the human beings, never touched them.

And when Gordon Collier had advanced on him . . .

Collier stared at the man called John. Was he telepathic, or had he picked up his story before he ever came through the door? Was he listening in on his thoughts even now?

That was unimportant, he realized suddenly. That was a blind alley. It made no practical difference. What counted was a simple fact: the alien could not touch him. And, presumably, it wasn't armed; that would have counterbalanced the danger factor.

It was very cold in the room. Gordon Collier felt a sick thrill in the pit of his stomach.

". . . to fill both your houses and the air bubble beyond. It will be alive . . ."

There was danger for the alien here. There *had* to be. Gordon Collier smiled slowly, feeling the sweat come again to his hands. There could be but one source for that danger.

Himself.

He saw the picture. It was quite clear. All that build-up, all the sounds and the rain and the wind, had been designed to test man in a beautiful laboratory situation. If man proved amenable to "typing," then he was next on the food list.

Pigs.

If he didn't crack, if he fought back even *here* and *now,* then the aliens would have to play their game elsewhere. Death wasn't fun, not even to an alien.

Death was basic.

Yes, it was quite clear what he had to do. He didn't know that he could do it, but he could try. He was weak on his legs and there was a cold shriek of memory that would not stay buried in his mind. He bit his lip until he felt the salt taste of blood in his mouth. He was totally unprotected now, and he knew the price he would have to pay.

He smiled again and walked slowly toward the man called John, step by steady step.

Gordon Collier lived an eternity while he crossed the room. He felt as though he were trapped in a nightmare that kept repeating itself over and over and over again.

The six dead eyes at the bridge table followed him.

"Stop," said John.

Gordon Collier kept coming.

The man called John slid out of his chair and backed away. His blue eyes were cold with fear and fury.

"Stop," he said, his voice too high.

Gordon Collier kept coming.

That was when John—changed.

Gordon Collier screamed—and kept on walking. He shaped his screaming lips into a smile and kept on walking. He felt the sickness surge within him and he kept on walking.

Closer and closer and *closer*.

He screamed and while he screamed his mind clamped on one thought and did not let go: *if that seething liquid hell is hideous to me, then I am equally hideous to it.*

He kept walking. He kept his eyes open. His foot stepped into the convulsive muck on the floor. He stopped. He screamed louder. He reached out his hand to *touch* it. It bubbled icily . . .

He knew that he would touch it if it killed him.

The thing—cracked. It contracted with lightning speed into half its former area. It got away. It boiled furiously. It shot into a corner and stained the wall. It tried to climb. It heaved and palpitated. It stopped, advanced, wavered, advanced—

And retreated.

It flowed convulsively, wriggling, under the door.

Gordon Collier screamed again and again. He looked at the three dead-alive statues at the bridge table and sobbed. He was wrenched apart.

But he had won.

He collapsed on the floor, sobbing. His face fell into the mound of dry gray ashes by the armchair.

He had won. The thought was for far away . . .

One of the statues that had been his wife stirred and somehow struggled to her feet. She padded into the bedroom and got a blanket. She placed it gently over his sobbing body.

"Poor dear," said Helen. "He's had a hard day."

Outside, there was a whistle and a roar, and then the pale light of dawn flowed in and filled the sky.

The five months passed, and little seemed changed.

There was only one little white cottage now, and it was on Earth. It snuggled into the Illinois countryside. It had been shutters and crisp curtains on the windows. It had knick-knacks on the mantelpiece over the fireplace. It had a fragment of cozy poetry, caught in a dime-store frame . . .

Gordon Collier was alone now, and the loneliness was a tangible thing. His mind was almost gone, and he knew that it was gone. He knew that they had put him here to shelter him, to protect him, until he should be strong enough to take the therapy as Helen and Bart and Mary had taken it.

But he knew that he would never be strong enough, never again.

They pitied him. Perhaps, they even felt contempt for him. Hadn't he failed them, despite all their work, all their expert conditioning? Hadn't he gone to pieces with the others and reduced himself to uselessness?

They had read the last notation in the equipment room. Odd that a meteor could unnerve a man so!

He walked across the green grass to the white picket fence. He stood there, soaking up the sun. He heard voices—children's voices. There they were, three of them, hurrying across the meadow. He wanted to call to them, but they were far away and he knew that his voice would not carry.

He stood by the white fence for a very long time.

When darkness came, and the first stars appeared above him, Gordon Collier turned and walked slowly up the path, back to the warmth, and to the little white cottage that waited to take him in.